HOPE AND VENGEANCE

SAA THALARR SERIES, BOOK ONE

CONNIE SUTTLE

Print Second Edition (2018)
Print ISBN: 1-63478-070-1
Print ISBN-13: 978-1-63478-070-4
eBook ISBN: 1-93975-927-7
eBook ISBN-13: 978-1-93975-927-6

Published by:
SubtleDemon Publishing, LLC
PO Box 95696
Oklahoma City, OK 73143

Cover art by Renée Barratt @ The Cover Counts

To Walter, Joe, Larry, Lee, Dianne, Sarah and Mark.
Thank you.

ACKNOWLEDGMENTS

As always, this book is the result of collaboration. If it weren't for the support of my editor, my cover artist and my beta readers, it would be less than it is. All mistakes, as usual, are mine and no other's.

About the Author:
Connie Suttle lives in Oklahoma with her husband and a conglomerate of cats. They have finally banded together to make their demands, which has proven disconcerting to all humans involved.

You may find Connie in the following ways:
Facebook: Connie Suttle Author
Twitter: @subtledemon
Website and Blog: subtledemon.com

Blood Destiny Series:

Blood Wager

Blood Passage

Blood Sense

Blood Domination

Blood Royal

Blood Queen

Blood Rebellion

Blood War

Blood Redemption

Blood Reunion

Blood Destiny Series Boxed Set (Books 1-10)

Blood Recall

Blood Alliance*

Legend of the Ir'Indicti Series:

Bumble

Shadowed

Target

Vendetta

Destroyer

Legend of the Ir'Inditi Boxed Set

High Demon Series:

Demon Lost

Demon Revealed

Demon's King

Demon's Quest

Demon's Revenge

Demon's Dream

God Wars Series:

Blood Double

Blood Trouble

Blood Revolution

Blood Love

Blood Finale

Saa Thalarr Series:

Hope and Vengeance

Wyvern and Company

Observe and Protect*

First Ordinance Series:

Finder

Keeper

BlackWing

SpellBreaker

WhiteWing

≈

R-D Series:

Cloud Dust

Cloud Invasion

Cloud Rebel

≈

Latter Day Demons Series:

Hot Demon in the City

A Demon's Work is Never Done

A Demon's Due

≈

Seattle Elementals Series:

Your Money's Worth

Worth Your While*

≈

BlackWing Pirates Series

MindSighted

MindMage

MindRogue

MindMaster*

≈

Black Rose Sorceress Series

The Rose Mark

Rose and Thorn

Black Rose Queen

Queen of Thorns and Roses

Future Wars Series

Buffer Zone

Black Zone*

Other Titles from SubtleDemon Publishing:

Malefactor

Transgressor

Underhanded*

by Joe Scholes

*Forthcoming

CHAPTER 1

"I have already assigned this task to Russell," I said.

"And I am assigning it to you." Xavier, my sire, ignored me as he sat at his desk, leaning back in an excessively expensive leather chair to stare at the original Monet hanging on the opposite wall.

Xavier was impeccably dressed as always, in a navy-blue suit that complimented his eyes. Dark-blond hair was carefully cut and styled to flatter his features and his hands received a manicure once a week. Human women frequently sought him out, and he treated them as dirt beneath his heel. Sadly, he treated most vampires much the same.

Tonight, he refused to meet my eyes as he spoke, choosing instead to explore the impressionistic light Monet depicted in one of his many large paintings of water lilies. Xavier acquired it directly from the artist, shortly after it was completed and signed. He'd purchased it because it held light on its two-dimensional surface, something that neither of us could ever experience in the flesh—unless we wished to die.

"Saxom is behind this reassignment," I muttered, displaying an unusual bit of anger. After all, I'd worked very hard the past two hundred seventeen years to eliminate emotions and facial expressions —especially in my dealings with anything vampire.

Saxom, a member of the Vampire Council and second only to Wlodek, seldom did anything that failed to annoy me—at least on some level. I only used Saxom's name away from his presence, too; he preferred an unofficial title, instead—*the Seer*. The few times I'd had personal contact with him, I'd come away with an oily feeling of revulsion clinging to my clothes and skin.

"Adam, you may be surprised to know that it wasn't the Seer behind this decision. As he is a member of the Council and Wlodek's second-in-command, I order you to display proper respect and never voice your opinion of him to anyone except me." Xavier placed compulsion and I shuddered as his pale-blue eyes bored into mine. A sire's compulsion is impossible for any vampire to ignore, so I was forced to obey anytime Xavier commanded me.

Of Xavier's two living vampire children, I found it more difficult to accept his commands. Russell, my vampire sibling, is younger than I and also an Enforcer for the Council. He, though, has an easier time with Xavier, as Xavier knew of him before he was turned. I, having been a complete stranger, lacked the attention Xavier lavished on his youngest.

Now, having skills few others did, I'd been made Chief of Enforcers more than a century earlier, after Gavin Montegue vacated the position to become Wlodek's Chief Assassin. Xavier was instrumental in putting me forward for the Chief's spot—he and Wlodek were very close. Xavier, too, trained Russell and me to be Enforcers from the beginning. We learned fighting techniques and tactics from him, along with our first lessons on how to be properly vampire.

Turning away from my thoughts and hiding my distaste for Xavier's compulsion as well as I could, I asked the logical question. "Who, then?"

"Merrill."

That was unexpected. Saxom, yes—Merrill, no. Merrill seldom concerned himself with Council business. He never attended Council meetings, but often met with Wlodek at Wlodek's manor. I'd heard from associates that Merrill was sometimes consulted regarding hearings or executions, but I had no idea whether anything the mysterious vampire offered swayed Wlodek's opinions at all. Still, Merrill's reticence over these matters did little to quell the rumors that swirled and eddied about him.

Legend had it that he was older than many thought and more powerful than most imagined. I'd once heard the theory that he was a King Vampire, something mythical to most of my kind, but I'd only heard that theory once and certainly hadn't repeated it. Surely, if he were a King, then he'd have the position at the center of the Council's table instead of Wlodek.

"Call Russell immediately and tell him to take your assignment in Madrid. I expect you to be on the jet tomorrow evening. Contact me when you arrive in Texas." Xavier's dismissal was brusque as he turned his gaze away from me and back to the Monet. I spun without a word and stalked from his study.

The manor was badly deteriorated. Rot and other smells of ruin drifted past me as I studied my ancestral home. Barely twenty miles away from Xavier's mansion in Kent, I'd chosen to drive by before I returned to London and prepared for my trip to the U.S. The last offer I'd made on the place—in excess of three million pounds and twice its worth—had been refused.

"Father, I am trying," I whispered into the air. My father had been dead for a very long time—since 1799, in fact. I'd heard rumors that he, my mother and my younger brother Justin had never gotten over my disappearance. If not for Xavier, I would have contacted them. Many times.

With Justin's death in 1847, I was forced to cease my attempts at breaking Xavier's orders. Justin's family still lived, but they'd sold the manor immediately following his death and moved to the London townhouse. His descendants were scattered across the globe and I no longer searched them out; it was useless to do so.

The manor now lay in the hands of an eccentric and aging bastard who cared nothing for the property and was content to let it die. I despised him. Sighing, I turned and slid into my Jaguar, closing the door and starting the engine. The manor was currently a lost cause and I had many things to do before sunrise. Xavier's command had placed a decidedly unappreciated knot in my schedule.

"Adam, what is he doing?" Russell, nearly a century younger than I, had never worried about hiding his emotions. He laughed, angered and annoyed as easily as when he'd been human. I'd phoned my vampire sibling shortly after I reached my London apartment, and Russell was just as puzzled over the change of plans as I.

"Russ, you know how things are. For some reason, Merrill has weighed in on this assignment. I don't recall that he's ever done anything like that. You and I suspect that Wlodek listens to him when he does speak, so there's nothing more to be said on the matter."

"It's still fucking strange." Russell never minced words, either.

"I'll grant you that."

"I was looking forward to Texas," Russell complained. "I bought a cowboy hat."

"You didn't." Russell, in his spare time, enjoyed barhopping and the women who invariably flocked around his six-six frame. The only thing that might be more entertaining to watch was when Russell and Will were sent on assignment together. I paired them up whenever possible, as it gave them a bit of enjoyment during what was often a dangerous and thankless occupation.

"Brother, this worries me," Russell went on. "Maybe Texas is more dangerous than we thought."

"It's a routine investigation," I countered. "Two bodies, which may or may not have been drained by a vampire." I flipped the file open as I spoke to Russell on my cell. Bite marks were on the throats of both victims, but the fang marks—if they were fang marks—were widely spaced and that was unusual. Any vampire, including the dimmest among us, knows to heal the marks after biting—even if vampire law is broken and the victim is killed afterward.

The killing of humans was against vampire law, because it might expose the race. Therefore, it only made sense to hide all evidence that any blood taking involved a vampire. Failure to do so would only bring Enforcers or Assassins, and the likelihood that the offending vampire would survive the incident was very small.

"A hundred pounds says there's something else they haven't told you," Russell countered.

"Xavier did say to call him when I arrived in Corpus Christi."

"See? You owe me already."

"That remains to be seen," I replied. "Take your cowboy hat to Madrid. Perhaps the women there will find it attractive."

"Will do, boss." Russell laughed and hung up.

"How do you expect me to feel about this?" Merrill felt helpless as he stared at Griffin. They'd been as close as brothers for fifteen hundred years, but this—this threatened everything, including Merrill's hopes and dreams. "I wish you'd never told me this. It was better not knowing the dream is dead."

"Sometimes our dreams must be set aside," Griffin replied, a depth to his eyes that Merrill was seldom allowed to see. "In order to preserve the greater good."

"Fuck the greater good," Merrill muttered.

"I did not say to give up your dreams forever," Griffin added enigmatically.

"I just arrived at the safe house. Has the Council not attended to this one in years?" I spoke with Xavier on my cell as I stared with distaste at my surroundings. The square, bunker-like accommodation was at least fifty years out of date, with avocado-colored appliances, Formica counter-tops and ugly, greenish linoleum flooring. Two bedrooms and a single bathroom, also woefully outdated, rounded out the underground portion of the only safe house in the Corpus Christi area.

"I'll make sure it's on the list for renovations," Xavier muttered dryly in my ear. "Meanwhile, it will do. I have other business to discuss with you, Adam, and I wish no interruptions." Silently I waited for Xavier to continue. When I failed to respond in any way, he sighed angrily and went on. "I didn't tell you earlier, as the situation has become delicate. One of the victims, Samuel Greene, was a werewolf belonging to the local Pack. Reports indicate he was night fishing with two human friends when he and one other was attacked and killed. The second human is still missing but presumed dead."

Xavier growled low when I failed to respond. "As you likely realize, the Grand Master is furious, since he received reports that the two recovered bodies were drained of blood and dumped in a nearby wildlife refuge. As this appears to be the work of a vampire, the Grand Master is demanding that Wlodek investigate and bring the offending vampire to justice. This could affect the peace treaty between the races, Adam. Now do you know why Wlodek and Merrill wished you to investigate this?"

If I could have, I'd have swallowed uncomfortably at Xavier's explanation. In place for less than twenty years, the fragile peace treaty between vampires and werewolves could collapse at any time, leading to open warfare between the races once more. With the technology available and the hate that remained between factions in both races, another war could have devastating results—not just for the weres and vamps, but for humans as well.

"There's another complication," Xavier added. I drew in a ragged breath. What could be more complicated than maintaining the peace between races? When I didn't respond, Xavier continued. "A local private investigator has become involved in these disappearances. The werewolves know where Samuel Greene is—they discovered his body first, then Bill Gordon's shortly after. There was no sign of Ray Wilson's body, although they have gone hunting for it several times. They desire our cooperation in locating Ray Wilson and investigating these murders. The Corpus Christi Pack is keeping the two bodies they have in storage until you can examine them. The humans have families, who are still searching for their missing. The local investigator has vowed to find them."

"I can easily work around him," I muttered when Xavier paused, expecting a response concerning the private investigator.

"*She* has already worked with the human families involved; the Greene family has refused to participate in her investigation," Xavier snapped. "For obvious reasons."

"Of course." I winced when Xavier said *she*. A female investigator. That could complicate matters.

"There's something else," Xavier said.

"And that is?"

"Her name is Anna—Anna Kay Madden, and according to her advertisements, she is a psychic investigator." I wanted to laugh at Xavier's statement. Most psychic detectives (in my opinion), were charlatans, out to bilk money from the hopeless.

"What do you want me to do about her?" I asked instead.

"Contact her. Wlodek insists upon it. Invite her to dinner or make an appointment. Find out what she knows, if anything, and proceed from there. If you believe she might be of some use, offer to work alongside her on the investigation. If she has nothing to offer, place compulsion and send her on her way. It's as simple as that."

It was never as simple as that, and Xavier knew as well as anyone that I preferred to work investigations alone or with vampire assistance only. As far as working an assignment with humans—I'd never done it and had no desire to begin now. "Stop grinding your teeth, Adam—I can hear it. Do this. I command it," Xavier said. "Keep me apprised of the situation as well. Send regular e-mails. I wish to know who—and what—Miss Anna Kay Madden is."

"I will keep you advised," I promised. I was under compulsion to do as Xavier commanded, even over the phone. That compulsion he'd laid long ago—to obey his every command no matter from where or how far away. If his voice demanded, I was compelled to obey. Did it aggravate me? On a daily basis. There was nothing to be done about it, however. Nothing at all.

"Good." Xavier ended the call. I swore and tossed my cell onto the pitifully outdated kitchen counter. It clattered across the Formica before sliding to a stop against the backsplash.

As it was nearing midnight and too late to contact the local Packmaster or the psychic detective, I stormed out of the bunker, flung myself through the trap door that led into the garage, climbed into my rented SUV and drove straight to the local 24-hour Walmart. Since I didn't have control over the investigation, I could at least control the dismal safe house.

By dawn, I had new faucets purchased for the kitchen and bathroom, new tile laid on the kitchen floor, new mattresses on the beds, new and freshly washed sheets on both and a coat of white appliance paint applied to an abysmally ugly stove and refrigerator. Resolving to get other things done as time and home improvement shop hours allowed, I went to bed and fell into a rejuvenating sleep.

"I have Thursday night open," the local Packmaster agreed to meet and allow me to examine the two bodies he had in storage. I was pleased to learn they'd been refrigerated—Roger Prewitt owned Prewitt's Seafood, in addition to a fleet of shrimp boats, which brought in local fish and shellfish. An old, walk-in refrigerator in one of his seafood shops was currently not in use, so he'd had the bodies stored there until the Council sent someone to investigate. We agreed on a time two hours past sundown, which gave me plenty of time to rise, shower and drive to Rockport, a small town north of Corpus Christi.

It was late August in south Texas, which meant it was hot and dry inland, hot and humid near the gulf. I detested those conditions already as I located the phone number for Anna K. Madden, also listed as Madden Investigations in the local directory. Her ad proclaimed her *The Investigator with an Edge,* as I punched the number into my cell. Hoping she'd still be available, I waited as the phone rang three times before receiving a response.

"Madden Investigations, Rita speaking," a melodic voice with a slight Spanish accent answered. "How may I help you?" Rita added.

"May I speak with Anna Kay Madden please?" I asked as pleasantly as I could.

"Hold please." Less than a minute later, another voice came on the line.

"This is Anna Madden. How may I help you?" she asked, her voice nearly breathless.

I held back from pointing out that she was the psychic one; shouldn't she know what my difficulty was? I didn't. "My name is Adam Chessman," I told her instead. "I am investigating the disappearances of three men, at the request of Samuel Greene's family. I understand you're also working the case. I'd like to meet with you over dinner and exchange notes, if that's possible."

"Where and when?" Her voice was now a bit more businesslike.

"Tomorrow evening—is nine-thirty too late?"

"No. Would you like to meet at Jorge's Restaurant? It's on Ocean Drive in Corpus Christi. I'll make reservations. I know the owner, so getting there at that time won't be a problem."

"That sounds fine," I agreed.

"Good. I'll see you there." She hung up. I ended the call, stared at my phone for a moment and then stuffed it in my pocket. If I hurried, I could make it to a local home improvement warehouse before they closed at ten.

By the time dawn came, there was new wood flooring down in the bedrooms and small sitting area, a new bathtub, vanity and sink in the bathroom, the new faucets were installed and boxes of ceramic tiles were piled in a kitchen corner, waiting to be installed on the bathroom walls surrounding the tub. Materials to replace the kitchen countertops were in the garage upstairs; I intended to get to that very soon.

~

Jorge's Restaurant was spelled out in green neon over a rustic wood façade. Located on the waters of Corpus Christi Bay, Jorge's appeared to be a popular restaurant for locals and tourists. I passed a crowd of vacationers leaving as I arrived, most of them dressed in shorts and print shirts.

Perhaps I was a bit snobbish, but I'd never worn shorts. Or print shirts, for that matter. Designer suits filled my closets, alongside custom-made shirts and Italian shoes. I'd never bought a pair of jeans or a pullover shirt in my life. Russell called me stiff and unrelenting at times. I ignored him and he laughed.

"I'm meeting someone," I informed the hostess. The girl wasn't old enough to serve alcohol in the restaurant, I noticed. That didn't keep her from attempting to fawn over me. If she knew what little interest I had in her, perhaps she might have saved herself the trouble.

"Female humans are for sex, not love," Xavier told me many times. "Take your pleasure with their blood and place compulsion to forget you and the act committed. It's the best way."

At first I thought him foolish, but after years passed and women died, I began to believe. No woman had been successfully turned vampire during my lifetime, and when I ventured to ask Xavier about it, he informed me that no female had survived the attempt in seven hundred years.

The last time I'd fantasized about taking a woman and making her mine—for as long as she lived, that is, was in Chicago during the 1920s. I'd seen her from a distance but failed to catch up to her. Her image lingered in my mind, still, and no other woman had compared to her since.

"Your name?" the girl asked, checking notes on a list and pulling me back to the present.

"Adam Chessman."

"Oh, you're the one meeting Anna," she gushed. "She came in not long ago. I think she's in the ladies' room. If you'll come with me, I'll show you to a table and tell her you're here."

The girl swung long, dyed-black hair suggestively as she led me to a table set against a wide, plate-glass window. Corpus Christi Bay gleamed in the moonlight beyond the restaurant, and reflections of street lamps glittered on its surface. If it weren't for the heat and humidity, the location might hold much appeal.

"It gets better during the winter months, but there's a lot of fog at times." A woman sat opposite me and accepted a glass of water from our waiter. "Thanks, James," she nodded at the young man. I forced myself not to stare—had she just snatched the words from my mind?

"I'm Anna Madden. Lyndsay told me you were here. Sorry to keep you waiting, Mr. Chessman," she apologized. Hazel eyes studied me as I remained silent. Pale brown hair swept her shoulders and she was pretty, no doubt about that. She was dressed in a silk print blouse neatly tucked into oatmeal-colored linen trousers. Little makeup adorned her face, but she didn't need it—her skin was clear and nearly flawless.

"How long have you been investigating these disappearances?" I asked bluntly. I have no idea why I was so rude. The only excuse I had was that she'd taken me off guard.

"Mr. Chessman, as long as we're being blunt," she searched my face briefly, "I have to admit I don't feel up to eating. I feel queasy. That's why I was in the ladies' room earlier."

"You don't feel well?"

"No, I'm sorry to say, and the idea of eating only makes things worse. Would you like to take a walk instead? There's a footpath running beside the water's edge, or we can sit on one of the benches scattered along the way."

"I don't feel like eating, either," I acknowledged. We vampires could consume human fare, but we had to eliminate it later—we had no way to digest it. Eating was a way to make humans believe we were the same as they. I preferred not to make the pretense, if I were honest.

"Good." She tossed a twenty on the table and stood. "I'll let them know on the way out," she sighed. I followed her to the hostess' stand, where she informed Lyndsay that we weren't staying. We walked through the door and into a humid, Corpus Christi night.

We followed the footpath in silence for several minutes; it led us very near the water and as we walked, I noticed that Anna Madden was much shorter than my six-four height. At least a foot shorter than I, she was also slender in build and I wondered at her chosen profession.

"Mr. Chessman," she began, "I know you came to investigate those three disappearances that the local media have covered. What you don't know," she looked up at me, "is that there are seventeen others missing as well."

Schooling my face, I led her to a nearby, slatted wood bench and gestured for her to sit. She sat on one end; I took the other, leaving empty space between us. "I have only been given information on three missing men," I pointed out while trying to control surging anger. My sources were usually reliable, so I was skeptical of Anna's claim and that made me want to growl at her.

"The three you know about are legal citizens," Anna looked over the waters of the bay, refusing to meet my gaze. I turned to the bay as well, where I could see a jellyfish hovering below the water's surface, its pale luminescence barely visible except to one of my kind. Waves lapped regularly at the shoreline, lending a soft rhythm to the night.

Anna's words, however, forced my breath to halt for a moment, while my anger disappeared. What she'd said was a terrifying possibility, and worry now replaced my anger. If this was the work of vampires, we could have serial killers on our hands. That's never a good thing.

"You're saying that seventeen others—perhaps in the U.S. illegally, are also missing?" I asked.

"That's right. And all of them have connections to Hartshorne Oil."

"One of the refineries located outside the city?" I'd done my homework on the jet when I'd made the journey to south Texas— Hartshorne Oil and several other petroleum companies comprised the larger business concerns in the area.

"Yes."

"How do you know about these people? I have no information on them," I admitted reluctantly.

"Do you think their families are going to rush forward and report a missing person if that person isn't here with proper documentation? I believe the Hartshorne refinery in Corpus Christi has been experiencing cash flow problems, so undocumented workers would be cheaper to hire and easier to pay under the table."

That troubled me. "You're suggesting that this problem is more widespread than the authorities believe?"

"Yes."

"Who would mind if they disappeared?" I asked, testing her. I knew illegal immigrants and undocumented workers were a touchy subject with many states and among American politicians.

"Adam, they're human beings, and if they're being murdered—or worse, then I have a problem with that."

"Ah. Who brought this to your attention?"

"My assistant, Rita. One of her cousins is missing, along with the others. I get information through her."

"Is she also here illegally?"

"No. Rita was born here. Manuelo wasn't."

"Did he work for Hartshorne Oil?"

"Yes. Until the night he disappeared. Manuelo called his neighbor from Hartshorne because he worried he'd left his front door unlocked. That was at two in the morning. He never came home after his shift. If my guess is correct, Hartshorne is hiding his records and the records of many others. Rita convinced two families to speak with me—she told them I would not bring the authorities to their door. Both missing men worked for Hartshorne, and I was told the other fourteen did as well." Anna now stared at her hands. "Those men have families. If not here, back in Mexico. The ones responsible for this must be stopped." She turned to search my eyes. I felt as if she were testing me, now.

"Is anyone else searching for these men?" I asked.

"Rita's brother, Rick. Also born here, in case you're concerned. But he can only search after work—he has a job at a local transmission shop."

"So, no bodies have been found—for any of these missing men?" I watched as she dropped her gaze to her hands again.

"No bodies. Not yet."

"You think they're still alive?"

"I can't answer that."

Usually, I have a good sense of truth and lie. Her statement made me think she was answering truthfully—but with an evasive truth. "What do you suggest we do about it, then?" I asked softly.

"Look for all of them," she shrugged. "Somebody is preying on these people, because they know it will be difficult to prove anything. They're getting away with it, too, since nobody will come forward and report these disappearances. The kink in their plans came when the three you were sent to investigate disappeared."

I knew, as well as she, that the three men I'd been given information on worked for the same refinery and disappeared on the same night. Everything was connected to Hartshorne Oil; I just didn't know when the seventeen undocumented workers disappeared.

"Do you have dates of disappearances?" I asked.

"Yes. Rick got the information and gave it to Rita. It's at my office."

"Might I come and take a look?"

"Of course. Do you want to come tonight?"

"Tomorrow will do. I have other things requiring my attention tonight." I planned to make an unscheduled visit to Hartshorne Oil. "Is eight-thirty too late?"

"No. That's fine," she nodded without looking at me.

"This ship channel—where the three disappeared—has that been thoroughly searched for the third body?"

"Yes. Several times. Nothing has been found—not even the boat. The last search was done with dogs along the shoreline. They found nothing."

"Are we sure they went fishing?" Something about that didn't ring true—in the police reports and from a witness' account.

"Bill Gordon's boat is missing. That's what I do know," Anna said.

Bill Gordon was one of the two bodies locked in the local Packmaster's freezer. The other was Sam Greene, the werewolf. The third missing man, Ray Wilson, hadn't turned up anywhere. Bill Gordon's wife reported her husband missing the day after his night fishing expedition.

Ray Wilson's family had already called in, however, when he failed to return home. Sam Greene's wife alerted her Packmaster—she was also werewolf, and Roger Prewitt, Packmaster for the Corpus Christi Pack, had sent wolves out searching immediately. They'd found two bodies sinking into knee-deep mud in a swamp. They'd gone out a second and third time, searching for Ray Wilson, but they couldn't find a scent to track.

"I was planning to speak with Bill Gordon's wife," I said. "I don't suppose you've had contact with her?"

"I called her yesterday. She said to come by anytime," Anna replied. "We can go tomorrow after you look at the records I have. I'll call her and let her know it'll be late when we get there."

"I would appreciate that," I said. I studied her unobtrusively—she was avoiding my gaze. That puzzled me, as most women didn't mind looking in my direction. So much so, at times, that I was often forced to place compulsion. This one didn't look to be a problem.

I was surprised to find myself willing to work with her. Before tonight, I wouldn't have considered it. Still, things could sour quickly. If so, there was always compulsion—and I hadn't seen a single piece of evidence that gave me any idea she was the psychic she claimed to be, a bit of good guessing aside.

"I'm not a particularly good guesser," She turned to me once more. "I'm good with possibilities and absolutes." She stood, letting me know that somehow, I'd offended her. And possibilities and absolutes? I had no idea what that meant. She'd certainly picked those thoughts straight from my mind, however, and that sent a worried tingle through me. I would be forced to report this to Xavier and police my thoughts better.

"I'll walk you to your car," I offered. It was the polite (and gentlemanly) thing to do.

"It's not necessary," she informed me coldly and walked away. I caught up with her. She walked faster; I lengthened my stride. It made me wonder why I was bothering. I hadn't bothered with a woman—not for a very long while.

Her automobile was a small import—a hybrid. Plucking the keys from her fingers, I opened the door for her. Without a word, she slid into the driver's seat. Reaching in, I leaned over her and inserted the key before pulling the seat belt and buckling her in.

"Safety first, huh?" she looked at me as I pulled back.

"Always," I said, a slight smile tugging at my mouth. "Drive carefully," I added as I shut her door.

"Always," she echoed my words. I waited until she drove out of the parking lot before going to my rental and climbing in.

Hartshorne Oil was located two miles outside Corpus Christi's city limits. I parked on a deserted farm road half a mile from the refinery entrance, hid my keys beneath the mat and concentrated on turning to mist. It takes roughly five minutes for me to become mist, but that talent is rare and highly sought by the Council.

Xavier always said it was quite the blessing that I'd developed the ability after my turning. He'd found me late one evening, bleeding to death on a dark London street after I'd been attacked by six men. Those men had stolen my money purse, my boots and my human life.

Pulling my thoughts away from a very great tragedy in my life, I focused on my misting. Once it was completed, I flew in a direct line toward the refinery. Misting is employed for stealth only, as it takes much too long to make the change. Another vampire would have ample time to destroy a mister in the minutes it took to turn. There are only three known misters in the vampire community, and all three work for the Council.

Passing high over the refinery, I could see men on the ground, large storage tanks, pipes and equipment, lighted towers and buildings. Shifting toward a single-story building with many automobiles parked around it, I lowered my mist to slip cautiously behind two men walking through the entrance. Inside, I found a lobby of sorts as I floated behind the two, both of whom were speaking Spanish. They were discussing a trip to Mexico, to visit family.

A dimly lit corridor was their destination, where rows of time cards were mounted on a wall. A faint beep echoed as each swiped an employee card through a machine. If I'd had a mouth at the moment, I would have smiled. They were clocking in. There were records somewhere. This was a job for Joey.

CHAPTER 2

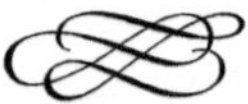

*A*fter returning to the safe house, I sent a message to Xavier, asking him to send Joey as quickly as possible. I ground my teeth when I reported on Anna Madden; perfect recall was one of my gifts after becoming vampire. I did—and didn't—appreciate its accuracy.

Joey Showalter was the Council's expert on computers and information technology. He'd been responsible for bringing the Council into the modern age. Prior to Joey's turning, Charles, Wlodek's assistant, had taken handwritten notes at Council meetings. Now, Charles had the latest in technology, access to records everywhere and took notes on a laptop. The Council supplied all Assassins and Enforcers with laptops. I'd taught myself how to use mine, but after meeting Joey, I was much better with it.

Joey was also openly gay, didn't mind that I wasn't and never lacked for companionship. The vampire community, being male almost exclusively, had a much healthier outlook regarding their gay compatriots.

As soon as I sent the message to Xavier, he instant-messaged me back.

What do you mean, she read your mind? I could almost hear the demand in Xavier's nonverbal question.

I said it seemed that she read my mind, I tapped out. *I can't say that for certain.*

Then I suggest you keep a watch on her, and be sure to let me know of other unusual behavior. Immediately.

Of course, Xavier. I never called him father. Yes, he was my sire, but he wasn't my father. I'd had a very good father, once; his memory remained unclouded in my mind. Xavier would never hear that word from me—not willingly, at least—and I think it angered him at times. I didn't care.

I will send Joey tomorrow. Will advise later on arrival time.

Thank you, I entered. Xavier never acknowledged my thanks. He merely ignored them as unnecessary.

With several hours remaining before sunrise, I chose to contact the only two vampires in the Corpus Christi area, asking them to meet with me at a local, twenty-four-hour coffee shop.

When I arrived, there were only two vehicles in the small parking lot of The Cracked Cup, located not far from the marina. A waitress and one customer were inside as I walked through the door. Choosing a corner booth away from the door, I nodded as the waitress held up the coffeepot.

Grabbing a cup from a shelf behind the counter, the waitress made her way to my table. I imagined that she'd held the same position for years uncounted, and judging by her gray hair and wrinkles, appeared to be in her mid-sixties.

"Can I get anything for you besides coffee?" she asked as she set the cup down and poured coffee efficiently.

"No, thank you," I replied.

"You're British."

"Yes, I am."

"I love British accents."

"So do I."

"I'm guessing you're not here for pleasure, then."

"You are correct."

"Enjoy your coffee. And your stay." She turned to move away.

"Two more will be joining me," I said.

"I'll bring more cups when they get here." She offered a smile, which I didn't return.

Ten minutes later, Jeff Garner and Kyle Williams walked through the door. I recognized them as vampires by scent. They came to sit opposite me while the waitress dutifully brought the coffeepot and two more cups. Kyle nodded and Jeff thanked the waitress politely. She walked away, barely offering me a glance.

"I'm Adam Chessman," I introduced myself after the waitress returned to the counter and resumed her conversation with the human patron.

"Jeff Garner," Jeff held out his hand. I took it out of necessity. Jeff was five-eight with a round face, brown hair, blue eyes and a deferential demeanor. Kyle Williams, slightly taller than Jeff and rail thin with black hair, was more reticent and didn't introduce himself. I'd given him my name over the phone when I called, and he hadn't failed to see my reaction to Jeff's gesture.

"What's this about?" Kyle asked instead, going straight to the purpose of our meeting.

"This." I'd brought the file of photographs with me—the ones depicting the bodies and their bite marks. "The local Pack suspects this is a vampire's work. Know anything about that?"

"Are these the ones on the news—those three who went fishing and didn't come back?" Jeff examined the top photograph carefully before replacing it in the folder.

"Yes."

"The punctures are too far apart." Jeff's blue eyes studied my face, silently asking if I hadn't recognized the same thing.

"I think so, too," I agreed. "Upon what do you base your opinion?"

"A medical one," he replied. "I have two medical degrees, and I've worked in the field for the past seventy years."

"So this is an expert opinion, then," I stared at Jeff, forcing him to lower his eyes. "Why doesn't the Council have this information on you?" I'd read his file. No data on medical training was in any part of it.

"Because the Council scares the bejeezus out of him, and all the other vampire physicians are forced to work for the Council." Kyle's words made me turn swiftly in his direction. He was right—there were only seventeen vampire physicians and they labored under the Council's thumb. Many of them were research biologists who also held medical degrees.

"If you cooperate with me while I'm here, I'll keep that information to myself," I offered.

"We'll cooperate," Jeff promised quickly, his voice and his eyes begging me to keep my word.

"We didn't have anything to do with those murders," Kyle said. "If that's what you're asking. We have alibis. Jeff was working his job at the hospital and I was in San Antonio. My hotel receipt." Kyle drew a slip of paper from a pocket and slid it across the table.

"A lover?" I queried, lifting the receipt and reading it.

"While I might consider that less than your business on a normal day, today, my answer is yes. He is also vampire, but I will only give his name if it becomes necessary."

"It won't be necessary." I'd gotten a good look at Kyle and Jeff's teeth. There wasn't any way their fangs were spaced far enough apart to inflict the wounds found on the bodies.

"Are we done?" Jeff's gaze was hopeful.

"You're done." I nodded.

"We, ah, won't leave town, as usual, and will be at your beck and call, should there be need." Kyle rose swiftly and followed Jeff from the café.

Madden Investigations was located on Mustang Island, two miles south of Port Aransas. I was surprised when the GPS on my rental took me to a condominium located on the barrier island—I expected something closer to town and farther from the beach. Miss Madden had the best of both worlds—her business doubled as her residence, and she had an unhindered view of the gulf.

Riding the elevator to the third floor where the condo was located, I pressed the doorbell and waited for her to answer. Her assistant, Rita, came to the door.

"Buenas noches, Mr. Chessman," Rita stood aside and invited me in.

"Rita, go home, your children are waiting," Anna stood inside the reception area as Rita led me inside the condo. Two desks occupied the space beyond, with plate-glass windows beside the second desk. A lovely view of the gulf lay outside those windows.

"Are you sure, Anna?" Rita asked. She was concerned about leaving her employer alone with me, I could tell. Rita was in her early thirties and quite pretty, with dark hair, a slightly round face and beautiful, full lips.

"Rita, we'll be fine," Anna assured her. Tonight, Anna was dressed in dark denim jeans and a blue silk blouse. Her hair was pulled back in a French braid, but a few tendrils had escaped and framed her face attractively. My fingers itched to brush it back. I wondered at my sudden desire to touch her, before quelling it.

"If you are sure," Rita said hesitantly.

"I'm sure."

"Call if you need something," Rita said, gathering her purse from a desk drawer.

"I will. Give your babies a hug from me."

"I will," Rita said. I watched Anna, who watched as Rita pulled her purse strap over a shoulder and walked toward the door. With my enhanced hearing, I could hear her footsteps echo long after she closed the condo door behind her.

"I worry about her," Anna murmured, walking toward her desk and lifting a thin stack of papers off it. "Here's the information on the disappearances," she said, handing the papers to me. "You're welcome to sit here and go over it, or you can come into the kitchen. I was about to mix a protein drink."

"A protein drink?" That puzzled me.

"According to a friend, I'm not getting enough protein," she said. "I'm vegetarian, so that can be a problem if I don't take time to eat properly."

"I'll come to the kitchen with you," I said. I was curious to see the rest of the condo, anyway.

I was led through a connecting door, which separated the business from the residence, and I found the second portion adequate. The kitchen was clean and quite neat, with very little cluttering the countertops. I watched in fascination as Anna dumped a scoop of pale powder into a blender before adding a handful of blueberries, half a banana and two cups of soymilk. The blender did its work quickly and I was thankful for that—it emitted a high-pitched whine, which I found annoying.

Anna went to the plate-glass window opposite the kitchen and stared through it at the gulf beyond while drinking her concoction. I went through the information she'd given me. The seventeen undocumented employees disappeared over a two-month period, the first occurring in late June, the most recent only five days earlier. Someone had listed the names on an original document, but I held a copy and those names had been carefully marked out.

"How am I supposed to help locate these, if I only have dates of disappearances?" I went to stand next to Anna.

"You're not here to investigate their disappearances," Anna said softly. "That's my job. Do you see those lights out there?" She tapped the window in front of us.

I did see them—lights from several offshore drilling rigs winked in the deeper waters of the gulf. I estimated they were perhaps two miles from shore. "Yes," I said. "Why?"

"Two of them are owned by Hartshorne Oil," Anna explained. "And I heard from someone that the crews on both platforms were fired today. All of them came ashore. None of them were happy. Replacement crews were sent out immediately."

"You think the replacements were undocumented?" I stared at Anna, who was still looking at the Gulf, her eyes locked on the two oil platforms.

"Or worse," she shrugged. I had no idea what she meant. "Come on, we should leave now if we're going to see Bill Gordon's wife tonight."

~

"Do you have Mrs. Gordon's address?" I asked as we climbed into my SUV.

"Yes. It's on Herring Lane—just go over the causeway toward Corpus and turn left behind the Fishing Shack. Her house is actually in the Flour Bluff area." The seat belt clicked as she buckled herself in. She'd done it quickly, before I had time to do it for her—and I'd been thinking about it. I had no way to explain it—this desire to keep her as safe as I could.

Instead, I started the engine and put the SUV in gear. Anna and I didn't talk on the drive toward Corpus Christi. She kept staring through the passenger-side window, although there wasn't much to see. On the west side of the two-lane highway was marshland covered in tall grasses, eventually ending in the ship channel.

The ship channel is a waterway separating the island from the mainland. Maintained by the Port of Corpus Christi, it services the naval ships from the local base and the commercial freighters coming into the free-trade zone. Not surprisingly, most of the trade is in petroleum products.

I didn't feel uncomfortable with Anna's silence; in fact, it helped tremendously that she wasn't a chatterbox. She wore no perfume and the scent of her body wash was muted and pleasant to my nose. I found myself glancing in her direction often, instead of keeping my eyes on the road. Eventually, I pulled my gaze away from her and concentrated on my driving.

"Is this where we turn?" I asked.

She brought her attention back to me. "Yes. Left—here," she directed. "Now, go down about four blocks, you'll see Herring Lane. Her house is third on the left."

"You've been here before?"

"Yes. I drove past yesterday, just to check things out."

I pulled into the driveway she indicated and shut off the engine.

The house was small; a white frame in desperate need of paint. The metal screen on the screen door was rusty and pulling away from its frame in the top corners. Anna knocked on the door, causing a dog in a neighbor's yard to bark.

It took Mrs. Gordon a few moments to answer the door. She wore a faded blue tank top and cutoff jeans, frayed around the bottoms. She was tall, thin and thirty-ish with a narrow face. Her hair was dyed an unnatural shade of red and smoke curled from the cigarette she held in one red-nailed hand as she opened the screen door with the other.

Anna introduced herself, then gave my name as a fellow investigator. Mrs. Gordon invited us inside, asking us to call her Kirby Lee. She had a southern accent and informed us that she and her husband were originally from Georgia, but Bill had moved them around often, looking for work. Prior to arriving in Corpus Christi, they'd lived in Oklahoma, where Bill had been employed as an oil rig hand.

Kirby Lee's living room was small and untidy. I had no desire to see her kitchen, and when she offered us a beer or soft drinks, we declined. She got a beer for herself and sat drinking and smoking while she answered our questions.

"When did you first know your husband was missing?" I asked her as gently as I could. If I'd been alone, compulsion would be placed and answers gotten quickly, but I had no desire to show that to Anna. I'd be forced to place compulsion on her as well.

"When he didn't bring his sorry ass home the next morning," Kirby Lee answered, taking a drag from her cigarette. This was the second she'd lit since we'd been there. She didn't seem upset that her husband was gone—and to her knowledge, quite possibly dead.

"Did you notify the police then?" Anna joined in.

"Yeah. They said he'd have to be gone more'n twenty-four hours before they started lookin', though." She sipped her beer. "I called 'em again the next day. They finally started to take me serious."

"Did you notify Hartshorne that he wouldn't be in to work?" Anna continued.

"Nope. Never called 'em. And they never called me. The police called and talked to somebody there, though. Then the news channels got ahold of it. I reckon the families of Bill's fishin' buddies talked to 'em."

"The families of Ray Wilson and Sam Greene?" I interjected.

"Yeah. Don't know 'em personally. Bill worked with 'em. Went fishin' with 'em. That's all I know." She finished the beer and rose to shuffle into the kitchen for another, the flip-flops she wore slapping against her heels as she walked.

Anna and I glanced quickly at one another; her eyebrows arched slightly before she turned away. Kirby Lee came back and sat across from us again.

"So, you say they called in sick to go fishing on the ship channel the night they disappeared?" I continued my questioning.

"Well, Bill said they did. They hitched the boat up to Bill's truck and drove off. That's the last I saw of any of 'em." She lit a third cigarette.

"Was Bill doing anything out of the ordinary before he disappeared?" Anna asked.

"Not that I noticed, 'course I didn't see much of him—he was either workin', fishin' or sleepin'."

"Are you employed, Kirby Lee?" I asked her.

"Not for the past six months," she replied. "Worked for a while at the grocery store over by the Fishing Shack. I could walk to work since Bill had the truck. Got into an argument with a nasty customer —got fired for it. Haven't looked for a job since then." She took another swallow of beer.

"So, how are you?" I was unable to finish the question because Anna laid her hand over mine. I'd been about to ask Kirby Lee how she was supporting herself, but Anna's touch stopped me.

"May we take a look at the garage where the boat was kept?" Anna asked instead. I barely managed to cover the confusion I felt at this odd turn.

Kirby Lee sat for a few seconds as if thinking it over, before nodding. "Sure." She led us through the kitchen, which I'd known I didn't want to see, and it was everything I'd imagined it would be—and worse. Dirty dishes were piled in the sink and strewn across every flat surface, and it reeked. I held my breath as we walked through it.

A door led from the kitchen into the attached garage. Kirby Lee flipped the light switch and we stepped down into what surely must have been the cleanest part of the house. Clearly, this was Bill Gordon's domain. Tools hung in neat rows on pegboards fastened to the walls, along with four life jackets and a shop broom. The floor was clean—what I could see of it. A new, red Honda sedan covered most of it.

"Wow. Nice car," Anna admired the automobile.

The compliment loosened Kirby Lee up. She'd tensed noticeably when Anna asked to see the garage. I'd felt a bit of fear from her as she guided us into the garage and wondered at her reaction.

"Yeah. I needed something to get around in."

"Well, you have wonderful taste. Bet it gets great mileage," Anna observed.

Kirby Lee relaxed further. "Sure does. After all this is over, I'm headin' back to Georgia. I figure after this amount of time, Bill's not gonna come back." She didn't sound upset at all.

"What do you think happened to him?" Anna asked the big question.

Kirby Lee stared at her for a few moments before she answered. "Don't know," she said coldly. "Accident, maybe. Could be the body just hasn't washed up yet." She was clearly through with us, and began to herd us into the house. We left shortly afterward. I thanked her for her assistance and let her know that we'd notify her if we found anything. She was opening another beer on the front porch as she watched us drive away.

"I don't think those boys went fishin'," Anna said in a Kirby Lee imitation. She sighed and blinked concerned hazel eyes at me.

I met her gaze briefly, then turned my attention back to the road. I didn't think they had, either, and I told her so. A man who was as fastidious about his boat and tools as Bill Gordon appeared to be wouldn't leave life jackets hanging on a peg in his garage. I also knew that Kirby Lee was correct on at least one point—Bill Gordon wouldn't be coming back. I didn't tell Anna that. There was time enough later for that information.

"I'm going to talk to some of her neighbors—I don't think Bill and Kirby Lee were fond of each other," Anna interrupted my thoughts. "I'll try to do that soon. Where are we going now?" she asked, changing the subject abruptly when I turned west on South Padre Island Drive instead of going east toward her condo.

"To meet a friend."

"Oh."

We drove westward until we reached the exit for the airport, turning off onto a side road before reaching the terminal.

"This is where the private jets are parked," Anna informed me, leaning forward to gaze out her window. She was curious but determined not to push.

"Yes, it is," I confirmed. I almost smiled. Almost.

I pulled to a stop near the hangar where the Council's private jet had landed, and climbed from the truck. Anna hesitated a moment, then exited the SUV as well. I saw Joey in the distance, talking with an airport employee. Probably setting up a date.

Joey was shorter than I, around five-seven, with reddish-blond hair that curled slightly. He kept it short. Nearly everyone found him quite attractive, and he was never without a date unless he wished to be. He turned and saw me, waved in his usual grand manner and then loped toward us. He spread his arms wide and gave me an exuberant hug.

"AAAdam!" he shouted with delight. Joey always greeted me this way. I'd learned long ago to stand still and accept the affection with stoicism.

After Joey completed his usual five-second hug, he turned to Anna. "Well, aren't you the cutest thing!" he gushed.

Anna cut her eyes toward me, then turned back to Joey. I introduced him. "Anna, this is Joey Showalter. Joey, this is Anna Madden." I completed the obligatory.

"Joseph David, it's a pleasure to meet you," Anna held out her hand. I went cold at her words. I hadn't given her Joey's middle name. She knew it anyway. Joey thought nothing of it—I'm sure he imagined I'd given her the information already. Schooling my face into the vampire mask, I resolved not to cringe as I realized this information would be passed to Xavier—against my will.

❧

"You're vegetarian?" Joey was very curious as we watched Anna consume a salad with walnuts and tiny mandarin oranges later. Joey was the one to ask Anna if she'd eaten—it hadn't crossed my mind. I watched covertly as Joey and Anna talked as if they were old friends. Joey has an easy way with people, and Anna opened up to him quickly.

"Yes. For a long time," Anna speared a tiny orange wedge and ate it with a smile.

"What made you decide to become vegetarian?" Joey asked.

"It was a necessity—I can feel the animal's death if I consume meat," Anna sighed as she lifted a forkful of greens to her mouth.

"Really? Bizarre," Joey breathed, fascinated. "Were you always a psychic?" No doubt, Xavier had briefed Joey before sending him away from London.

"I'm not psychic," Anna set down her fork. Joey's question upset her, and her answer upset me.

"So the ad—all of it is a lie?" Joey sat back in the booth we'd been given at the restaurant. He was disappointed, I could tell, and I wanted to ask why the pretense, when she repeated what she'd said to me the first night we met.

"I'm good with possibilities and absolutes," she said. "Some people might interpret that as psychic. What I have isn't psychic ability. Being psychic isn't an exact science," she added, dropping her gaze to her lap.

"You have an exact science?" Joey leaned forward, intensely curious again.

29

"As exact as you can get," she sighed. "Adam, I'm ready to go home, now."

"But you haven't finished your salad," Joey tried to convince her to stay and answer more questions. He'd made her uncomfortable, somehow, and her appetite had fled.

"Joey, no more questions. Miss Madden is tired, it's late and you and I have work to do," I cautioned.

Adam, she knew my middle name. I know you didn't tell her, Joey sent mindspeech. He'd noticed after all, just as I had. I should know better. Joey was a bit of a genius, when all was said and done. He and I had discovered (by accident) that we could mindspeak one another. That talent was a secret we both kept from my sire and the Council. I could only imagine what they might do to both of us if they learned we had the gift and deliberately kept it from them.

According to Council records, Joey's sire, whose original name was Timerius before he changed it, had walked into the sun a year after Joey was made. Joey was now fourteen years old as a vampire and had been under the Council's thumb since Timerius' death. The first time he'd been sent to assist me, I'd grumbled about it, only to learn that Joey wasn't a burden. And we'd stumbled onto the fact we could mindspeak—I'd picked up his broadcasted thoughts quickly. We'd decided to keep the information to ourselves and seldom employed mindspeech.

Anna slid out of the booth with Joey close behind. I followed swiftly as Anna walked toward the door, before recalling I hadn't paid for the meal and drinks. Joey and I had only ordered wine, claiming we weren't hungry. We weren't; both of us had fed earlier. I shouldn't have worried, Anna handed cash to our waitress on the way out. I realized she hadn't let me pay either time we'd gone to a restaurant. Somehow, that bothered me.

"I didn't mean to upset you," Joey apologized when Anna exited the SUV the moment I stopped outside her condo. She hadn't said a word on the drive to Port Aransas.

"I know," Anna hesitated with a sigh. "I have to go." I watched as she walked away from us. Joey and I waited until she'd gone inside the ground-floor entrance.

"I didn't mean to do that," Joey rubbed his forehead as I jerked the SUV into gear and drove away.

~

"I'll create a diversion while you slip in and unlock the door." Joey and I were both dressed in dark clothing for our trip to Hartshorne Oil. Roy Cheek, CEO, was our target. Actually, his office and computer were our targets for the evening. Joey could hack into almost anything, and we were going to Hartshorne Oil after a brief stop at the safe house for a change of clothing. Joey was good at providing a slight disturbance while I misted beneath doors or through keyholes. It was easy enough to let him in afterward, to gather needed information.

It didn't take long and the diversion wasn't much—Joey set off a car alarm right outside our targeted building and slipped inside once the security guard left the building to investigate. I'd misted beneath the CEO's office door before coming back to myself and unlocking the door from the inside. Joey was there quickly; I locked the door behind him.

"How unimaginative." Joey found Roy Cheek's passwords on a slip of paper taped to the underside of a desk drawer. "And here I thought it might be a challenge." He was already tapping away on Cheek's desktop computer. I waited patiently as Joey copied files onto a flash drive. "Adam, look at this." He'd found something.

Names, all of them Hispanic in origin, were listed, with a date beside them. "Joey, these dates correspond to those on a list Anna showed me." I knelt beside Joey's chair and examined names that coincided with dates employees had gone missing.

"Here," Joey pulled up another list—this one showing that each date was a date that particular employee was scheduled to be paid.

"They're going missing right before they're scheduled to be paid, probably in cash," I muttered.

"And this is probably why." Joey pointed me to a third file—a personal one, belonging to Roy Cheek. It listed gambling debts, totaling in the hundreds of thousands.

"He's hiring undocumented workers, offering to pay them in cash, getting the work out of them and then conveniently disposing of them, somehow, so he can keep the cash for gambling or paying gambling debts," I pieced it together. "But why would he kill three local residents in the middle of all this? And it still doesn't explain the bite marks or drained blood."

"Do you think the three locals found out about it, somehow?" Joey asked.

"Possibly, but Kirby Lee Gordon swears her husband went night fishing with the other two. Something about this bothers me," I rose from my kneeling position. "Copy all those files, Joey, and we'll look at them when we get to the safe house."

"You got it." Joey finished his work and pulled the flash drive out before shutting down the computer. "There. He'll never know we were here."

Joey and I wore gloves—that was standard in any investigation. Leave no trace behind—we'd been taught that early on. I allowed Joey to leave first, then locked the door from the inside and concentrated on turning to mist. Neither Cheek nor the security guard would ever know we'd been there.

"This doesn't explain the bite marks on the bodies," Xavier pointed out when I phoned him and explained what we'd found. Dawn was approaching in England and Xavier would be forced to end the conversation quickly.

"I know," I said between clenched teeth. Nearly two hundred twenty years after my turning, Xavier still treated me like an ignorant dolt.

"Then find an answer," Xavier's voice was clipped as he rang off. I cursed softly as I tossed my cell onto the kitchen counter.

"Thanks for updating the bathroom. It's less ugly now," Joey said from his chair at the tiny kitchen table. He continued to wade through records filched from Roy Cheek's computer on his laptop.

Much of Joey's luggage had been equipment. There were no bag limits on the Council's jet and the back of the SUV had been filled with Joey's things when I picked him up. A portable printer was connected to his laptop and he'd printed several lists, correlating names and dates of disappearances. I now had a more comprehensive list than the one Anna had shown me.

"You're welcome," I muttered to Joey. Xavier's words still rankled, and this wasn't the first time Joey had overheard Xavier dressing me down. I was Chief of Enforcers but in Xavier's eyes, I would always be his inept child. Joey was politely telling me, in a backhanded way, that anything Xavier said was worth ignoring.

"I know you love me," Joey teased, keeping his eyes on the laptop screen. I laughed.

Joey and I stared at the huge black man who stood inside Anna's condo when we arrived the following evening. Anna introduced him as Lion Kleander. Taller than I was by three inches and built of solid muscle, Lion handed me a look that might have made me quail if I hadn't been vampire.

"Lion is helping with the investigation," Anna informed me after inviting us to sit at her small table. "He's been asking Kirby Lee's neighbors what they saw." Joey and I sat and listened as Lion explained that a teen boy had seen someone backing Bill Gordon's boat out of the garage the night before Bill's disappearance.

"It wasn't Bill Gordon," Lion's voice was deep and even. He didn't have an accent; nevertheless, I felt (and I couldn't explain why) that English wasn't Lion's first language. "And then something changed hands between the stranger and Kirby Lee," Lion added.

"Why don't the police have this information?" I asked. It hadn't been in the report I'd been given.

"The kid who saw the transaction sneaked out to meet with friends, and he smelled of marijuana." Lion flashed a wide grin. "I got the idea he'd be in trouble with the law and his parents if he volunteered that information."

"Then how did you convince him?" Joey asked. He and I were wondering how (without compulsion) Lion had gotten the information.

"You'd be amazed what a gift card to the local electronics store will accomplish," Lion's deep chuckle rumbled in his chest.

"So, Kirby Lee may have sold her husband's boat," I worked through the information we'd been given.

"And we know, just by looking at the garage, how much he loved his boat," Anna's hazel eyes locked with mine.

"You think she sold the boat to put a down payment on her new car, because she didn't have a job. How did she get approval for the loan?" I asked. "They wouldn't have approved the loan without collateral of some kind. And when did she get the car?"

"She purchased the car two days after her husband was reported missing, so she didn't use his information to secure the loan," Lion said. "But we don't have an answer as to how she managed to buy the car."

"That may be the question we answer next," Anna sighed. "In the meantime, there's this." She shoved a newspaper in my direction.

"What's this?" I asked, lifting the paper. An article was circled in red on the front page of a Corpus Christi newspaper.

"The EPA is investigating Hartshorne Oil, that's what," Lion replied. "Seems they're oh, how do you put this—polluting everything in sight."

"They're cutting corners on keeping that shit from leaking into the air and soil," Anna muttered. I was shocked to hear profanity from her. "To save money," she added grimly.

I read the article, which stated that the Hartshorne refinery in Corpus Christi could be shut down if demands for a cleanup weren't met. Hartshorne's corporate officials were puzzled over the whole investigation and Roy Cheek, in an interview, claimed the refinery was doing everything it could to keep pollution at a minimum. At the end of the interview, Cheek accused the EPA of launching a witch-hunt and threatened to sue them.

"Cheek's trying to keep them away from the refinery," Joey muttered, reading over my shoulder. *Should we tell them what we found?* He asked mentally.

Not yet, I cautioned. *Let's see what else they have first.* I had an idea that Anna hadn't told me everything.

"I want to drive down Padre Island tonight; I caught something on the police scanner—somebody reported bits of fiberglass washing ashore. I want to make sure it isn't Bill Gordon's boat," Anna stood and stretched. As she'd been sitting next to me, I almost reached out a hand to rub her back. The urge was automatic—almost reflex. I forced my hand to stay where it was.

"I plan to go to the auto dealership and ask questions," Lion said.

"Joey, go with Lion," I ordered, making decisions quickly. "I'll go with Miss Madden to search for debris." I wanted to make sure we would receive all the information collected by these two. And I would be forced to inform Xavier that another investigator was now muddying the waters.

"May I tag along?" Joey asked Lion. I hadn't bothered to ask; I'd become used to handing orders to those who served with me.

"Sure, kid," Lion grinned. Even with Joey's vampire strength, I imagined that Lion could sweep him off his feet with a single swipe of a very large and powerful hand. I blinked away the image and turned to Anna.

"May I come with you?" I asked.

"I was hoping someone would," she offered dryly.

Padre Island National Seashore is a national park, and we paid to drive onto the beach. Past a certain point, however, you are discouraged from driving on the beach unless you have a four-wheel-drive vehicle. The sand is too loose and the environment too wild for anything else. Anna and I drove onto the loose sand of the beach, traveled down its length for nearly four miles and still had another mile to go to reach our destination when Anna finally spoke.

"Stop the car, stop the car," she shouted. I hit the brakes while the SUV slid to a stop in loose sand. Not waiting to provide an explanation, Anna unbuckled her seat belt in a blink and straddled my lap in almost as much time. Slapping my seat belt when it didn't open immediately, she jerked my door open and pulled me from the driver's seat. "Run, you overgrown oaf!" she shouted and grasping my hand, proceeded to pull me away from the vehicle. When I was reluctant to break into a trot behind her, she shouted again. "Run!" She jerked on my hand urgently. I ran, without really knowing why. We'd gotten perhaps a hundred yards from the SUV when it exploded behind us, knocking us to the sand and sending bits of metal and debris raining down around us.

CHAPTER 3

*L*ifting myself off Anna, I groaned and sat up, the explosion still ringing in my ears. Anna was slower to rise; her face was smudged with dirt and sand clung to her clothing as she brushed hair away from her face.

"How did you know," I rasped before shaking my head and turning away. The gulf waters continued to sweep the sand behind us, oblivious to the near-loss of two lives.

I sighed. Bombs will kill vampires if the explosion is near enough. Whoever had set the explosives in my SUV intended for us to die. Somehow, Anna Madden had known of it beforehand and gotten us to safety before the explosion occurred.

"I'm sorry, my ears are still not right," Anna shook her head at me.

"Give them a moment," I leaned closer to say. She nodded. I struggled to my feet, then offered her a hand. Her fingers trembled slightly as she accepted my assistance.

After a brief disagreement over what to do first, we walked the last mile (in the dark) to find bits of fiberglass washing ashore. I called Xavier while we walked; surprisingly enough, he didn't ask many questions and agreed to arrange for another rental. I knew he'd demand an accounting later, when I was alone. I didn't look forward to it.

"See this," Anna pointed to a broken piece of fiberglass that had washed ashore. "The last three numbers match those on Bill Gordon's boat."

"Why would someone destroy it after going to so much trouble to buy it?" I asked as we began our trek back to the bombed SUV.

"Because everybody is looking for it, now," Anna shrugged. We left the piece on the sand where we'd found it; the local authorities would find it in the morning. My current worry was what to do with the remains of the SUV.

"I'll take care of it," Anna sighed as we approached the wreckage. The axle was a twisted pile of metal but still intact. It was the only thing that remained in one piece. Pulling a cell from the pocket of her jeans, Anna dialed a number.

Half an hour later, the local sheriff, a park ranger and two deputies climbed from an SUV marked with Corpus Christi PD decals on each side. The sheriff was young, perhaps in his mid-thirties, and he and Anna knew one another. She hadn't wanted to contact him, I could tell, as he touched her shoulder. She carefully stepped away. Just as well; I wanted to toss him into the gulf for putting a hand on her.

"What have you done this time to piss someone off, Anna?" he asked as he and his deputies surveyed my bombed rental. The park ranger ignored us and began photographing the scene.

"Only the usual," she shrugged.

"And who is this?" The sheriff now looked in my direction.

"Someone who is helping with my current caseload," she replied. "Adam, this is Sheriff Paul Anderson," Anna made introductions. I was obligated to shake hands with him. I wanted to growl as I did so. Schooling my face, I muttered pleasantries instead.

"Plates registered to a rental company," one of the deputies held up the remains of the SUV's license plate.

"Adam rented a four-wheel-drive to drive down the beach. One might assume that whoever is targeting me has seen us together. Therefore," Anna didn't finish her sentence.

"Therefore they made sure to cover all their bases," Sheriff Anderson supplied. "Where is your car, Anna?"

"In the parking lot where it normally sits, outside my condo," she replied.

"I'll send someone out to look at it," the sheriff offered. Anna nodded a reply. Eventually, after answering numerous questions for the official report, another vehicle arrived to take us away.

"So, Anna," Sheriff Anderson said as he prepared to close Anna's door. "Were those pieces washing up on the beach parts of Bill Gordon's boat?"

"Yes," she replied and pulled the door shut herself, leaving Sheriff Anderson standing there, wearing a puzzled frown.

"Where are you going?" I demanded later, after we cleaned up inside her condo. Our officer had dropped us off there and driven away. My suit was ruined—it bore stains from seaweed and anything else littering the beach. Anna changed clothes and looked much better than I did as she collected her car keys from a bowl on the kitchen island.

"Adam, I'm going for a drink. I don't normally do that, but tonight, I need one," she snapped, hazel eyes flashing a challenge in my direction. "If you want to come, then leave that jacket behind, roll up your shirt sleeves and let's go."

"The bars are only open for another hour," I pointed out as I dumped my ruined suit coat onto a barstool.

"Then I'll have to work fast to get drunk, won't I?" she offered a tight, false smile. I left a message on Joey's cell as we walked out the door.

The Beach Bum Bar hummed with late-night business. Shoes and shirts for men were optional, and many had taken advantage. Women wore bikini tops in many instances, and most of the patrons were in various stages of inebriation when Anna and I walked in. Country music thumped from an old-fashioned jukebox in a corner and few paid attention as we made our way to the bar and slid onto barstools.

"Anna, what brings you here? I haven't seen you in a year," the bartender said, setting napkins down in front of us.

"A close call," she admitted with a sigh. "I'll have a bloody Mary. Heavy on the vodka, Lonnie."

"Got it. And you?" He turned green eyes in my direction. Lonnie had sun-bleached, short brown hair, laugh lines and was in his early forties. He'd smiled too much at Anna, in my opinion.

"I'll have the same, with only a splash of vodka. *Lonnie.*"

"Right-O, mate." Lonnie mimicked an Australian accent—badly. It wasn't the first time an American mistook my British accent for Australian. Truly, they had no ear for such. After my second century, I'd learned to ignore it. Before, it made me angry and often resulted in unnecessary compulsion and gleeful thoughts of the offender's death.

"You were serious, weren't you?" I stared as Anna drank half her bloody Mary in seconds.

"I wasn't kidding," she turned hazel eyes on me. "Alcohol destroys my shields, and I pick up all kinds of garbage. I believe you'd call that rubbish." She tipped her glass and finished off the rest of the drink, slapped the glass on the bar and nodded at Lonnie to bring her another.

Leaning against the bar, I watched her drink two more. Lonnie had been more than generous with the vodka and Anna's gaze was hazy as she stared at me.

"Adam," she motioned with a hand, asking me to move closer.

"What?" I leaned in, getting a whiff of tomato juice.

"You see that man at the end of the bar—the one with the blue shirt?" Anna hiccupped, making the corner of my mouth curl slightly.

"Yes, I noticed him earlier." I hoped she could hear me; the music was still loud inside the bar.

"You need to stop him. He's really drunk. If you don't stop him, he'll walk out of here, get in his truck and drive away. He'll kill a car full of kids two miles from here."

"What?" I now stared at Anna in alarm. "What do you expect me to do about it?" I leaned in closer to ask.

"Adam, you can do this. I know you can do this. Just keep him from driving away, all right?" Anna hiccupped again.

"I'm supposed to take you seriously when you're drunk enough to hiccup?" I leaned away to search her face.

"Please, Adam?" She begged me with her eyes and her words. Cursing under my breath and wondering what might have possessed me to even consider it, I followed the man outside when he slid off his barstool.

"You will sleep this off in your truck." I deftly plucked keys from shaking fingers as the drunk stared at me. The compulsion would hold, although he was completely pissed. Just to make sure, however, I tossed his keys into a weed-covered empty lot next door. He'd never find them in his current state.

Smelling of sweat and bourbon, the man obediently fumbled with the door of his truck. Sighing, I opened it for him, ordered him to roll down his window halfway and watched him climb inside the vehicle. As ordered, he fell asleep the moment his head dropped against the headrest. Closing the door on him, I left him snoring behind the wheel and went in search of Anna.

"Anna?" I leaned my mouth close to her ear—she'd propped her forehead against the bar.

"Adam, I'm drunk." She slurred her words.

"I know. I could smell you from the door," I teased.

"Hmmph," she muttered.

"Come on." I slapped a hundred on the bar and lifted her in a fireman's carry over my shoulder. We left the bar amid shouts and cheers.

"Here, you should drink this." I lifted a glass of water to Anna's lips. "It'll help with the headache tomorrow."

"Have some experience in the drunk department?" Anna had

trouble focusing on my face. I'd set her on the sofa inside her condo, after driving her home. She'd slept most of the way, only waking for a few moments as I carried her into the condo.

"Long ago," I admitted. It had been; the last time I recalled being drunk had been with my younger brother at his stag party in 1790, only a few weeks before I was made vampire. I was twenty-seven when I was turned and until that time, my father worried that I'd never find a wife. Justin, my younger brother by two years, married first. My father, as it turned out, was right all along.

"I'll sleep here." Anna curled up on the sofa.

"I'll find a blanket," I murmured. After rummaging through a hall closet and finding nothing except a vacuum and a few jackets, I located Anna's bedroom. An extra blanket was tucked inside a cupboard within the walk-in closet. It surprised me, that closet. I expected more clothes to be hanging there. Instead, it was barely half-full, and I counted only six pairs of shoes.

"Were you disappointed?" Anna mumbled when I draped the blanket over her.

"No, sweetheart. Your keys are on the counter. Pleasant dreams." I walked away from her and closed the condo door softly behind me. I'd called her sweetheart. Where had that come from? Squaring my shoulders, I walked toward the stairwell, turned to mist when I determined I wasn't under camera surveillance and misted to Corpus Christi.

"Somebody was out late last night," Joey sang as I opened the fridge to extract a unit of blood the following evening. I stared at Joey over the refrigerator door.

"And you weren't out late as well?" I nipped the top off the unit and drank.

"I had a date. After Lion and I got done at the car dealership, anyway. I had an excuse. What's yours?" Joey's smile was smug as he watched me drink my meal.

"I also have an excuse," I retorted after emptying the bag and tossing it in a recycle bin. "Anna and I were almost blown to bits. Somebody put a bomb on my rental."

"What?" Joey stood abruptly, his mouth open in surprise.

"Exactly what I said. Xavier is arranging for another rental, and I'm sure there was a bit of difficulty with the rental agency." I smiled at the thought of Xavier having to explain everything.

"I can get us a rental if there's a problem," Joey sat down again. He'd been working at his laptop on the tiny kitchen table.

"Go ahead. It wouldn't hurt to have two," I nodded.

"I was thinking about checking on Roy Cheek again," Joey said. "The EPA shut down the refinery earlier today."

"What?" I was now the one surprised. I strode to Joey's side and read over his shoulder. He'd pulled up the online version of the local newspaper; the headline plainly stated that Hartshorne Oil's Corpus Christi refinery had closed that afternoon. The drilling platforms were still working, however, and plans were made to transport oil to another refinery in Louisiana.

"Anna was concerned about the work crews on the platforms. Too bad they weren't shut down, too," I remarked.

"What do you have planned for tonight?" Joey asked.

"I have an appointment with the local Packmaster. He has two of the bodies stored in a walk-in freezer. I'm going to examine them and take a few photographs."

"If you don't need me, I'll do some Roy Cheek watching."

"Go ahead. Rent two vehicles—use my credit card for mine," I pulled out my wallet and tossed a card on the table.

"All right," Joey said and pulled up a car rental website. "What do you want?"

"Get another SUV with four-wheel-drive. The last one came in handy."

"Until it got bombed," Joey snickered. "How close were you when it detonated?"

"I would have been in it, if not for Anna," I muttered and raked a hand through my hair. "I need to brush my teeth and call Xavier,"

I added.

I wasn't particularly enthusiastic about having the necessary conversation with Xavier. Anna's behavior was certainly far from normal, and whether she thought of herself as psychic or not, she certainly held talents associated with that gift. I worried that Xavier might be more interested in her than I wanted him to be.

I stared at myself in the bathroom mirror before brushing my teeth. I had my father's nearly black hair and my mother's gray eyes. When I was still human, I'd had no lack of female companions—if I wanted them. My brother often teased me about it; his hair, like my mother's, was a lighter brown. I often left the flock of tittering women with him and went to the stables to see to my horses.

The last night of my human life, I'd missed a dinner with my brother and his new wife. I'd ignored the invitation, choosing to tend one of my horses when the farrier could have done the same. I often regretted that final decision. I'd been caught in the streets late that evening and my human life had ended. Three days later, I'd awakened vampire and thirsty for blood.

"Xavier, I have a meeting with the Packmaster. I'm sorry I can't explain these occurrences better to you. I can only report what I've seen and heard." Xavier kept asking questions about Anna Madden, and I'd run out of explanations.

"But do you believe her to be psychic? You know how important this information might be, Adam." Xavier's voice was curt as I flung open the door of my rental. Joey and I had run into Corpus Christi after he'd made reservations for a rental for both of us. It hadn't taken long—vampires run quite fast.

"I have no idea, Xavier. This bears greater scrutiny, I believe."

"Then watch her carefully and report everything to me."

"I will," I acquiesced reluctantly.

He ended the call, preventing me from forcing the end of the conversation. I sighed, tossed my phone onto the seat of the SUV and climbed inside. Packmaster Roger Prewitt's Seafood Shop was my destination for the evening.

~

Prewitt's shop was a squat, square building with a concrete façade on the front. In the back, where I parked the SUV, it was downright ugly. Pushing the unimaginative architecture from my mind, I slipped my keys beneath the mat, rolled the window down an inch and shut the door. A new, green Ford truck was parked close by and someone climbed out of it when I walked away from my SUV. He was werewolf; I knew by the scent.

"Roger Prewitt," he held out a hand. I took it.

The Corpus Christi Packmaster was dark-haired and dark-eyed, but many werewolves were. He was of medium height, but looked to be lean and well-muscled. I wasn't surprised; werewolf Packmasters had to be damn tough to keep their position in the Pack. According to my records, the Corpus Christi Pack had thirty-four members. Thirty-three, actually, since one of them was dead.

"Sam Greene's widow says Sam told her Bill Gordon's boat was stolen, but that Bill thought he knew where it might be," Prewitt explained as he unlocked the back door of his business. "I know the police have a different story," he added as he led me inside the dim interior.

"That almost fits other information I've gotten recently," I said. "I heard from another source that Bill Gordon's wife may have sold the boat so she could put a down payment on a car. She was already planning to leave her husband, I think, and selling his boat was the way she chose to start."

"That could be, I guess," Prewitt nodded. I followed him down a narrow hall, where he produced a second key to unlock the walk-in freezer. "We've kept the bodies here since they were found."

Both bodies were lined up on wide, wooden tables inside the freezer. I examined the bite marks on both. "This doesn't look like the work of a vampire, Packmaster," I pointed out. "These punctures are too far apart."

"I thought so, too, but I'm no expert on these things," he admitted.

"Was there any smell of blood around the bodies when they were discovered?" I asked.

"None. They were killed elsewhere; I'm certain of it. Whoever left them in the wildlife refuge was likely hoping they'd be consumed by predators or swallowed by the swamp."

"And no evidence turned up anywhere on the ship channel, where they were reported to have gone fishing?"

"Nothing. I've sent my best trackers out several times, but they had to be careful not to tread on the local authorities' toes."

"Understood."

"Can a vampire really drink somebody dry?" Prewitt's eyes met mine briefly.

"That's a common misconception," I muttered. "We can't. The best of us can only consume two or three pints at most. If a vampire wants to allow someone to bleed to death, they often slash the throat to hide fang marks. Allowing someone to bleed to death from two small punctures is a very slow process, leaving more than enough time for them to be caught in the act. With the spacing of these wounds, I'm inclined to believe this is something else," I replied.

"But what? I want to give the Grand Master an answer tonight, if I can."

"I'm sorry, but this is something I haven't seen before," I admitted. "We'll have to investigate further. I'll ask Wlodek's assistant to contact the Grand Master, and if he wishes to speak with me personally, here's my card." I handed over a card that bore only my cell number.

"I'll ask him to call," Prewitt nodded. "Do you need more time with the bodies?"

"Just a few photographs." I pulled a tiny camera from my pocket and snapped close-ups of the wounds. "There. That should do it." I pocketed the camera. "You can dispose of the bodies now, if you want."

"I'll do it tomorrow night. We'll weight the bodies and dump them twenty miles out in the gulf."

"Good enough," I agreed. Prewitt locked the freezer door behind him and I followed silently toward the back door. My cell phone rang as Prewitt opened the back door and stepped through it. All hell broke loose after that.

~

"What do you suppose is happening?" Merrill turned his gaze on Griffin, who sat inside his study. Griffin had poured wine for both of them, then sat in one of Merrill's wingback chairs, savoring the drink.

"I can't tell you. You know that already."

"There are times, brother, when I'd like to tell you to fuck the rules." Merrill leveled a piercing blue gaze on Griffin.

"We are forced to abide by the rules, Merrill. Just as you are forced to abide by those set down by the Council. All I can say is have patience."

"I have patience. More than enough patience. Patience for two thousand years, Griffin."

"I know."

~

Eight werewolves jumped us at once, and Prewitt died quickly, his throat torn out and still in human form. My claws and fangs were out and I'd already decapitated two wolves, but the others were better at strategy. My left arm was practically useless; skin and muscle hung off the bone in shreds after I'd been attacked from both sides. Both my legs were nearly in the same shape; two more wolves had attacked while I was busy killing the first two.

I'd backed against the wall of Prewitt's ugly building, to keep them from assaulting me on that side. Werewolves preferred to attack vampires in packs—it was easier to bring them down that way. I might have been able to fight off four or five, but I was severely injured and six still growled and paced about me, looking for any opportunity to strike. I was a dead vampire and I knew it; it was only a matter of time.

Four of the six stepped forward, preparing to attack when a snort came from behind them. I jerked my head up—I'd been concentrating on the enemy before me to the exclusion of everything else. What arrived surprised me greatly—most animals would run for their lives from werewolves. They recognized the danger and knew to flee. A white horse stood behind the werewolves, and I wasn't sure how or why that might be.

One of the werewolves turned and growled, intending to warn the animal away, I think. The horse's ears twitched as a hoof lifted and pawed the ground in challenge. Knowing horses as I did, I knew this one to be in its prime, with a long white mane and tail lifting in the breeze, its muscles rippling in the light provided by a nearby streetlamp. No horse was a match for a werewolf, however, and now the horse and I looked to be victims of the six surrounding me.

"Run," I whispered, my breath short. The horse shook its head and pawed the ground again. One of the werewolves growled, then leapt at the horse. Fully expecting its throat to be slashed, instead I stared in shock as the werewolf was kicked aside. It yelped once and lay still when it hit the ground. How had the horse moved so fast? I hadn't seen it, and could only imagine that my mind was playing tricks on me after I'd lost so much blood.

"Well, now," I stood straighter. "Looks like a fairer fight." Another werewolf hit the dirt after attacking the horse, and I swept out my hand, decapitating a werewolf who'd turned to watch.

"How did you know?" I woke briefly as Joey steered my rental into the safe house garage. He and the two Corpus Christi vampires had shown up as the last werewolf died. Joey had lifted me into my rental after I'd been checked briefly by Jeff, who demanded that I be taken back to the safe house quickly. The horse had disappeared the moment the last werewolf fell, leaving me with Joey and the others.

"Got a call from Anna," Joey muttered as he left the driver's side and trotted over to pull me from the vehicle. "This isn't gonna be fun for a while, Adam. They have to scrub all the werewolf saliva out of your wounds, and it's gonna hurt."

"I know." Wearily I closed my eyes as Joey lifted me easily and carried me down the steps leading into the safe house.

Werewolf saliva is poison to any vampire. Enough of it will kill a vampire if it isn't washed out of the wounds—the vampire's healing reflex will attempt to close the wound, locking the saliva inside to infect the flesh around it.

Death by werewolf saliva isn't pretty, either; I'd seen photographs of puddles of dissolving flesh after an attack by werewolves. My vision swam and I lost consciousness for a while, until Jeff began scrubbing my ripped flesh with a stiff brush and peroxide. The screams—my screams—started then.

"He's fighting us," I heard Joey's voice and footsteps. "We have to get the wounds cleaned out."

"I know. Let me help."

Anna's voice. What the fuck was she doing here? Not only did she not need to see this, it was dangerous. For us, as well as her. Plus, she now knew the location of the safe house. In my foggy consciousness, I promised myself that I'd punch Joey for bringing Anna here the moment I was able. My vision was blurry, but I recognized Anna's face and scent as she leaned over me.

"Adam, you'll feel better in a minute. I promise," she said to me. As confused as I was, I had no idea, short of staking or beheading, if anything might make me feel better.

"Hold still," she soothed and settled onto the bed beside me. Surprisingly, Anna lowered her forehead until it touched mine. What happened after that I have no words to explain. The pain fled and I was floating away. The last thing I heard before I was gone completely was Anna's voice, asking Jeff to continue his efforts.

I woke on clean sheets, my wounds almost healed. Only a few red marks remained where I'd been ripped apart—I examined my arms carefully to make sure. Vampires heal quickly, but the wounds I'd suffered should have kept me down for days. Instead, I was nearly whole and felt surprisingly good.

Sitting up in bed, I discovered the strangest sight. Anna was sitting on the floor beside my bed, her head leaning against the side of my mattress. She was asleep. I frowned.

Had she witnessed the rejuvenating process, where I'd stopped breathing as the sun came up? If she had, we could all be in trouble. I didn't want to place compulsion; somehow that felt repugnant to me, although it could prove necessary.

Another thought wriggled its way into my brain. She was there. I was there. My body was certainly awakening. Reaching out carefully so as not to startle her, I gently traced her cheek with a finger before leaning in to place a kiss. That alarmed her and it took every bit of speed I could muster to keep her from getting away from me.

"Here, now, where might you be going?" I allowed the accent to come through in my voice. Anna's green eyes were frightened, I saw that immediately as I held her tightly and pulled her body over mine.

"Adam, no," she whimpered and struggled against me.

"But your wiggling is giving me ideas." I smiled, attempting to calm her. Fear enveloped her, and I had no idea where it had come from, unless she had seen things the night before that might require compulsion.

"Adam," she dropped her forehead onto my chest and went still.

"Anna?" I stroked her hair carefully. It was fine and soft as silk against my hand. I couldn't recall the last time I'd touched any woman's hair, and I wanted to bury my nose in Anna's.

"Adam, I," she hesitated. "I don't have any good memories of sex," she added eventually before lifting her head.

"What?" I blinked at her. She was trembling, now, and that worried me.

"I just don't." She attempted to push herself away from me. My arms tightened about her in reflex.

"It was bad every time?" I studied her face—she was terrified.

"There was only once," she closed her eyes in remembered pain. "It wasn't, well, consensual."

I think it was at that moment I first vowed to find the bastard who raped her and make him dead—in a very painful way. When Anna's body shivered against mine, I wanted to kill the bastard twice. Once for raping her, and the second time for making her afraid of me.

"Then we'll take this slow," I whispered, rolling over and taking Anna with me until her body was partially beneath mine. "When you're ready, I'll love you properly and you'll have better memories. I guarantee it. For now, I'll settle for a few kisses, followed by an extremely cold shower." I breathed in her scent and nuzzled her ear before placing the first kiss at a sensitive spot beneath her earlobe.

"Adam," she began.

"Shhh, sweetheart. I'm not done kissing. This makes that nasty, cold shower more bearable." I placed another kiss on her forehead. The tip of her nose was next and then, when my mouth took hers, she closed her eyes with a sigh.

CHAPTER 4

I waited until the required cold shower was over before contacting Xavier. I had things to report and some of those things I was more than reluctant to reveal. I'd left Anna sleeping in my bed—she'd snuggled beneath the covers when I rose for the evening, and had somehow managed to fall asleep while I showered.

Joey hovered while I dialed Xavier on my phone—I knew my sire wouldn't want to hear what I had to say in an e-mail. "Xavier," he barked an answer.

"Xavier, I was attacked by eight werewolves outside the Packmaster's business in Rockport, last night," I began. "Prewitt is dead and I would have been without a bit of help from an unusual source."

"We've gotten no information from the Grand Master," Xavier began, and I could hear him tapping keys on his laptop—likely contacting Wlodek while he and I spoke.

"I imagine these were rogues, angry over the fact that one of their own seems to have been killed by a vampire," I reported dryly. Joey, who'd taken a chair across from me at the tiny kitchen table, nodded his silent agreement. "Therefore, no report would have been made to the Grand Master, since the Packmaster failed to survive the attack."

"How badly were you injured?" Xavier demanded. "Werewolves will pay for attacking one of ours."

"Xavier, we're attempting to preserve the peace, not initiate another race war," I pointed out judiciously. Joey's head bobbed emphatically at my words. "And I was severely injured. That's the other thing I have to report. I received assistance from Joey and the two local vampires, but I might not have survived had Anna Madden not called Joey and told him I was in danger."

"She knew?"

"Somehow. She phoned him and told him I needed help. He and the two vampires from Corpus Christi showed up, along with a stray horse that appeared and fought at my side."

"A stray horse?"

"Yes. It was shocking, and I assure you I wasn't hallucinating when that happened."

"What did Miss Madden say to Joey when she called him?"

"Let me ask; he's right here." I lifted an eyebrow at Joey.

"She said to get the other two and go help Adam." Joey knew Xavier would hear his answer. I blinked at Joey in shock.

"You're sure she said to get the other two and help Adam?" Xavier's voice held a command. His compulsion wouldn't work with Joey over the phone, but I was older and more experienced than Joey, and if I laid compulsion, he'd be forced to answer anyway.

"She said 'Joseph, get those other two and get your asses to Rockport. Adam is in trouble,'" he quoted.

"I see," Xavier muttered. "Out of curiosity, what color was the horse?"

"White," I replied. I couldn't see why that might make a difference, but I answered the question anyway.

"I will get back to you on this," Xavier said and ended the call. I was more than grateful that he did so; otherwise I'd have to admit that Anna was not only at the safe house in Corpus Christi, but that she knew where it was and was currently asleep in my bed.

If I were honest with myself, that's exactly where I wanted her to be.

~

"Where are you going?" I demanded when Anna walked out of my bedroom half an hour before sunrise.

"Back to my condo. I run on the beach most mornings," she said, shoving hair behind an ear and blinking at me. Joey, who'd been doing research all night and sharing information on Hartshorne Oil and Roy Cheek, CEO, stared as I blocked Anna from leaving through the only door into the safe house basement.

It was one thing that she knew where the safe house was, another to let her out again. Every vampire knew it wasn't safe to reveal a hiding place to a human unless compulsion was placed.

"Adam, it won't do a damn bit of good to do that," Anna stated flatly. "You can try, but it'll be wasted effort."

"What will be wasted effort?" I asked, but fear was already crawling up my spine. Vampires handled those who weren't susceptible to compulsion in one of two ways—the first was to attempt the turn. The second was to kill them outright.

"Adam, I'm not about to tell anybody. Let's just leave it at that, okay?" She sounded tired but resolute.

"Tell anybody what?" Joey sounded breathless. He knew, just as I did, what could happen.

"That you're vampires. I have to go. I have things to do." Anna pulled the strap of her purse more securely over a shoulder and crossed arms over her chest.

"Bloody hell," Joey muttered.

I have no idea how Anna managed to get around me and out the door before I could catch her, but she did. I can only attribute it to my shock and the ensuing immobility it created. Joey and I jerked when the door slammed behind her, followed shortly by the sound of her car's engine starting and then tires crunching on gravel as she backed out of the driveway.

"Now what?" Joey turned to me. "Daylight's in ten minutes. There's no way we can go after her."

"She saved my fucking life last night, and we're going to repay that how?" I stared back at Joey.

"I hate this," Joey muttered.

The fog was thicker over the beaches of Mustang Island. Bob Dougal stood just a few feet from where the tide swept the sand, casting his line far into the gulf water. Since he'd retired, fishing was how he occupied his time and was the reason he'd moved to the area after retirement.

His line whizzed as it flew through the air before landing in the water with a soft plop. The sun was barely clearing the horizon and he'd already been fishing for an hour. Two good-sized fish were in his cooler and he was looking to hook more.

The remains of a six-pack rested next to his beach chair; he'd brought beer with him to help pass the time. There were still two left as he crumpled his latest empty and tossed in into the tackle box.

A light fog thinned around him as the sun rose farther into the sky. Bob settled his pole into the stand he'd stuck in the sand, then went back to his chair to wait for the fish to bite again. Bending down, he pulled another beer from the plastic ring, then lifted his head when he heard a swishing in the surf.

He looked up, expecting to see a tourist wading through the water on an early-morning walk. He didn't want them to get tangled in his fishing line, so he rose from his chair to warn them away. Bob's eyes widened in surprise; instead of a tourist, a white horse walked out of the gulf toward him.

Drops of seawater hit him in the face as the horse shook its damp mane. The animal was now so close he could touch it if he wanted. Bob lifted his hand, unable to stop himself. The horse flinched away, blinking a deep-blue eye at him.

Then, before his fingers could reach its muzzle, the horse turned quickly on its hind legs and trotted south along the beach, wet sand muffling its hooves, the fog swiftly closing around it. Bob blinked a few times, wondering if he'd fallen asleep or imagined it. He dropped his gaze to the sand of the beach and watched as the few remaining hoof prints were washed away by the tide.

~

Joey and I knocked on Anna's condo door shortly after nightfall. We knew two things after waking at sunset—one, Roy Cheek had gone to Shreveport on a gambling expedition and two, we had to do something about Anna.

"Come in," Anna opened the door for us and walked away. Her movements were stiff—she expected an attack. I have no idea why, but I felt that the next few minutes might determine my fate in some way.

"Anna, we don't want to hurt you," Joey began before I could find words to speak.

"I know that." Her shoulders drooped.

Joey, what are you doing? I hissed mentally.

The right thing, he snapped back. "Anna, all we need is something— some kind of reassurance that you won't let our secret out," Joey began.

I watched her as she turned toward us, almost in slow motion. The breath caught in my throat as she actually turned—into the white horse that saved me two nights earlier.

Joey gaped before whistling and breathing the word *shapeshifter.* If there were any guarantee that we might be safe with her, it would be because she held an equally important secret. This was something I could take to Xavier, and stave off any desire he might have to convince Wlodek that her death was required.

There wasn't any way I could deliver her death—not of my own will, anyway. Joey, I knew, felt the same. Before I could stop myself, I closed the distance between us and brushed Anna's ears. Her animal snorted softly as she jerked away from me.

"We're not gonna hurt you," Joey soothed, holding out a hand.

"How do I know that?" Anna was back. She turned abruptly away from both of us and stalked toward the glass windows overlooking the gulf. "Roy Cheek went to Shreveport earlier today. Here." She handed a folder to me.

"What's this?" I took the folder and opened it. Inside lay a single photograph—of Roy Cheek. He stood next to a late model luxury car and looked ready to climb inside. Beside him was another man I didn't recognize. On the opposite side of the car, with the door also open, stood Kirby Lee Gordon.

"What the bloody hell?" I muttered.

"Lion figures she and Cheek have been, well," Anna shrugged. She was still tense, that was easy enough to see, and still frightened.

"Do you think she and Cheek may have planned her husband's disappearance?" I asked, keeping the conversation on safer ground and hoping to calm Anna at the same time. "Perhaps Cheek intended to leave the state with her? Kirby Lee told us she planned to return to Georgia."

"That would explain her vehicle purchase—if they planned this from the beginning and he helped her buy the car," Joey took the photograph from me and studied it. "But who's the other guy?"

"Somebody I thought was dead," Anna sighed. "And I don't think he's human, now."

"What does that mean?" Joey asked.

"It means I have to go to Shreveport. You're welcome to come along if you want."

I had no idea she'd chartered a private jet to Shreveport. Her bags were already packed and waiting. Joey and I held a thirty-second mental conversation before deciding to travel with her. We only needed to drop by the safe house, throw clothes in a bag and head to the airport.

"Who is this?" I asked, tapping the photograph. Joey offered to drive us to the airport in my SUV—we'd decided to park it at the airport and leave Anna's hybrid in the safe house garage. I felt strangely unfettered, leaving town with Anna and Joey while realizing I hadn't had the urge to contact Xavier even once. I'd waited patiently for Anna to tell me who the strange man in the photograph was, but she'd withheld the information—until now.

"It's Manuelo," she sighed. "Rita's cousin. I don't know how to tell her this." She'd leaned forward, poking her head between the two front seats so we could talk.

"What's wrong with him?" Joey asked. "You said before that he might not be human, but I have no idea what that means."

"I'll explain it better if we catch up with him," Anna breathed and leaned back in her seat. "If he really isn't human anymore, we'll have to kill him."

"Sweetheart?" Anna had fallen asleep in the seat beside me half an hour before we landed.

"Huh?" She blinked sleepily at me.

"Ready to get off this flying tin and chase Roy Cheek?" I offered a lazy grin. I think I'd smiled more in the last three hours than I had in the past century. Joey had certainly noticed—he'd sent mindspeech twice during the trip as he, Anna and I talked.

We'd discussed Hartshorne Oil and Cheek's gambling debts, certainly, but in between, Joey kept us entertained and made Anna laugh.

Adam's got a girlfriend, Joey's mindspeech sang in my head.

Sod off, I returned.

Somebody's grumpy.

Somebody doesn't know grumpy, I replied. *Somebody may find out very soon.*

Gotta catch me first. Joey grabbed his carry-on and raced toward the door.

"Are you going after him?" Anna asked dryly.

"There's no need," I shrugged. "The room reservations are in my name."

Joey managed to discover where Cheek was staying, so I'd reserved rooms for us at the same casino hotel. Anna wanted a separate room. I lied and told her there were only two available. All I had to do now was convince her to share my bed. And make sure nobody disturbed Joey and me while we slept during the day.

"Don't worry, I'll make sure you're safe," Anna smiled at me.

"And I'll do the same for you." Leaning in, I kissed her lightly before drawing away and unbuckling my seat belt. "I've never been to Shreveport. What might you suppose there is to do, here? Other than chasing criminally inclined polluters?"

"Do you gamble?" She blinked at me innocently.

"No."

"Watch American football?"

"Definitely no."

"Go swimming at waterparks?"

"Not in this lifetime."

"Then there's nothing to do." I laughed aloud at her reply.

"What I have is two rooms with a connecting door, with two beds in each room," the frazzled desk clerk informed us later. I didn't want that—I wanted one king-sized bed in each room. There wasn't anything I could do, unless I wanted to carry sleeping patrons out of their rooms and dump them in the hall.

"Adam, it's okay," Anna placed her hand on my arm.

"Then it'll do," I nodded to the desk clerk and handed over my credit card.

"At least it's livable," Joey muttered as we examined both rooms a short while later. Cheek hadn't chosen the best casino hotel in Shreveport, that much was evident. If the rooms hadn't been clean, I'd have gone elsewhere. Anna was exhausted, I knew that, and she hadn't eaten, either. I was about to remedy that.

"Sweetheart, there's an all-night diner downstairs," I said. "Leave the bags, I'll take you to dinner and then get you in bed. Joey and I can look for Cheek after that."

"Are you sure?" Anna turned to me, concern in her eyes.

"You're not worried for Joey and me, are you?" I pulled her against me.

"A little," she muffled against my chest.

"Don't be. We've done this before."

"Adam," she leaned her head back to look me in the eye, "you may not have done this—exactly—before. Be careful, all right?"

"I'll just expect my horse to get me out of a jam," I grinned at her.

"Schmuck," she tapped my chest as she moved away.

"Did you know that schmuck in Yiddish actually means penis?" Joey informed us.

"Joey." I glared at him. Anna laughed. I realized I enjoyed that sound very much.

"Adam's smiling," Joey grinned.

"Not for long." I schooled my face into the vampire non-expression. Joey scooted out the door as quickly as he could, making Anna laugh again.

My hand was at the small of Anna's back as we waited for a server to lead us to a table inside the diner. I wanted to put my arms around her, but resisted the urge. I'd do that later, when we had privacy.

The diner was less than half-full at three in the morning, and I'd already studied all the patrons by the time the waitress arrived to show us to an empty table. Roy Cheek wasn't there, and Joey, who'd gone to the casino to look for Cheek, hadn't found him, either. He'd sent mindspeech, informing me that he was going to check the poker room next. I told him to be careful and use compulsion sparingly.

Anna and I took seats at a booth just as Joey sent mindspeech again. *Cheek's in the poker room,* Joey reported. *With a big pile of chips in front of him. Kirby Lee and that other man are sitting outside at slot machines, but they're not playing. She looks normal and fidgety, but the man —Adam, I think there's something wrong with him.*

Why do you say that? I accepted the menu from our waitress with a nod of thanks.

He's sitting there, completely still. Not moving at all. That's just not natural.

Are they talking? Manuelo and Kirby Lee? I reminded Joey of the man's name, and briefly pondered his kinship to Rita, Anna's assistant. Something was definitely wrong, here.

He's not talking. Kirby Lee talked with a man who sat down to play the slot machine next to hers, but he got up and left after a few minutes. Are you going to tell Anna?

After we order. The waitress is hovering.

Adam, you dog. Is she pretty?

Joey, stop.

Adam's got it ba-ad, Joey responded.

Joey. I put as much sternness as I could into my reply.

I've just never seen you get interested in anybody, and we work together a lot.

There was nobody worth my interest, I returned, my mental voice cold. *Stop teasing. We have work to do.*

Yeah, but it's boring, watching these two. I don't want to be obvious about watching them, so I put money in a penny machine. I haven't won anything so far, but I'm only playing a penny per spin.

Up your bet. I'll pay you back.

You got it.

"I'll just have coffee and the special," I handed the menu back to the waitress. She was pretty, but I had no interest in her. Anna sat across from me, and that's exactly what I wanted.

"I'll have the veggie burger," Anna handed her menu back.

"Mustard or Mayo?" the waitress asked.

"Mayo. Please."

Anna and I watched as the waitress walked away, swinging her hips slightly. If she knew how many times I'd seen that suggestive walk and ignored it, she wouldn't have made the attempt.

Pulling out my cell phone, I dialed Joey. *Pretend I don't already know what's going on,* I sent as the phone rang. *This is for Anna's benefit.*

Gotcha, Joey said, before answering his phone. He proceeded to tell me everything he'd already told me. I rang off and turned to Anna.

"Joey found Cheek in the poker room, and it looks as if he's winning," I said. "He says Manuelo and Kirby Lee are sitting outside the room at slot machines, but they're not gambling. Joey says that Manuelo hasn't spoken, but Kirby Lee talked to a gambler for a while."

"Manuelo may not be able to speak," Anna muttered, turning her head away.

"How can that be?" I asked.

"He may not be human. Not anymore."

"How can that be?" I repeated. In my experience, the only way to make a human not a human but still alive was to turn him vampire, and we had a photograph of this one in daylight. That couldn't be. Besides, Joey would have scented a vampire.

Joey, I sent, *did you get any unusual scent off Manuelo?*

He's wearing cologne, but there's something odd underneath, Joey responded. *Why?*

Odd? How? Have you smelled anything like it before? What about Kirby Lee?

Kirby Lee smells human, although she's wearing perfume. Manuelo, though, I don't know what that smell is. So far, I've lost a hundred dollars of your money.

Move to a different machine, but stay close to the targets.

Will do.

The special turned out to be pot roast. In my human life, I might have enjoyed it. As a vampire, it was extremely difficult putting any part of it in my mouth. I chewed methodically, distracting myself by watching Anna and going over what Joey told me.

I couldn't tell Anna about the scent—that would betray the mindspeech I had with Joey. There wasn't any way I wanted that secret out; Wlodek would punish both of us for hiding such a desirable talent from him and the Council.

"Adam, you can stop chewing, I think that bite's done for," Anna said. She wasn't looking at me when I blinked at her, she was stacking crisps on her plate instead.

I swallowed with difficulty before nodding as she looked up at me. "I'm done, then." I shook my head at my plate—I'd gotten through half of it while I considered my current set of problems. I still hadn't heard anything from Xavier regarding the Corpus Christi Pack and the rogue werewolves.

"I'm ready whenever you are," Anna said, breaking into my thoughts.

"You only ate half your food," I pointed out.

"I could say the same for you. But I won't."

"That is much appreciated." I waved to the waitress, to bring the check. At least Anna let me pay this time.

"Sweetheart, you need to get in bed," I whispered against Anna's ear as she watched Kirby Lee and Manuelo from a distance.

"Yeah. Joey, stop playing that machine," Anna said. Joey turned to her in surprise. We'd been standing behind him for fifteen minutes, pretending to watch him play while we surreptitiously watched our targets.

"But," Joey sounded confused.

"Move to this one over here." Anna indicated another slot machine a row over. We'd still have a view of our targets, so I nodded to Joey. We moved. Anna handed Joey a hundred-dollar bill and told him to play the maximum bet. He slid the bill into the slot. He and I were both surprised when he hit a jackpot for a thousand dollars around sixty dollars in.

"I don't think Cheek is going to move from his spot as long as he's winning and as long as the casino lets him sit there and gamble," Anna said as I escorted her into the elevator a few minutes later. I'd cashed in Joey's winning ticket so he could keep gambling, and Anna and I left him there, at another machine she picked out.

"Sweetheart, you look exhausted," I murmured, pulling her against me as the elevator doors closed.

"I am tired," she admitted.

"Then you won't fight me if I do this." I leaned down to kiss her. I wasn't satisfied with a quick peck. This was a real kiss. A deep kiss. My tongue probing her mouth, exploring the scent and taste of her. She whimpered. I stroked the back of her neck gently to calm her before pulling away.

"I won't hurt you," I whispered. "You can count on that."

"Adam, I," she began, concern in her eyes as I leaned against the back wall of the elevator.

"It'll take time, sweetheart. I understand that. Just don't shut me out, all right?" I offered her a smile. "Sex is meant to be pleasurable. A consensual give-and-take between us."

"Adam, I'm not saying I don't want it. It just scares me. Brings up bad memories."

"I know. We just have to find a way to get you past that." The elevator doors opened and I ushered her out. The door to our shared room was at the end of the hall, near the stairs.

"Brush your teeth, I'll be right back," I said, once we were inside the room. After the bathroom door was closed, I walked through the connecting door into Joey's room, heading straight for the toilet. There, I eliminated the food I'd eaten earlier, rinsed out my mouth with Joey's mouthwash and went back to find Anna.

"Nice," I smothered a grin. Anna was dressed in a white T-shirt easily four sizes too big and pajama bottoms decorated with small tigers.

"Don't laugh, a friend bought these for me," she huffed, pointing at the pajama bottoms.

"We won't need this," I said, jerking the bedspread off the bed and tossing it in a corner. Those things were generally crawling with bacteria anyway.

"What if I get cold?"

"I'll send Joey to buy you a blanket."

"Adam, don't approach Cheek, all right? Just watch him for now. We need the ones behind him, in addition to him and his minions downstairs."

"What might be behind him?" I asked.

"Can we talk about this later?" She yawned, reminding me of my manners.

"Sure. Get in bed, I'll tuck you in."

The bed creaked when I sat on it. "Anna," I said, "We may argue and disagree. Most couples do. But I will never, ever, force you. I will never ask for anything you can't give. Deal?"

"Deal," she whispered.

"Good." I leaned in for a quick kiss before pulling away. "Pleasant dreams," I said, and turned out the light.

"Any change?" I took a seat beside Joey, who handed me another ticket —this one for seven-hundred-fifty dollars.

"Anna knows how to pick slot machines," Joey said, pressing the button again. "I don't understand why she isn't the richest person ever, if she can do this."

"I don't understand it either, except that she does have a serious secret to hide."

"There's that," Joey agreed. "Kirby Lee got up to visit the restroom, but that's it. Oh, and she got a soda from the cocktail waitress."

"How is Cheek getting along?"

"Still winning," Joey said. "I hear some groaning from time to time. That lets me know he's won another hand."

"I'll go stand by the door for a moment," I said. "I'll be right back." I walked away from Joey, making it almost to the door leading into the poker room as a gambler came out.

"Tell me what's going on in there," I laid compulsion. The man was middle aged, slightly overweight and looked to be a professional at gambling.

"That asshole is taking everybody's money. I don't know how, but I think he's cheating," the man said.

"How much has he won?"

"He's sitting on half a million right now. I lost fifty grand in there."

"High-stakes?"

"It is now."

"Has he said anything?"

"Not much. Talked about taking his winnings to another tournament across town. The winner there gets an automatic entry into the big tournament in Las Vegas next week."

"How long will the casino let him play?"

"Probably another four hours or so. Figure he'll quit just before that and sleep for a while. Unless he's an idiot."

"I haven't seen much evidence otherwise," I muttered.

"What?"

"Nothing. Thank you for the information. You'll forget you spoke with me."

"Sure thing." The man walked away.

"Cheek's up more than half a million," I said, taking the chair next to Joey's slot machine. "Placed compulsion on the gambler who walked out. He says the casino will probably let Cheek play for another four hours before forcing him to stop. He also says he thinks Cheek is cheating, but didn't know how he was doing it."

"I know you're already thinking this, but this is really weird. Anna isn't telling us everything, either. I really like her, Adam. I don't want to see her get hurt. What do you think the Council is going to do when this is over?"

"I'm worried about what they might do before this is over."

"You're not very reassuring, you know that?"

"You don't know Xavier as I do. Or Wlodek, for that matter."

"True. What do you think might happen?" Joey sounded worried.

"I don't want to tell you because frankly, I don't want to even consider what might come of this."

"I've never seen you this concerned about any human."

"I've never been this concerned about any human."

"Daylight in two hours," Joey said as his watched chimed softly.

"I know. I don't like this. I like it less that Anna won't have enough sleep when she rises to take watch."

Adam, Joey sent. *There's a werewolf over there. Just walked in.*

I see him. He's walking this way. He has our scent.

I'm ready, Joey responded, pulling his hands away from the slot machine and allowing his claws to slide out about an inch.

"Hello," the werewolf nodded to both of us. "I'm Daniel Carey. William Winkler, the Dallas Packmaster, asked me to meet with you."

CHAPTER 5

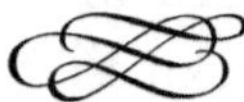

"**I** doubt he's going anywhere, at least for an hour or two," Daniel said after a quick survey of the poker room. "Winkler was contacted by the Grand Master, after he was informed of the attack by rogue members of the Corpus Christi Pack."

"They killed their Packmaster first," I said. "Should this conversation be more private? Joey can keep watch until daybreak."

"We can go to my room—if you want," Daniel offered.

"Joey," I nodded to him. Joey nodded back. I followed Daniel out of the casino.

Once the door was closed on Daniel's room, I rounded on him. "How the hell did you know where we were?" I snapped.

"I believe Wlodek offered that information to the Grand Master."

"Fucking credit cards," I muttered. I wanted to curse Xavier, too, who'd likely traced my charges for the Head of the Council, but I kept that to myself. There wasn't any need to let this wolf know of disagreements with my own kind.

"I want to know what information you have," Daniel said. "So the Dallas Packmaster and the Grand Master can be fully informed."

"It was no vampire," I said, raking fingers through my hair in frustration. "The fangs were too far apart for it to be a vampire."

"Then what was it?"

"I don't have an answer for that. Anna may, but you'll walk carefully around her or you'll regret it."

"Is that a threat?"

"Look, I'm trying to solve this, Anna has answers and we may not get them if we use force, all right?"

"I've never believed in psychics. Especially psychic detectives," Daniel growled.

"She says she's not psychic. I don't know what she is, but she knows things that I can't begin to explain."

"Then I want to meet her."

"She's sleeping right now."

"She'll be up come daylight, unless I miss my guess. We can wake her now and I can talk to her with you present, or I can wait for sunrise and ask questions by myself. You should know not to place compulsion. I have assurances from the Grand Master, through Wlodek."

"Who are you?" I countered, narrowing my eyes at him.

"Naval Intelligence," he replied. "That's my day job."

"Please tell me the U.S. Government isn't involved."

"They're not. I'm doing this as a favor to the Grand Master and the Dallas Packmaster, who runs his own investigations through Winkler Security."

"I'm familiar with Winkler Security."

"Then I don't need to explain that to you. Let's go speak with Anna Madden."

"I'm up," Anna said when Daniel and I walked through the door. Not only was she up, she was showered and dressed.

"Anna, this is," I began.

"Daniel Carey. Works for Naval Intelligence. Also a werewolf. How's that work out on full moons, Mr. Carey?" Anna frowned at him.

"Damn," Daniel muttered. "How did you know that?"

"I know plenty," Anna said, crossing arms tightly over her chest. "What killed your werewolf compatriot, Sam Greene, is known as a kapirus. They're not local. They're water demons, which are amphibians that prefer fresh water, but they'll swim in saltwater if they have to. They drink the blood of mammals. To them, the blood of a humanoid is a delicacy. I imagine a werewolf's blood is quite rich and tasty, too. Is there anything else you'd like to know?" She rounded on both of us.

"What does Roy Cheek have to do with this?" Daniel asked.

"Well, the kapirus is just a distraction," Anna said, walking to the window and peering out. Thankfully, it was still dark. That wouldn't remain true for much longer, however.

"A distraction? I don't understand," Daniel said.

"A distraction from the real enemy," Anna sighed. "Spawn. And their maker. For now, they're our real enemy."

"Spawn?" I asked the question, as Daniel registered disbelief at Anna's statement.

"Enemy spawn. I can't say the name of the enemy," She added. "Some people call spawn demons, because they choose not to say spawn or just don't know any better. Spawn are not demons. Only demons are demons. Adam, daylight is coming."

"I know." *Joey, get up here.*

On my way, he returned.

My eyes snapped open just before sunset. I wake early, nowadays, but usually my mind isn't racing at five hundred miles per hour when I wake. I barely recalled climbing into bed the night before, fully dressed because I couldn't wait any longer. I'd left Anna in the room with a werewolf, too, and I didn't like that at all.

Joey? I sent.

Huh? His reply was sleepy. I always woke first.

I'll be there in a minute. At least we were safe. Sitting up, I pushed hair off my forehead and looked around, hoping Anna had left a note for me. I found nothing. Dragging my cell from a pocket, I dialed her number. There was no reply—it went straight to voicemail. Muttering obscenities, I stood, examined my clothing, changed in the time it takes to blink twice and went to haul Joey out of bed.

~

"If he's harmed her, I guarantee the Grand Master will get an earful," I fumed as we walked to the front desk. "Do you have any messages for me?" I asked and gave the desk clerk my name.

"This," I was handed an envelope. Ripping it open, I read the following.

Cell phone dead—sorry. Daniel on trail of rogues seen in town earlier. Cheek got thrown out of hotel for being greedy and trying to stay too long. Is up at least 1 mil. Moved to Mine Town. I have rental.

Anna.

Muttering further obscenities under my breath, I hauled Joey out of the hotel to find a taxi.

"He's been here all day. I think they're about to send him packing, too. He never bothered to move into a room here," Anna said the moment Joey and I arrived. Like us, she'd sat at a slot machine, playing it now and then.

"Anna, I really want to yell at you right now," I hissed, sitting beside her.

"I know. Adam, how fast can you run?"

"What?" I was in the middle of a rant, and she wanted to know how fast I might run?

"Daniel's in trouble," she said and stood abruptly. "Cheek's not going anywhere we can't find him. I'm going. You can stay if you want." She walked swiftly away from me.

"Joey, stay," I commanded before following Anna. "I'll show you how fast I run," I grabbed Anna's arm when I caught up with her. "Where are we going?"

She named an old train bridge across from one of the casinos. The bridge was constructed of rusty iron and covered in kudzu. Once we were outside and covered by darkness, I lifted her and ran as fast as I could.

Daniel was already wolf when we arrived, and he was bleeding after fighting off four other werewolves. He was effective as a fighter, I could see that clearly, but he'd started with seven opponents. Three were dead around him as he faced the others, all of whom were in better shape.

"Well, well," I set Anna down and walked toward Daniel. "I've seen these tactics before."

Four wolves turned toward me and growled. Yes, they recognized my scent. "Aren't you operating against the Grand Master's wishes?" I asked. In my peripheral vision, I watched Anna change. I felt Daniel and I might take down this horde, but it never hurt to have backup.

"Look, either turn yourselves in or join your dead friends," I said, holding my hands away from my body and letting my claws slide out. Daniel growled at my side when the first creature stepped from the river.

Adam, watch out, Joey shouted in my mind. Somehow, he'd known to join the fight, although I hadn't told him where we were. At least fifty creatures, some of them resembling the humans they'd once been, others only bearing the faintest resemblance to anything human, fought us on the banks of the Red River. The nearby road was deserted, and we were far enough down a steep embankment that it wouldn't have mattered anyway.

This was no fight for humans, after all. The creatures only fell after we took their heads. Daniel ended up fighting off werewolves while Joey, Anna and I fought spawn. Now I knew what she was talking about. What Manuelo was turning into. What Roy Cheek had allied himself with. I needed more information, however, and I'd have to call Xavier.

If we survived.

Slicing off another head, I ducked as the creature exploded in a rain of forceful, black dust. Nothing I'd ever encountered died in such a way. Usually it was messy—a death brought about by beheading. Only a vampire left ash behind, and it didn't explode when it died.

Anna—I barely had time to glance in her direction from time to time. I didn't understand how she was doing it, but if anything got close to her, it was either kicked away or exploded. Eventually, I determined that spawn near her hind legs got kicked. Anything near her head exploded. I had no idea why, and no time at the moment to figure out the mystery.

More coming, Joey shouted mentally as another wave rolled onto the bank. Some of these—yes—they resembled trolls. Seven and eight-foot trolls. They stomped onto the wet, slippery bank, their clawed feet sinking into the mire beneath their weight and giving them traction. How the hell were we supposed to fight them?

Joey, get away, I sent. *Get to safety and let Charles and Wlodek know what we're dealing with*. With four large trolls attacking, in addition to the spawn rolling out of the river, I had no idea how any of us might survive unless we could get away.

Not leaving, Joey returned, slicing off another head. I recognized the one he'd killed—Ray Wilson's image flashed through my mind as his body exploded in a rain of black sand. Two more took his place, forcing Joey to back up. If the cavalry hadn't shown up, we'd have died, I imagine.

I almost died anyway when the giant black lion joined the fray, followed by a tall, Asian man with a long, black braid down his back and a steel blade in each hand. Yes, I stared for a moment as the lion snapped off heads with claws and jaws, while the Asian man's blades flew so fast they blurred in my vision.

The trolls? Anna took care of them. Their explosions when they died were more forceful than the smaller versions. Joey screamed when one of the explosions knocked him down. Several spawn leapt at him. I shouldn't have worried, although if my heart still worked it would have stopped then. The lion leapt to Joey's aid, grasping attacking spawn in his jaws and flinging them toward the Asian, who cut them neatly in midair, relieving them of their heads as deftly as any sushi chef cutting shrimp.

The battle took about an hour. Or perhaps it was only a few minutes, it happened so swift and furiously. Daniel's wolf, bleeding profusely, stood and panted as I surveyed the wreckage about me.

"We'll have to get rid of the werewolf bodies," Anna muttered as she walked toward me.

"Or the pieces," Joey said, gingerly toeing the head of a werewolf and watching it roll down the bank a short distance. We couldn't dump them in the river like that—they'd be found and human suspicions would be raised.

"Hold on," Daniel sighed, coming back to himself. He was naked and bleeding as he walked toward a nearby tree. Lifting a pair of jeans from a pile of clothing, he pulled a cell phone from a pocket and dialed a number. I heard clearly when William Winkler answered the phone.

"Got into a scrape with seven rogues and a shit-load of something else," Daniel reported. "Need body disposal."

"I have triangulation on your phone. I'll have somebody there in a few." The call was ended.

"Anna?" I turned to her. She was back to herself and decidedly not naked. I only thought to wonder at that then. The black lion? Like Anna, he became himself. No wonder he was called Lion. That's exactly what he was.

"Adam, you already know Lion," Anna nodded to the tall, muscular black man. "This is Dragon." She introduced the Asian man.

Does that mean? Joey asked, his sending almost breathless.

I don't have the slightest idea, I replied as I held out my hand to the man with two blades strapped to his back. What I did know is this—he only wore a black leather vest over black leather pants, and his chest and arms were covered in tattoos. Those tattoos were all red dragons.

"I brought your blade with me, just in case," Dragon nodded to Anna.

"I hope I don't need it," Anna said. "Look, I'll see to Daniel, if you want to report to Pheligar."

"Done," Dragon said. He and Lion began walking up the

embankment. I might not have admitted it to anyone right then, but those two were perhaps the most dangerous men I'd ever met in my life. At least one of them was a shapeshifter. The other? I was content to wait to learn about him.

Joey was already attempting to help with Daniel's wounds. Anna went to assist. Together, they helped Daniel dress. As a werewolf, he'd heal fast enough, and I'll admit I stared when he lifted a pistol off the ground and stuffed it into the back of his jeans.

"Didn't want to call attention to the fight with gunshots," he admitted as he walked stiffly in my direction. "Got information yesterday from the human wife of one of the rogues you killed in Corpus, Chessman," he nodded wearily at me.

"What information is that?" I asked.

"The rogues who attacked you were associated with a Pack in Mexico. They've been running a little side business, hauling undocumented immigrants into Texas for a fee, after promising them work with Roy Cheek and Hartshorne Oil. Winkler's sent some of his bunch in that direction, but Juarez is no place for anybody on the right side of the law. I figure these were sent to kill me after I pulled the confession out of the human woman." I watched as blood soaked through his shirt from numerous wounds and shook my head.

"That's fucked up," Joey mumbled. "Who knows how many paid to get into the country to work for Cheek, and then ended up dead?"

"I need to get back to my truck," Daniel said, painfully rotating an arm to loosen it.

"You're coming with us," Anna insisted. "I'll clean out those wounds and you can sleep in Joey's room. We'll drive you to the casino. Joey can take the extra bed in our room, to give you privacy."

"Sounds good," Daniel nodded. "My truck is parked a quarter of a mile south of here, just off the road." He flexed his shoulder again, which popped audibly.

"I'll give you a lift there," Anna said and turned to her alter ego. Daniel barely blinked when I tossed him onto her back, although that was a place I longed to be. I hadn't been riding in a long time.

~

"Look, I can't repay this debt," Daniel said later after Anna and Joey finished cleaning his wounds and putting him to bed.

"What debt?" Anna said. "You owe me nothing. I'm just helping a friend."

"Then I thank you for that," he muttered. Anna and Joey followed me through the connecting door and I shut it quietly between us.

"Sweetheart, go to bed," I said. "I don't think you've slept four hours out of the last forty-eight."

"What about Roy Cheek?" she asked.

"Joey and I have time to change clothes and check on the bastard. Then we'll come back here and go to bed. You'll stay in bed. That's an order."

"Really?"

"As much as I can order," I said, pulling her against me. All of us looked as if we'd fought a war, which in reality, we probably had. At least the opening battle of it, and if that was any indication, we had a very hard road ahead of us.

"I want a bath first," she muffled against my chest.

"I do, too. Want to shower together?"

"Hey," Joey said. "I'm right here."

"You will not be offended. Admit it," I said.

"Nah. Just wanted to tease you."

"Adam," Anna sighed.

"Come on, it's just a shower. You're tired. It'll save time."

"Sure."

I deliberately misinterpreted her sarcasm. Lifting her quickly, I carried her into the bathroom and shut the door. Before she could complain, I'd razored stained and torn clothing off her with shortened claws before tossing the fabric into the bin. She was just as perfect as I imagined—I watched her shamelessly while I undressed. After a few moments of attempting to cover up, she gave up with a sigh and turned on the taps.

The shower took longer than it should have, but there was no sex, just a lot of touching as I washed her body thoroughly.

"Adam, that's not normal," Anna blinked at my erection.

"Most women have no complaints," I said. "It'll fit, and I'll make sure it feels good, too. Now, I get to kiss these before we get out." I lifted her, encouraged her to wrap her legs around my waist and kissed both nipples. We were so close, but she wasn't ready.

I dried her off, too, before tending to myself. "Want to touch?" I still sported an erection—I couldn't convince my body to behave.

"Adam."

"Come on." I took her hand. She didn't protest when I wrapped her fingers around my penis. I didn't complain either, when her hand moved. "Like my John Thomas, do you?" I grinned.

"This is so soft—the skin," she touched the head.

"Meant to be. My body, inside yours. Treating it as it should be treated. Not meant to harm," I explained. "Gentle, when necessary. Rougher if requested." I grinned again.

"What about you? What do you want?" She took her hand away. I wanted to protest at the loss of warmth. I didn't.

"I'll let you know what I want. If you don't want that, it'll be all right."

"That doesn't embarrass you?"

"Sweetheart, it is extremely difficult to embarrass a vampire more than one hundred years old."

"I'm going to bed." I watched as she slipped on the oversized T-shirt, which hung halfway to her knees.

"No bottoms," I pleaded.

"Fine." She walked out of the bathroom, the neck of the T sliding off a shoulder. I turned and grinned at myself in the mirror before stalking after her, wearing nothing. Joey had seen me naked before. Now, Anna had, too. I intended to sleep that way, when Joey and I returned after checking on Cheek.

Anna didn't say a word as I sat on the side of the bed to dress.

"Go to sleep, baby," I breathed against her temple before leaving the room. Joey had taken a shower in record time while I dressed, and he followed, closing the door softly behind us.

~

Cheek hadn't moved from his seat at the poker table, so Joey and I left after half an hour. We had less than an hour to get back to our hotel, and I wanted to savor being in bed with Anna as long as possible before the rejuvenating sleep claimed me.

Joey checked on Daniel while I undressed and slid into bed. Likely, I'd go to sleep with a smile on my face. Leaning in, I pulled Anna against me and covered as much of her body with mine as I could. This was the way any vampire protected his mate. An enemy would be forced to kill me to get to her.

~

"I hear from the werewolves that you were attacked, and still no word from you? Adam, it has been three nights with no contact." Xavier was furious. "Wlodek expects a report as well. What have you been doing with your time? Tell me. Immediately."

I stared at my cell phone before ending the call and tossing the infernal device onto the bed. I'd awakened to find Anna missing from my embrace. At least she'd left a note this time.

Gone with Daniel to meet with local pack, the message read. I'd crumpled it in my hand—if that werewolf thought to move in on my territory, he'd have a fight on his hands. My cell phone rang again. This time, it was Charles calling.

"Charles?" I snapped.

"I hear you had a bit of a problem." Charles was always smoothly unrattled. *About everything.*

"We did. We're not hurt, thanks to Anna and a werewolf sent by the Grand Master. Anna says these things that attacked us are spawn, whatever that means, and that the creature that bit Sam Greene and the others is a type of water demon called a kapirus."

"We haven't been attacked by spawn in centuries," Wlodek said. He'd been listening to our conversation. "What did they look like?"

"They came out of the water to attack us. Some of them looked human. Others had darker, scalier skin. None of them spoke; they just attacked. We had to take their heads to kill them."

Wlodek cursed in Greek, then. I only understood half his words. "Are there more of them?" he eventually asked in English.

"I assume so, and these appeared to be allied with several rogue werewolves. We were fighting them by the river when the spawn appeared."

"I've not heard of a kapirus before," Wlodek muttered.

"Anna says they're not local."

"What does that mean?"

"I don't know, and she isn't here to ask at the moment, Honored One."

"I hear she's a shapeshifter. The Grand Master's report says she's a white horse. Is that correct?"

"Yes. And quite adept at fighting rogue werewolves as well as spawn."

"I have no idea how a shapeshifter might know of these things—no shapeshifter is old enough to have knowledge of them."

I found myself wondering at Wlodek's words—he was old enough to recall spawn. I didn't push for answers, however. It was inevitably a mistake to push the Head of the Council on anything.

"How well does her psychic ability work?" Wlodek asked. I froze.

"She says she isn't psychic," I replied.

"Then what does she do? She seems to know too damn much for her own good."

"She says she's good with possibilities and absolutes." I repeated Anna's words.

"What in the name of creation is that supposed to mean?"

"I don't know, Honored One."

"She certainly knows too much," another voice spoke. Wlodek had our conversation on speaker, and if I'd thought I was cold earlier, this froze my very blood and marrow. The Seer was there. Saxom. The one I trusted least had heard everything I'd said.

"What do you suggest?" Wlodek asked. It took a moment to realize he wasn't asking me.

"I suggest we attempt to turn her," Saxom replied. He sounded almost gleeful to me, and I didn't like that at all. "Her talents would enhance our race, don't you agree? Xavier says she managed to help Adam heal after the attack by rogue werewolves, and this ability—whatever it is—to know things would be an obvious advantage for us. Adam can bring her to us, and we can make the attempt in a safe place."

"And if the turn isn't successful? You know this will likely fail," Wlodek responded.

"It is inevitable, don't you think? As you said, Honored One, she knows too much. I suggest we wait to make the attempt. If my vision is correct, then Chessman and Showalter should continue to follow this Cheek person. I see that there will be a trip to Las Vegas very soon. After their return to Corpus Christi, should they survive, then we consider the appropriate time to bring her here and make the attempt."

Saxom's ability to see into the future at times had earned him the title of Seer among the vampire race. He was employing his ability now, evidently.

"Who will do this? Chessman has no experience at turning." They spoke of me as if I weren't listening to their conversation.

"Chessman's sire has much experience," Saxom pointed out. My breath caught. Not only were they intending to gamble with Anna's life, they wanted Xavier to do it. I wanted to explode. Shout at the Head of the Council and his second-in-command. If Anna survived, my sire would have control of her. Female vampires, unless they were extremely old and powerful, were few and shut away from the rest of the vampire world. Xavier would achieve a coup if he had one of his own.

Not only did I despise Xavier as my sire, I'd despise him more for destroying Anna's life for the benefit of the vampire race. He'd take full credit, too, I had no doubt. Somehow, I had to protect Anna. With my sire's involvement, I had no idea how that might be accomplished.

"Adam, you will keep this information from her, do you hear?" Wlodek commanded.

"Yes, Honored One." Frantically, I searched my brain for a way to disobey that command. There had to be something. Some way to save her.

"Keep me and your sire informed." Wlodek ended the call.

"That's fucked up," Joey said. He was sitting cross-legged on his bed, blinking at me. He'd heard the entire conversation.

"Fucked up sounds mild compared to what this really is," I growled. "Get dressed. We need to find Anna and check on Roy Cheek."

~

"Adam, you know we can't let them do this." Joey's gaze was pointed toward the lights on the bridge we crossed as we drove toward Cheek's newest gambling spot.

"Joey, I want you to stay out of this. If anybody goes down for trying to protect her, I don't want it to be you."

"I think there may be a way. I can't tell you right now, but hear me out when the time comes, all right?"

"I promise to hear you out. Will you promise to stay out of it if I don't think it's a good idea?"

"Deal. I don't like it, but we don't have much choice." He hunched his shoulders, and I knew he considered what might happen—all I had to do is lay compulsion and he'd be forced to obey me. I didn't like doing that unless there was no other option; Joey was like a son to me.

Joey's cell rang as I prepared to pull into the parking garage at the Casino. Anna was calling. "Joey," she said, "Cheek's moved to the Sea Serpent Casino, where the tournament is being held."

"On our way," Joey said. "Anything else?"

"The local pack is hunting spawn, but they haven't found anything.

I think we cleared out what they sent after us, but that doesn't mean there won't be more, later."

"Anna, can you hear me?" I asked.

"I can hear you."

"Good. Where is Daniel now?"

"With the local Packmaster. They've pulled in some of the Baton Rouge pack to help with the hunt. If they don't find anything here, they'll wait for the Grand Master's response on Daniel's request to send some to Corpus Christi. The Pack there is in flux, since several members went rogue and their Packmaster is dead."

"Has there been a challenge? Is the Second still alive?"

"He isn't—I believe you killed him in Rockport. It's my guess he's the one who took the Packmaster down. We have other problems, too. Looks like there's a splinter faction in the werewolf community that's trying to destroy the peace treaty, so they're putting out information that a vampire killed one of theirs, and then another vampire—you— killed several others. The Grand Master is having a hard time getting the proper information out to combat the rumors."

I cursed. In Spanish and Italian. "I agree," Anna said when I was done. "We need to find the kapirus, I think. This whole thing is going viral, and not in a good way. It's driving a wedge into the werewolf community, and you probably realize what the repercussions might be if that happens."

"It means their civil war will likely be televised," Joey muttered. "It'll only be a matter of time before the vamps and shifters are outed, too."

"Exactly. Humans will panic and nobody will be safe."

"Anna, do you have Cheek in your sights?" I asked, changing the subject.

"Yes. Manuelo and Kirby Lee, too. Manuelo hasn't started the change, and that's a good thing."

"The change?"

"The change the spawn infection causes. They retain their human appearance for around two or three weeks. After that, the skin sloughs away, leaving leathery, scaly skin behind. Just before that happens, though, they get hungry. They'll eat anything humanoid in sight."

"There's a feeding frenzy?" Joey asked. "Like sharks?"

"Similar," Anna agreed.

"I'm pulling into the casino parking garage," I interrupted. "We'll discuss this later. When does the tournament start?"

"Tomorrow night. I figure Cheek has to stop gambling soon, to sleep and shower before it starts."

"Has he lost?"

"Very little. It's as if he's playing smarter than usual, losing some here and there so the casino won't be so suspicious."

"This isn't the sharpest knife in the drawer," Joey muttered while I parked.

"I agree," Anna said.

"Anna, we'll see you in a few." I reached over and tapped Joey's phone, ending the call. "Joey, don't even think about that discussion I had with Wlodek while we're around her, do you hear me?"

"This is scary," Joey murmured, stuffing the phone in a pocket of his jeans.

"We'll get through this." I hugged him and discovered he was trembling slightly. We were both beginning to care for Anna, and I had no idea where that road would lead.

Thanks for the hug. I needed it, Joey sent as we stepped out of the rental.

I know. I crooked an elbow around his neck and hugged him again as we walked toward the parking garage elevator.

"Sweetheart?" I leaned down to give Anna a kiss. She was sitting at the usual slot machine, playing now and then. I was surprised Kirby Lee never glanced in our direction. She kept her eyes pointed toward the poker room, now, whereas she'd at least looked about her the first two nights.

"She's exhausted, but Cheek probably wants her out here to stand guard," Anna said, pulling my thoughts away with ease. That sent a shiver of fear down my spine, but I schooled my face and hid my concern.

"So he doesn't sleep, she doesn't sleep? What about Manuelo?" Joey asked.

"They do what they're told. They really don't need a lot of sleep anyway—the viral reaction is a little on the hyperactive side," Anna said.

"Then why force Kirby Lee to stay up?"

"Because Cheek doesn't trust what Manuelo is," she informed me.

"An uneasy truce?" I asked.

"You could say that."

"It's logical," Joey agreed. "I wouldn't trust that, either, after seeing what we fought last night."

"He's greedy," Anna said. "This is his way of getting what he wants, and their way to get what they want."

"What do they want?" Joey asked.

"Everything," Anna shrugged. "Earth will be nothing more than a living buffet if things go their way."

"Do they eat vampires?"

"No. They'll kill you if they can. After all, they're rivals for the same food source."

"Will they eat all the humans?"

"Yes and no. They'll turn some to build up their army, but if they succeed, Earth will be overrun. Look, Cheek's leaving."

He was. I studied him covertly as he collected Kirby Lee and Manuelo before heading toward the door. The hotel was connected to the casino, and I assumed he'd already reserved a room.

"He does have a room—on the third floor," Anna confirmed.

"Should we take him while he's asleep?" Joey asked.

"No. He's our connection to the kapirus—and the bigger and badder," Anna said.

"There's bigger and badder?" Joey's voice quavered.

"There's always bigger and badder," Anna said. "Somebody brought the spawn here—or made them after he got here."

"How do we handle anything worse than what we saw last night?" Joey sounded worried.

"Let me deal with it," Anna said simply. "Let's go. Cheek's going to sleep the rest of the night and half the day tomorrow, before he has to get up, eat and get ready for the tournament."

"Feel like going to a water park?" I teased, attempting to lighten the mood.

"No. I think we need to pay Daniel's way into the poker tournament," she said.

~

"I've been known to play poker," Daniel said later, after learning I'd paid his ten-thousand-dollar entry fee in the high-stakes poker tournament. "This will get us a front row seat to see how Cheek is cheating."

"You're convinced he's cheating?"

"He's cheating. This guy is known for losing. You don't have a winning streak like this without having some sort of edge."

"I'm surprised this casino allowed him to keep gambling, then," I said.

"Oh, they're looking," Anna interjected. "They just can't find anything. To them, he looks clean."

"How do you think he's cheating, then?" I asked her.

"Adam, I don't want to speculate at this time."

"But you do have suspicions?"

"Of course I do. I just can't explain them right now. It's too dangerous."

We were in a hotel room at the Sea Serpent, on the second floor. Surprisingly, Anna reserved one room for us, and an adjoining room for Joey. At least she didn't mind sleeping with me—our room held a king-sized bed.

Daniel took a room across the hall; I still watched him suspiciously from time to time, although he and Anna didn't appear to have any interest in one another—except a professional one.

"I'm going to bed; I need to sleep for a while," Anna announced. "Cheek isn't going anywhere, and his allies know that. They'll probably lie low while he's down."

"What about the ones we killed? Won't the ones who sent them be looking for us?" Joey asked.

"They expect some resistance," Anna said. "And the loss of a few of their youngest is of little concern. They likely believe vampires, werewolves and shapeshifters took down what they sent to help the rogue wolves take Daniel. Those things would have stayed in the water if we hadn't shown up to help. Those last four rogues could have taken Daniel down."

"They would have," Daniel admitted reluctantly. "I can handle four, maybe five, but seven was out of my league. The Grand Master sends his thanks, by the way."

"Tell him he's welcome," I nodded to Daniel.

"Look, you guys talk if you want, I'm getting into my jammies and going to bed." Anna walked toward the bathroom.

"I need sleep, too," Daniel agreed.

"Joey and I will keep an eye on things," I said. "We'll wake you if anything important happens."

"Thanks." Daniel headed toward the door. "You're good in a fight—all of you," he acknowledged. We watched him walk through the door and close it behind him. It was becoming harder and harder not to like the werewolf, and I had little love for most of that race. Things were changing—I realized that. I just had no idea how many more changes might lie in wait.

CHAPTER 6

"Anna?" I nuzzled her cheek and neck when I crawled into bed just before daylight. I received a sleepy *hmmm?* in response.

"We really need to get on the same schedule," I murmured before kissing the side of her neck and settling onto my back. While I had time—and energy—to fuck, Anna was still exhausted from too little sleep. She and Daniel would have to rise after a while and prepare for their part of this investigation.

Stay safe, I sent to her, knowing she wouldn't hear my mindspeech.

"Okay," she mumbled before rolling over and curling into a ball. I only wondered at that for a moment—she hadn't heard me, she'd merely read me as she usually did. I stared at the ceiling after that until daybreak forced my eyes closed.

"What is happening?" Xavier demanded the moment I answered my cell phone.

"The werewolf is doing well in the tournament, but Cheek is still ahead. Anna is inside, in the audience," I replied, working to keep the contempt from my voice.

"Keep me apprised." The call ended abruptly.

"He really is an asshole," Joey said beside me. We sat in the sports bar, watching the tournament on one of several large screens there. Only a small audience was allowed inside the ballroom where the tournament was held, and all the seats were full. Once in a while, cameras panned the audience. Kirby Lee and Manuelo were also there.

Joey and I had drinks in front of us, but neither of us bothered to pretend we were drinking. "Anna was right to enter Daniel in the tournament," Joey nodded. "Looks like you'll get your money back. He's in third place at the moment."

"And still no clue as to how Cheek is cheating," I muttered. The tournament was down to the last four players, and the fourth was almost out. Third place was a guaranteed fifty thousand, so Joey was probably right. He usually was whenever math or numbers were involved.

"Maybe Anna or Daniel knows something," Joey sighed. "Looks like we'll be going to Vegas, just like the pruney old bastard said."

"Ask Anna to pick out a machine there for you to play," I ruffled his hair. "I hear they may pay better."

"There's a thought," Joey brightened momentarily. "I've never been to Vegas."

"I haven't been in fifty-seven years," I said. "I hear it's changed since then."

"That was before I was born," Joey leaned his chin on his arms while keeping his eyes on the screen in front of us. "There on vacation?"

"Assignment," I said. "A younger vamp thought to make money the easy way—by taking it from criminals. He was dangerously close to exposing us, in addition to murdering his way through crime bosses."

"Interesting. You'll have to tell me that story, sometime."

"Not much to tell. Took him down the second night I was there."

"You're tough to fool," Joey said.

"Except in this case," I replied. "I still don't know what the hell is going on. I've never seen spawn before, but Wlodek and some of the others have. It puzzles me that they haven't bothered to tell me about them until now—when they show up again."

"I have resources. Maybe I can get some information for you," Joey offered.

"If you can, without raising suspicions," I said.

"I'll work on it. Look, number four is out."

The fourth-place player was headed for the door—he'd lost while Joey and I talked. He still made money—the top ten finishers did. He'd be interviewed by a television crew before he got away, just as the rest of them would.

"I wonder where this kapirus thing is, and how often it eats," Joey said. "If it eats often, then more people ought to be disappearing."

"A fair point," I agreed. "We'll have to ask Anna to see if she knows."

"What did you want to ask Anna?" Lion took a seat next to Joey and slapped him hard on the back while grinning hugely.

"Uh, how often a kapirus eats," Joey said, offering Lion an answering grin. Lion's slap on the back was nothing to a vampire, and he likely knew that.

"They eat roughly once every two or three weeks. That means it won't be long before this one goes hunting again. Unless the enemy has made arrangements to feed it—if that happens, look for it to be an enemy of the enemy, and possibly one of our warm-blooded allies."

"You mean they may have trapped someone already, to feed to that thing?"

"Easy way to torture them and get rid of them too," Lion shrugged.

"How do you know all these things? I hear that no shapeshifter is old enough to recall the last time spawn were here."

"I'm not surprised the vamps would see things that way," Lion shook his head. "At times, they can be just as shortsighted as anybody else. No offense meant, of course."

"None taken."

"I see our werewolf is doing well," Lion turned to the monitor on the opposite wall.

"Daniel's doing really well. If things were normal, he'd probably be winning," Joey said.

"Things are definitely not normal, kid," Lion said.

"Where do you think the kapirus is?" I asked.

"No telling. Could be still in the Corpus area, but my guess is he'll want fresh water. Farther inland, there are lakes, plus the river in San Antonio. He can stay out of water for a few hours at a time, but doesn't like it. Those things prefer to lounge in soft, freshwater mud instead of sand and salt water."

"Anna says they're not local," Joey offered.

"They're not."

"How not local?"

"As in not from Earth not local," Lion explained.

"You're joking, aren't you?" Joey said.

"No."

Adam, the hair on my arms is standing up, Joey sent.

Mine, too, I replied. *Do you think he's telling the truth?*

"My kind can't lie," Lion said. "We may make origami out of the truth, but we don't lie." That statement made the hair on the back of my neck rise. "Look, if you know what's good for you, you'll take care of our girl in there." The camera panned the audience for a moment, and passed over Anna. "No matter what," Lion added. With that, he rose and walked out of the sports bar.

"What the hell is that supposed to mean?" Joey asked.

"I don't know, but I intend to keep her as safe as I can."

"I want to, too."

"Look, the guy in second place is going all in. Adam, Daniel has a better hand." Joey almost bounced in his seat.

"You think Daniel might fold?" I gripped the sleeve of Joey's shirt as we watched the tension build on the screen.

"He's not folding," Joey whispered in excitement. "Oh my gosh, Daniel's gonna move into second place." He would, Cheek had folded early and waited for the outcome of this hand. The current second-place player had a full house, aces over queens. He thought he'd win. Daniel held four tens.

"Look, they're laying out their cards. He won. Daniel won." Joey's eyes widened as he grinned at me. "He'll make a hundred grand off this."

"You're assuming Cheek will win?"

"Yeah." Joey deflated. "I figure he will, because he's cheating. Daniel would take him, otherwise."

"He certainly has a feel for the game. Likely a scent, too."

"I always heard dogs could smell fear," Joey agreed.

"Perhaps our werewolf there has an especially sensitive nose."

"That doesn't matter, unless you have a hand to back it up and know how to play the game," Joey countered.

"There's my genius." I ruffled his hair.

"Oh, sure. The genius who doesn't know what the hell is going on," Joey's shoulders slumped. "The closest I could come when I researched kapirus is a kappa, and that's a mythical creature from Japan that responds to politeness. I get the idea that this kapirus thing won't bother with being polite."

"Seems he can drain more than one human at a time, too," I acknowledged. "That means he's rather on the large side."

"You're not making me feel better about it," Joey mumbled. "He took out a werewolf and two humans. You know the werewolf would be stronger and better able to protect himself, but he died, just like the others."

"You killed Ray Wilson," I pointed out. "Although he was one of those things we fought on the riverbank, so he wasn't human."

"I don't want to tell Wlodek that," Joey shivered.

"Let's shelve that topic for now," I suggested, turning back to the monitor. Another hand was dealt, and Roy Cheek placed a bet.

"I knew he'd win," Daniel said later, handing me a stack of U.S. currency. He'd taken the hundred thousand second-place prize. "That's my buy-in—to pay you back."

"Thanks." I handed the money to Joey, who forgot to breathe for a moment before shoving it into a pocket. "Where's Anna?"

"Here." Anna walked up behind me and tapped me on the shoulder. "Cheek is covered in reporters and casino security right now, getting his picture taken. He'll get a round-trip ticket to Las Vegas, along with the winnings and the automatic entry into the tournament there next week."

"You think he'll go back to Corpus?" Daniel asked.

"I doubt it. I think he'll be on the first plane that can carry him to Nevada," Anna shook her head. "He'll gamble and have a high old time before the tournament starts in a week."

"Should we follow him?" Joey asked, moving to give Anna a hug. "We missed you."

"Joey, I was only away from you for one night," Anna hugged him back.

"Yeah. But it was a whole night," Joey whined. "And we have to go to bed soon."

"What's the move from the locals?" I turned to Daniel.

"I need to check in with them," he replied. "And with Winkler and the Grand Master. You may be out for the day by the time I hear back."

"Then we'll talk at sundown," I said. "Joey, Anna needs something to eat. I think we have time for that before bed." I offered Daniel a nod, took Anna's elbow and steered her toward the nearest twenty-four-hour restaurant in the casino.

"I'm almost too tired to eat," Anna sighed as she studied the menu. "They don't even have a veggie burger here. I guess it's French fries or a baked potato and salad."

"You always have trouble finding something to eat?" Joey asked.

"A lot of the time, yes," she agreed. "They even have bacon in their green beans." She flopped the menu on the tabletop with a sigh. "I need to find a place that sells protein powder."

"Do we need to follow our spawn-loving CEO to Vegas?" Joey asked, changing the subject.

"Yeah. I don't have enough clothes with me," Anna buried her face against my shoulder.

"I have money," Joey grinned, patting his pocket.

"Joey, that's for your savings account," I countered. "And for showing up to help the other night. Use my credit card for anything Anna needs."

"I can buy for myself," Anna leaned away from me.

"And spoil my shopping spree? No way," Joey fussed. "We can shop in Vegas. That'll be awesome."

"Use my card," I said, pulling Anna close again. "I owe her my life."

"Adam, you don't owe me anything," Anna said later when I lay beside her on our bed and settled her in the crook of my arm.

"I beg to differ." Leaning in, I kissed her. Then kissed her a second time. The fucking sun rose at that moment and that's all I remembered until nightfall.

"Cheek is already in Las Vegas," Anna said. She'd walked back in the room shortly after I showered and dressed. I wouldn't have been as calm as I was if she hadn't left a note for me on her side of the bed.

She was learning. I smiled at her, although her words weren't what elicited my response. "I'll make reservations," I said.

"Already done." She handed an envelope to me. It contained flight information for her, Joey and me. "We have to be at the airport in an hour, and we change flights in Dallas."

"Not a problem," I said. "I just have to throw everything back in my carry-all."

Half an hour later, we were on our way to the airport. Joey sat in the back seat of the rental, his laptop bag clutched possessively in his arms. I'd discovered years ago that he really had no care for his clothing—it was his technology he clung to the tightest.

"Pack all your cords?" I teased, giving him a quick glance over my shoulder.

"I have my cords, and extras," Joey grinned. He was excited to go to Las Vegas. I'll admit I was happy to go anywhere with Anna, but there was a job to do.

I'd wakened earlier to an e-mail from Xavier, instructing me to be more forthcoming with information on Anna. Evidently, he'd heard from Wlodek and was looking forward to gambling with Anna's life. The bastard wanted photographs, too. I'd ground my teeth over that bit of information.

After dropping off the rental, I took Anna's bag, hooked mine onto it and pulled it toward the terminal. We had a small carrier for the flight to Dallas, where we'd connect with a larger carrier for the trip to Las Vegas. I hated small planes, but there'd been little choice at such short notice.

"It's a short flight from here to Dallas," Anna said as Daniel walked up beside us, a duffle draped over a shoulder.

"You coming with us?" Joey asked.

Stop staring at his ass, I ordered sternly.

I can't help it, Joey whined back.

"Stopping in Dallas to speak with the Packmaster, then likely heading back to Corpus to quell a rebellion within the ranks."

"Why don't you go for Packmaster?" Joey asked.

"Corpus isn't my desired destination," Daniel said. "I like it better farther north, with cooler temperatures. I can stay as long as I'm stationed there, but that could change, too."

"Seconds aren't held to such stringent rules," Anna offered quietly.

"I'll consider that," Daniel grinned. "Thanks for adding me to the reservation list," he told her. "Saved me the trouble."

"My pleasure," Anna replied.

The trip to Dallas was understandably turbulent, in a smaller plane that barely held Joey's laptop case in the overhead bin. We said good-bye to Daniel at the Dallas airport and took the tram to another terminal, where a much larger plane waited for us. We'd arrive in Las Vegas shortly after midnight, local time, which meant a longer night for Joey and me.

"Can you sleep on the plane?" I asked as I pulled Anna's seat belt around her and buckled it.

"It's not easy, but I can try," she said. "I really am tired, but I'd like to track down Cheek and company before I go to bed in Vegas."

"I just got information from the UK—there's a place waiting for us in Las Vegas," I said. Charles had sent the combinations to get into a safe house in the area.

"Good. I didn't know where you wanted to stay, so I didn't make reservations," Anna covered a yawn.

"I want you with me, that's what I want," I nuzzled her ear. "Want me to order anything from the flight attendant for you?"

"Tomato juice, no ice," she mumbled, leaning her head on my shoulder. She had the window seat; I had the aisle, while Joey sat on the aisle across from me. I preferred it this way—anyone would have to go through me to get to her. I knew she could likely take care of herself, but I felt protective, and I couldn't begin to explain that.

"Close your eyes, sweetheart. I've got this," I murmured against her hair.

Adam and Anna, sitting in a tree, k-i-s-s-i-n-g, Joey sang in my head.

Adam and Joey, running through the dell. Joey better run fast, or Adam will give him hell, I shot back.

Gonna be quiet now, Joey promised.

For your own good.

True. I allowed a small smile—I'd smiled frequently after meeting Joey, and smiled more since meeting Anna. Before I'd met Joey, I'd have said I was busy purging everything human from myself. That no longer held true. Joey's youth had affected me in a positive way and that, I felt, helped a great deal in my relationship with Anna.

Many of the older vamps I knew had very little human about them. Gavin, Wlodek's Chief Assassin, was one of those. I had a reputation among the vampires, but Gavin's was much more pronounced. I seldom spoke to him unless it was absolutely necessary, as he could quell almost any other vamp with just a look.

Anna was already asleep when the plane taxied for takeoff, so I soothed her during a bump on our way through the clouds over Dallas.

~

"Better than the last one," Joey nodded, looking about the safe house basement. He was right; this was a vast improvement over the two-bedroom in Corpus Christi. This one was completely updated, with granite countertops in the kitchen, stainless-steel appliances and en-suite bathrooms to go with the three bedrooms.

"This is nice," Anna agreed, blinking in the soft light of the kitchen.

"Off to bed for you," I attempted to scoot her toward the largest bedroom.

"No, we have to find Roy," she countered. "We have to check on Manuelo. If he goes through the change, then the tourists won't be safe."

"Let us find him," Joey coaxed. "You really do need sleep—you look exhausted."

"I'll sleep better after I've seen him," she argued.

"Come on, then. Let's find the bastard, then put Anna in bed." I lifted her in my arms before she could protest and ran up the narrow steps leading to the ground floor of the home.

We finally found the bugger—and his entourage—at the Emperor's Palace. Cheek was throwing money around in the poker room as if he only had a week to live. As always, Kirby Lee and Manuelo were outside, waiting patiently. Manuelo scratched often at his neck, making Anna frown.

"If he holds out until the tournament is over, it'll be a record," she whispered.

"Is there some way they can delay the change?" Joey asked quietly beside her.

"If there is, I don't know about it. That doesn't mean it can't happen," she added quickly. "The enemy likes to confuse us as often as possible."

"Joey, stay here and watch, I'll take Anna back to the house," I said. "Call if anything changes."

"Okay. Uh, Anna," Joey began.

"Play this one over here," Anna gave him a weary smile. "You have money?"

"I have money."

"Good. Invest what you win in Apple stock," she said and allowed me to steer her toward the door.

Las Vegas in August is hot—even after midnight. I considered that I was used to cooler European temperatures, and the tourists didn't seem to mind. They still wandered up and down the strip with little regard to the time of day—or night. The town was a mecca for vampires, as it was open round the clock. It likely explained the reason our safe house was as modern as it was—there were several in the area and Charles had given us the best available.

I considered that as I drove our rental toward the safe house—the fact that other vampires were in the area, occupying other safe houses. Somehow, that troubled me, but I put it out of my mind and concentrated on my driving. Anna slept in the passenger seat while I negotiated highways that hadn't been on the drawing board the last time I was in the area.

"Sleep, sweetheart," I murmured against Anna's ear before placing a kiss. "You smell so good," I added. She did. Her blood, too, sang to me in a way I'd never experienced. So much so, at times, I was dizzy with it. I'd never been this close to a shifter before—perhaps they were all like that.

"Not," Anna mumbled.

"Stop reading my mind and go to sleep," I ordered.

"Not reading your mind," she blinked at me. "You're broadcasting your thoughts."

"What's the difference? Aren't you supposed to be asleep?" I arched an eyebrow at her.

"Adam, just don't take my blood unless I give permission, okay?"

"I won't," I promised. "I was going to ask, but that's down the road a ways. I won't hurt you, either. I guarantee it."

"I know. It still scares me."

"You're afraid of me?" I gripped her chin carefully between a thumb and forefinger.

"Uh, I'm really tired."

"Don't be afraid of me. Ever."

"I'll work on that."

Adam, he moved from the Emperor's Palace to the Amalfi, Joey sent. *That's where I am, now.*

On my way to pick you up—he won't get far. Looks as if he's spreading himself around so he won't win too much from one casino, I returned, rounding a corner and heading back to the strip. *Anna will likely keep track of him, come daylight.*

She's really good at this, isn't she?

Better than I could ever imagine.

I never thought we'd get cooperation like this from any of the daywalkers, let alone a shifter. Plus, she's awesome. I won twenty-two thousand dollars on that machine.

Is that the only reason you like her?

No. Hell no. She's just, I can't explain it. I've upset her and she still treats me like I'm somebody special. I was thinking about investing in Apple stock, but after she said that, I think we can guarantee it's a good thing.

Invest a hundred thousand for me, too, while you're at it.

Really? You think the information is that reliable?

I think it's gold, Joey. She hasn't steered you wrong once on those machines, has she?

No.

You know where that account is—the one I said you could use in emergencies? Use money from that one.

All right. I'll make my investment at the same time. Thanks, Adam.

Pulling into the parking garage now. I'll be there shortly.

~

"I heard a gambler say that Cheek is up by a lot," Joey reported when I sat beside him at a slot machine.

"Then he should quit soon," I said. "Do we know how long he was at the Emperor's Palace?"

"I heard four hours. He's been here for two, but these are bigger bettors."

"He'll probably work his way up and down the strip, then," I sighed. "Do you know where he's staying?"

"I placed compulsion on the desk clerk at the Emperor's Palace—he has rooms there—at least for now."

"Kirby Lee and Manuelo?" I could see them from where I was sitting. Manuelo was sitting still and not scratching—at least for the moment.

"She went to the bathroom and ordered a bottle of water from the cocktail waitress, but that's it. I heard her asking if she could get a sandwich, but the woman said they can't serve food out on the gambling floor. I can't believe she hasn't noticed you or Anna the whole time we've been following Cheek."

"It's as if she looks right past us," I agreed. We'd stayed back whenever we watched, but if Kirby Lee were halfway intelligent, she might have seen us by now.

"Adam, look. He's leaving." Cheek walked out of the poker room with several racks of chips in his hands. All the chips were black, orange or red. He'd done some heavy betting.

"Want to follow him, or go home?" I asked. "We've had a long day, although it's still three hours before daylight, local time."

"Let's go home. I want to do research on my laptop and drink half a bag of blood."

"Feeling it?" I offered him a smile.

"Yeah. All this worry and trying to keep my thoughts to myself whenever I talk to Anna? I'm wiped."

"I'm worried that she'll be sick when she finds the refrigerator filled with bagged blood."

"She saw the stuff in the fridge in Corpus Christi. Didn't say a word."

"What was she looking for?"

"A bottle of water. Said what was coming out of the sink looked rusty."

"Because the kitchen plumbing hasn't been updated in fifty years," I growled. Parking the rental in the safe house garage, I let the door down before tapping in the code to get through the kitchen door.

The upper floor may have been used a time or two for lavish evening parties, but apart from that, it barely looked to have ever been inhabited. Joey and I walked straight past all of it, heading toward the master bedroom and the door in the closet floor.

Another keypad waited there, and I punched in a second code to lift the door. I wanted to slide into bed with Anna. I didn't intend to wake her—at least not yet.

Joey, Merrill's e-mail began, *what do you mean they're threatening the life of a shapeshifter? Call me. Immediately.*

"I had to sneak away to the top floor, and it's nearly daylight," Joey mumbled into his cell after dialing Merrill's number.

"This shapeshifter—what is she—exactly?"

"A white horse."

"Nothing else? Have you seen her fight?"

"I can't explain how she fights. She moves faster than any warmblood I've ever seen, including werewolves. She kicks hard, but if anything gets close to her head, it dies. Spawn—have you heard of them? They just explode."

"Joey, listen carefully. Don't allow anyone on the Council near her, understand me? Especially Saxom. Call immediately if things start to go wrong."

"Xavier has already been appointed to attempt the turn. They want to bring her back to England soon and do it there."

"Let me handle that."

"All right. I have to go. Now." Joey ended the call and raced for the trap door.

~

I'd heard Joey go out a few moments earlier, but he was back before I could worry about him. Anna murmured in my arms, so I settled her closer against me and closed my eyes against the rising sun.

~

"This is a bigger game than either of us," Merrill leaned against the wall in Wlodek's study two hours after nightfall, his arms crossed tightly and a hooded, angry expression on his face. Seldom had he allowed his sire to see any emotion in the past fifteen hundred years. He was showing temper now.

"You're asking me to let this go? To let her go?"

"Only you, Saxom and Xavier know this information. Chessman and Showalter can be controlled. It stops here."

"And should I choose to ignore your request?"

"Then I will not take blame for the consequences, because those will come. In ways you cannot begin to imagine."

"Then I choose to allow the Council to decide."

"Then you are a fool." Merrill swept angrily from the room. Wlodek watched as a sheet of paper lifted off his desk and floated to the floor.

~

"Adam?" Anna spoke my name softly as my eyes opened just before nightfall.

"Sweetheart?" I rolled over, offering her a smile—she stood beside the bed, gazing down at me.

"The media has caught up with our quarry. Some journalists have already latched onto the fact that he's here with Kirby Lee and another man they can't identify." She handed two newspapers to me as I sat up in bed.

"It was bound to happen," I rubbed my forehead before focusing on the article on the top paper.

"Yeah." Anna walked away from the bed, her head bowed in thought and arms crossed tightly over her chest. "I'm just worried about what might happen if any of those journalists get too close to Manuelo." She stopped talking when her cell phone rang.

"Hello?"

I heard clearly as Lion explained that there was evidence of spawn in Las Vegas.

CHAPTER 7

"Near the Air Force base," Lion informed us an hour later, at a coffee shop inside the Egyptian Casino. "Bodies mutilated and half-eaten. The authorities don't know what to make of it—they're saying wild dogs may be responsible, but the truth is, they just don't know."

"Anybody missing?" Anna asked. She didn't drink coffee often, but she was having a cup now.

"Six people reported missing in the past two days. That doesn't include the ones who were eaten." Lion passed a folder in my direction. It listed names and current addresses of all those missing. All six were male.

"They prefer women and children to eat," Anna sighed as I studied the names, committing them and their corresponding images to memory. My fingers stilled on the reports—all those attacked and killed had been women.

"That's not right," Joey joined the conversation.

"The meat is tender," Lion rubbed Joey's back. "These are predators. Never forget that."

"They don't remember they were human?"

"They have no memory. All they know to do is follow the orders of their maker."

"Does their maker have a memory?"

"If they live long enough," Anna shrugged. "It takes roughly five years to recall that they can speak. A few more years past that they'll remember some things, but by that time, they're so immersed in what they've become, it no longer matters."

"Those trolls we saw in Shreveport?" Joey asked.

"Were around twelve years old. They could have spoken if they wanted to, but you wouldn't have understood their language."

"Why?"

"Because they weren't from Earth, kid," Lion explained.

"Then how are they getting here? Who's shipping them in?"

"That's something we can't explain right now," Lion said. "You'll have to trust us. Anna, Dragon says to hop to Kansas City if it becomes necessary." I watched as he gave a slight nod in her direction. Somehow, I had the idea that this was something they'd already discussed between themselves while Joey and I had been sleeping.

"Adam, that is still hovering in the possibilities section. It hasn't become an absolute, yet."

"Remember Pheligar's warning," Lion nodded in Anna's direction a second time.

"I won't forget that." She sounded uncomfortable, and I couldn't explain it. Her pretty face was set and unreadable. I'd never seen that from her before. Something troubled her and I had no idea what it might be.

"I'm worried that everything might happen at once," Lion muttered, nodding and gazing into his coffee cup.

"I'm worried that the Powers That Be are worried," Anna responded. "I thought I'd be working alone on this. You see what that turned into." She swept out a hand.

"It means this is more important than anybody realized," Dragon said, nodding to me and pulling out a chair to sit on Lion's other side. Like before, he wore leather pants and boots, but the vest had been discarded in favor of a more conventional, white, long-sleeved shirt. The cuffs had been turned back, revealing a red dragon's head on each forearm. The teeth on both dragons gleamed against Dragon's skin, and I wondered at the skill needed to produce a tattoo of such quality.

"LaFranza," Dragon shrugged.

I had no idea who—or what—LaFranza was, so I remained silent.

"Pheligar says he's ready to transport Lynx and Tiger in if it's necessary. Wolf is still out on assignment."

"This is a mess," Anna mumbled, rubbing her forehead. My arm stole around her and I squeezed her shoulders solicitously. My mind worked furiously at the same time, attempting to decipher this conundrum. That didn't mean I wouldn't take every opportunity I could to touch Anna.

Adam, what's going on? Joey sounded upset, even in mindspeech.

I'm trying to determine that. Keep your ears open, son. We'll figure this out.

I like it when you call me that.

I know.

While he was human, Joey never had a father figure in his life. I knew that from reading his records, and his mother never said whom his biological father might be. I was happy to fill that role, as I'd never get a child of my own.

"Who's tracking the spawn from the killings?" Anna asked.

"I am," Lion said. "I'm heading back that way when I finish this." He held up his coffee cup.

"I'll keep an eye on things in Corpus Christi. Daniel went back to calm the Pack, and he's staying in touch." Dragon pulled a cell phone from his shirt pocket and laid it on the table.

"Want coffee?" I asked. Dragon hadn't ordered anything.

"He prefers tea so black and strong it can pump iron," Anna sighed. "They don't serve that here."

"I'll have water," Dragon nodded, his eyes hooded. He spared a slight smile for Anna, however. I signaled our waitress, who quickly brought a glass of water.

~

"This gets weirder every day," Joey flopped onto the sofa beside me.

I'd chosen to watch a rerun of the local news while Anna slept. We'd driven her back to the safe house after Dragon offered to keep an eye on Roy Cheek and his menagerie.

Roy was currently hiding in his hotel room at the Emperor's Palace—he'd been chased there by a pack of journalists. All of them wanted answers on his recent run of luck after Kirby Lee's husband disappeared and the refinery shut down in Corpus Christi.

The last thing Anna said to Dragon before we left the casino, was that she felt Roy's luck was about to run out. Dragon didn't reply, he'd merely given her an enigmatic nod.

"He's become too much of a liability, no matter what he did for them," I said aloud.

"What?" Joey asked.

"Cheek. Whatever deal he made with those things—the enemy, as Anna says—he's no longer useful to them. Too many people are following him around, now."

"You mean he's toast?"

"I think he was toast the moment he was approached by the enemy."

"I've seen at least fifty hits on the 'net, saying Kirby Lee murdered her husband, and fifty more saying Cheek did it so they could be together."

"Understandable, how they might arrive at that conclusion."

"How is Cheek connected? The police in Corpus think this is about a boat and a cheating wife. It's not. Why would the enemy come to Cheek for anything, other than a ready supply of fresh bodies that he wouldn't have to pay and nobody would go looking for? It can't be just that, can it?" Joey turned a worried gaze in my direction. "Surely they can round up their own food source."

"Let's look at our facts," I began. "Cheek hired undocumented workers, got them to work for him and then handed them over to the enemy before he had to pay them, so he could keep the money to gamble."

"Yeah. Then he made a big show out of the EPA closing the refinery in Corpus, over violations. The refinery is still closed," Joey said.

"True. Then, the Corpus Packmaster and I are attacked by rogue werewolves in Rockport. They intended to kill both of us. Anna shows up and I don't die."

"The first kink in their plans. They come looking for Daniel in Shreveport. We help him and again—you don't die. Daniel doesn't die, either."

"Because Anna, Lion and Dragon are there. I'm not sure we could have taken down the trolls, Joey. They were too big for us to handle."

"This is fucked up."

"You are correct."

At that moment, a flashing banner crossed the television screen, announcing breaking news. I stared as the words crawled across the bottom of the screen. If I'd thought things were complicated already, I was very, very wrong.

Body washes up on Port Aransas beach, the crawler announced. *Identified as Anna Kay Madden, a popular local investigator. Stay tuned to News Eleven for more details as they become available.*

"If that's Anna," Joey's eyes were huge as he blinked at me.

"Then who's sleeping in my bed?" I growled.

My cell phone buzzed as I stalked toward the bedroom, Joey stepping fearfully behind me. I ripped my pants pocket with partially formed claws as I pulled it out and glanced at the text.

The message was from Dragon. While I stared at the screen, a second message appeared—from Lion.

Harm her, Dragon's text read, and *I'll have your head so fast you'll never see it coming.*

Hurt our girl, Lion's text said, *and there won't be enough of you left to fill a matchbox.*

What the fuck? Joey read the texts over my shoulder.

"Where do you think you're going?" An eight-and-a-half-foot blue giant appeared before me. Joey shrieked. My cell phone clattered to the floor as I stared in shock.

~

I recalled the memory vividly. I'd been in Chicago in the 1920s, chasing a rogue. Louis Armstrong was playing at a club near my hotel, so I'd thought to go hear the music that everyone was talking about.

They stepped in front of me as I walked toward the line of humans waiting to get inside the venue. Three people. A tall, sandy-haired man with broad shoulders, who moved with the grace of a cat. A woman, only slightly shorter than he, with a tawny mane of hair that hung to her shoulders. Like the man, she moved with the grace of a stalking panther.

Out of place beside them stood a woman, perhaps five-three or four, with long, platinum hair down her back. It looked as if the gazelle had joined the lions for a night out. The fashion of the day was short, bobbed hair, so the pale-haired woman was doubly out of place.

She wasn't dressed in the fashion of the day, either, choosing to wear slacks and a jacket. I'd seen only a few women in pants up to that time, so her outfit puzzled me. My breath caught when she turned, offering her profile. She was beautiful. If my heart had been beating, it would have stopped at that moment, I was so taken with her.

I never took my eyes off her for the duration of Armstrong's performance. Following the group afterward, I meant to discover where she was staying. Intended to make her mine. Somehow, the three managed to elude me—a vampire. I hadn't had sex in more than ninety years after that night. I looked for her everywhere, but she'd disappeared for good, leaving me with only a memory.

Until now.

"Adam, if you'll stop woolgathering, I can explain."

This wasn't Anna. The blue giant stood next to her, frowning at me. He dwarfed the safe house basement and terrified Joey.

"Who are you?" I demanded, my voice a raspy growl. I was angry. More than angry. I'd been deceived—in the most devious manner possible. Was this a trick, too, that she was taking this form as her present appearance? Had she stolen the vision of the woman I'd seen so long ago, to confuse or upset me?

"Her name is Kiarra," the blue giant spoke.

"Pheligar, let me handle this," she said, raking fingers through long, platinum hair in frustration. "They did this on purpose," she added. "First they weighted the body and dumped it offshore before I arrived, then let it wash up now to cause problems."

"Because they suspect," Pheligar snapped. "While others might be able to change appearances, they suspect that you are what you are. They're calling you out."

"Then they'll expect the second Anna to show up and refute the findings. They'll expect the body to be altered to prove the authorities wrong. What if we don't do that? What if we let things stand as they are? Change the airline records. That's all it will take."

"I've already done that," Pheligar sniffed.

"Good. Anna can stay dead, now."

"Who the fuck are you?" I demanded a second time. They'd held a conversation while ignoring me, as if a vampire weren't a dangerous entity to either of them.

"I am Pheligar of the Larentii," Pheligar announced. "I can separate your particles if I find you annoying. Be silent."

"Pheligar, please leave. Adam and I need to talk," she said.

"I will separate your particles if you harm her," Pheligar said before he disappeared.

"That's the third threat I've gotten tonight," I growled, crossing my arms and staring at the woman before me. If I'd seen her on the street, I'd have followed her without question. She'd been with me for days, in disguise and obviously lying to me.

"This disgusts me," I flung out a hand and turned my back on her.

"If you'll let me explain," she began.

"I want nothing from you. You've done nothing but lie and misrepresent yourself," I said, walking toward the kitchen and snatching up the keys to the rental. "I'm leaving. Joey, are you coming with me?"

"Adam, I want to hear what she has to say," Joey's voice was timid as he begged me mentally to stay. I didn't respond to his mindspeech.

"Fine. Stay here and listen to the lies." I flung myself toward the stairs leading to the trap door overhead.

"Our kind can't lie." Lion took the barstool next to mine. I'd found a casino bar that was mostly empty and sat there, nursing a drink I had no intention of consuming while feeling sorry for myself.

"What kind is that?" I took a huge swallow of the bourbon I'd ordered.

"Our kind. I can't say the name, because the enemy is listening."

"Convenient." I slapped the glass on the bar and nodded for the bartender to fill it again.

"At the moment, it's completely inconvenient. Of all the times for this to happen," Lion shook his head. "I'll have a double," he said as the bartender held up the bottle of Jameson's in a silent query.

"For what to happen?"

"For Kiarra to find a mate."

"I'm not her mate."

"A day ago, I'd have said that's a lie."

"I might have said it, too. Things change."

"You don't turn feelings on and off, like a light switch," Lion pointed out philosophically. "I know you feel betrayed. All I can say is there's a reason for the subterfuge. A very good reason. Kee wouldn't hurt you like this if there were any way to avoid it."

"Sure." I emptied my glass a second time.

"She can do things for you that nobody else can do."

"Like what?"

"That's not my information to give. You need to talk to her."

"I don't care if your kind can't lie. I don't choose to believe you."

"She's saved your life three times. That doesn't mean anything?"

"Maybe it would be better if she hadn't."

"You don't mean that."

"Fuck you."

"Not gonna happen. I have a mate."

"Then leave. I'm not in the mood for any philosophical, motivational speeches."

"That's what I used to do," Lion said with a sigh. "Before. Know how old I am?"

"No, and I don't care."

"You should. Make a guess. Tell me how old I am."

"Fine. Shifters live around two hundred years, on average. You're one hundred seventeen."

"I'm sixteen thousand years old, give or take, allowing for variances in size and lengths of planetary rotations."

"That's a lie. I know," I held up a hand. "Your kind can't lie."

"We can't."

"Why are you here?"

"Because I wanted to talk. Dragon wants your head. I felt discretion was the better course of action."

"You think he can take me? A vampire?"

"With no trouble, and keep your voice down," Lion cautioned.

"Perfect. How old is he, by the way?"

"He's slightly younger—by a thousand years."

"This is a fucking joke," I muttered.

"I fail to see any humor in this situation." Lion shifted. I watched as the muscles beneath his shirt flexed and bulged as he settled himself more comfortably on the barstool. The leather seat creaked beneath his weight, and I considered that I might not get away if Lion chose to chase after me.

"You wouldn't. I've tracked and killed things that were faster than you." He emptied his glass and thumped it on the bar. "Daylight is in two hours. What will it be, Chessman? You know too much already. Now, I can take you out of the game, or you can continue to play along. Either way, you won't be upsetting Kiarra. Any more than you have already, anyway."

"I won't go down without a fight," I hissed.

"Oh, it won't be to the death. I can have you removed from the planet until this is over, though. Make your choice. Do it now. You won't get another opportunity. If Dragon comes, he won't be half as polite."

"If I go, then Joey comes with me."

"That's not what I hear. Joey's talking with Kee. He's staying."

"Fuck."

"Again, no, thank you. The way I see it, you're staying. You have a job to do and an adopted child to protect. Do it, Chessman. Who knows, maybe you'll have a change of heart."

"Doubt it. I don't like betrayals." I tossed a hundred on the bar, nodded to the bartender and slid off the barstool.

"Then you have a long, difficult way to go," Lion growled low and followed me out of the casino.

~

"He'll play along, but he doesn't like it," Lion announced as we stepped into the basement of the safe house.

Anna—*not Anna*, I reminded myself, rose from her seat at the kitchen table. She'd been crying, that was easy enough to see. Her nose and eyes were red. If I were more forgiving, I'd have said she was still beautiful. That no longer figured into the equation for me.

"Thanks, Lion," she said softly. "I've moved my things into the third bedroom. I'll have Pheligar remove the M'Fiyah when he comes back."

"Kee, don't do anything rash," Lion said.

"You think this is rash?" She tossed a hand helplessly. "No good deed goes unpunished." I watched as she walked down the hall toward the smallest bedroom in the safe house. The door closed behind her moments later.

"Someday, vampire, you're going to regret every minute of this,"

Lion said. "I have work to do." I watched him climb the steps to the trap door without a word.

~

"Adam, I don't want to interfere in your business," Joey began.

"Then don't."

"You don't know everything."

"I have no desire to listen." I stalked toward my bedroom, realizing that I was punishing myself, just as much as I was punishing Joey and the woman. I still couldn't bring myself to say her name. For me, the Anna I knew lay dead in Corpus Christi, and a changeling had taken her place.

~

"I have information that says the woman you've been working with is very much alive. I want photographs," Xavier insisted. He'd called almost the moment my eyes opened after sunset.

"That may prove difficult," I said. "We aren't on speaking terms at the moment."

"Go fuck yourself, vampire," Dragon pulled the cell phone from my hand and spoke to Xavier.

"Who is this?" I clearly heard Xavier's demand.

"Somebody you shouldn't mess with," Dragon responded.

"Your name?"

"I don't give out my name. Most people call me Dragon. Tell your puppet master that." Dragon ended the call, offered me a scowl and tossed the phone on the bed. Without a word and with his black braid swinging, he stalked out of my bedroom.

"What's going on?" I demanded as I walked into the kitchen. Joey sat at the kitchen island, morosely drinking a bag of blood.

"Cheek's dead," Joey muttered. "Manuelo went nuts. Killed Kirby Lee first, then attacked Cheek. At least he did it in an alley behind one of the casinos. Anna—Kiarra," he corrected himself, "had to kill him.

After that, a crowd of people was attacked outside a business in Summerlin. Fifteen died. The bodies were half-eaten when the police showed up."

"Cheek's body?" I asked.

"Mostly bones. He's at the coroner's, with Kirby Lee's bones. Manuelo devoured her, first. You were right—Cheek was a liability and they got rid of him and Kirby Lee—in a really gruesome way. The newspapers and TV stations are broadcasting that and nothing else. There's been a rush for the airport, and flights are jammed."

"What did she tell you?" I ignored her as she walked past us, on her way to the refrigerator.

"I can't tell you."

"Joey," I warned.

"He can't tell you. Knowledge of my race protects itself. If we don't tell you, nobody else can."

"You're joking?" I'd just broken a promise I'd made to myself not to speak to her.

"I'm not joking. My kind can't lie. If you'd stayed, or asked Lion appropriate questions, you might know a lot more than you do now. I've heard older vampires are more stubborn than jackasses. Now I know it's true."

"Did you just call me a jackass?"

"Yeah." She sipped the protein drink she'd pulled from the refrigerator before nodding her head. "I did call you a jackass. Jackass." She walked toward her bedroom without a backward glance.

"Adam," Joey hissed. "She's saved your ass. Three times. If you knew," he said.

"If I knew what? This changes nothing."

"I've been asked to set up another e-mail account for you," Joey ducked his head. "It's done, and I can get rid of the old one anytime you want."

"You should get a new phone, too," Dragon said, walking into the kitchen. "If I were you, I'd cut all ties with your sire."

"Because?" I snapped.

"Because it's the prudent thing to do." I blinked. I'd only seen

Merrill once, and he walked into the safe house basement as if he owned it, followed by a hazel-eyed, brown-haired man who was taller than I. I blinked again. Merrill has jet-black hair, piercing blue eyes and a commanding way about him that brooks no argument.

"What the hell?" I began.

"Hello, Father," Joey said, and went to hug Merrill.

"There's a reason for the subterfuge," Joey attempted to explain later. "I know the Council's records say Timerius turned me, but that's not true."

"I keep hearing that word—subterfuge. I tire of it," I huffed. I felt betrayed a second time.

"I don't wish to interfere with your relationship with my youngest," Merrill frowned. "It has done him a world of good."

At that moment, I wished I were old enough—and strong enough —to tell Merrill to go to hell. I couldn't. Instead, I kept my features in a smooth vampire mask while seething on the inside. Anna had lied. Joey had lied. The world was crumbling about me and I had nothing in my arsenal to fight back.

"We're moving. They know where you are. Leave your phone behind—that's how they're tracking you," Merrill informed me after I returned from a very long walk in the dark. If anyone—or anything had thought to accost me during that walk, they would have died.

"What about Joey's phone?" I snapped, narrowing my eyes at Merrill.

"Non-traceable." Joey waggled it at me. "I got you one, too."

"Won't this brand us rogues with the Council?" I demanded, my voice rough with anger.

"Let me handle that," Merrill said.

"Adam, I know you don't trust me anymore," she blinked sky-blue eyes at me. "But they're coming. We have to go."

"Why do you trust them?" I turned back to Merrill.

"They're the only ones you can trust right now," Merrill's voice and eyes were hard. "We're all dead if we don't get out now."

"What about my things?" I pointed to my bedroom.

"Everything except your laptop and phone is already moved," she sighed. "Joey transferred necessary files to a new laptop and wiped the old one—with help from Pheligar. Nobody will be able to use it again."

"I liked my laptop," I snapped.

"It's been bugged," Joey said. "The Council supplied the equipment, remember?"

"This is untenable," I rubbed my forehead. If I'd been human at that moment, I'd have had a migraine.

"They know your every move, and have, since you've been connected," Merrill said. "It's time you left them behind—until this is sorted. There's something else, too."

"What's that?"

"I remove all compulsion from you."

I'll admit to staring at Merrill as if he were a lunatic—until the compulsion drained from my mind. I felt as if I'd been freed from nearly three centuries of chains weighting me down.

"What the bloody hell?" I blinked at the older vampire.

"I can't remove your sire's compulsion. There are only two things that might accomplish that." Merrill turned away and walked toward the steps leading to the ground floor. "We don't have much time. Don't make me place compulsion on you to come along quietly."

"Where are we going?" I asked, begrudging every word I was forced to speak. The words were hissed through my teeth, since I regretted having to speak to anyone.

"Into the hills, for now. Kiarra and Griffin say there's unfinished business here." Dragon, who drove a van with Joey's and my belongings stuffed in the back, answered my question. Lion and I rode with him, while Joey, Merrill and she rode in a separate van with the one called Griffin. The rental was left behind at the safe house.

Halfway to our destination, the neighborhood containing the safe house exploded in a fireball behind us. I settled myself uncomfortable in my seat after that. Something was happening; I just had no idea what it was.

~

"The windows are blocked, so you'll be safe. I have to say, Adam, you're not the man I thought you were."

She stood inside my assigned bedroom, blinking at me in half-anger, half-confusion. My new quarters were in a large house in a relatively new subdivision located outside Las Vegas. Lion, Dragon, Merrill and Griffin had taken the house next door, leaving Joey, her and me in this one. I had no idea how they'd managed to take over these homes, but decided not to ask.

"You're not the woman I thought you were," I responded, my voice cold. Somewhere, what was left of my heart was weeping—reeling from this unwelcome revelation. I didn't feel right, either, but there was no way to explain it. I'd never been so willing to give my love, and it was all a lie.

"Touché," she sighed. "Let me know if you need anything. We'll likely need your help come sundown." With that, she left my bedroom, closing the door behind her. With an unhappy sigh, I lifted my bag onto the bed and began to unpack.

~

Kiarra's Journal

"You know it's compulsion from his sire, Kee."

"I don't care." I refused to look at Lion, though I knew he was speaking the truth. How could one vampire turn love off in another? It made absolutely no sense.

"I know your past. I know this is hard for you. There's a way around this, if you'll stop being stubborn."

"He has to cooperate, and in this condition, he won't. I don't want him to, either. It'll be almost like trading one compulsion for another, and I won't have anybody unless they want it—of their own free will."

"This is crazy." Lion rubbed a large hand over his face before turning dark eyes in my direction. "Look at me, Kee. Somewhere inside that rigid vampire is a man who loves you. You can't handle that. Admit it."

"I don't want to talk about it." I didn't, but he was right. I wasn't sure how to handle any of this, and things weren't going well on any other quarter, either. Seldom did the enemy make his presence known so openly. This defied all logic, and I was too exhausted to go *Looking* for a cause. If I were honest, I'd admit—at least to myself—that I needed Adam's care and support at the moment. I didn't have it and he couldn't give it.

"I don't want to bring up the subject of Joey again, but," Lion said.

"Lion, leave it, all right?"

"For now." He stalked out of my bedroom, leaving it feeling as cold and empty as my heart.

∾

"Where are we going?" I asked. I walked into the media room an hour after sundown, where it looked as if the others were preparing for war.

"This is a war," Lion said. "We have body armor for you, if you want it. Joey is already wearing his."

"We're going to Nelson," *she* informed me, strapping a blade in a sheath to her back.

"Formerly known as Eldorado?" I began. "What the bloody hell is out there?"

"Actually, we're stopping before we get to Nelson. We think the spawn are holed up in the mountains north and east of Nelson," Dragon said.

"You think? You don't know?" Yes, my temper was certainly evident in my voice.

"It's as close as you can get to certainty," Merrill snapped. "Stop being an idiot and get ready to go."

"Come on, it'll be like an attack of zombies. For real," Joey said. He wore his body armor over a T-shirt and jeans and seemed excited to be going.

"Whatever you do, don't let anything get close enough to bite," Lion warned. "I've never seen a vampire bitten so I don't know what the result might be, but I don't want to take any chances."

"I'll be fine," I muttered. The body armor I accepted, however. In my line of work, it always paid to be cautious.

"This is the middle of nowhere," Joey muttered, looking about us. We'd pulled off highway 165 and parked both vehicles in a ravine, hiding them from view. I noticed he'd gotten closer to me after we'd left the SUVs behind. Not closer to his sire—closer to *me*.

That meant something, even to my increasingly addled mind. Reaching out, I pulled him to me in a quick hug before letting him go. Yes, my mind felt clouded, and I couldn't explain that. During our trip, I'd begun to feel strange. The feeling had persisted and grown stronger as we approached our target.

I might have called it fear or at least trepidation, but something appeared to be blocking both emotions. That in itself unnerved me, but I determined to shut it out of my mind and concentrate on the work at hand.

We were spawn hunting. Not waiting for them to come to us as they'd done before; this time, we were initiating the attack. I still didn't understand how Dragon and the others knew where they might be, but I was determined to do my part.

"Stay sharp," Merrill warned me softly. "This isn't the first time I've hunted spawn." He was old enough to have seen them before. I filed that away in my mind.

Kiarra says there are several washes in the area that flood whenever it rains hard, Joey silently informed me. Glancing up, I saw clouds building over our heads at too rapid a rate.

Shouldn't we get out of this ravine, then? I smell rain coming, I returned.

"Get out of the ravine," the one called Griffin ordered. All of us scrambled for higher ground the moment clouds burst over our heads.

CHAPTER 8

I hate fighting in the rain, but this was no ordinary rain. It came so hard and heavy it was difficult to see the enemy, who fell on us the moment we scrambled out of the ravine. We had a difficult enough time fighting spawn, but that worsened when they were joined by rogue werewolves and vampires.

Yes, vampires had joined this fight, and I had little time to wonder at the fact that they fought alongside werewolves. Instead, my claws were bloodied from decapitating werewolves, and covered in spawn debris when they dusted, spraying their particles on anything nearby.

Rain continued to fall, turning spawn dust to black sludge on skin and clothing. Eventually, we gathered in a ring, conserving our energy to fight anything that approached us. "Don't let them breach the circle," Dragon shouted as a vampire almost got past Joey. He didn't have two centuries of fighting experience, as I did.

Merrill—I'd never seen another vampire fight as he did—with the exception, perhaps, of Gavin Montegue. "More coming," she shouted. I jerked my mind away from its wanderings and decapitated the spawn before me, who still looked very, very human. Thunder rumbled over our heads and heavier rain fell. The ravine behind us was overflowing, threatening one side of our fighting circle.

"Two steps to the east," Dragon shouted. His voice from the beginning held the timbre of command. Somewhere, somehow, he'd done this before. The spawn attacking us now were freshly turned; I could see and smell it on them. An occasional vampire thought to hide among them, but they couldn't fool any of us. My sleeves were tattered from slashes by enemy claws that nearly reached my skin on several occasions.

"Pull in tighter," Dragon yelled at us. "This is their last attack."

I had no time to pay attention to the allies about me; I only had time and energy to devote to what confronted me. With heavy rain still falling, I couldn't see past the spawn before me. We'd had no way to gauge the enemy's numbers by sight, so Dragon had to be using another sense to determine the size of their army.

How long had the enemy been making spawn? Where were they coming from? I'd not heard any reports of so many missing, although I did see several who were dressed for the desert—*in another country.*

"Last wave," Dragon said. I could hear the weariness in his voice as he made the call. With claws that felt as heavy as iron, I removed the head of a young boy. Perhaps fourteen, he was too young to die. Too young to be spawn. The enemy was ruthless in its selection of humans.

One more came. An old man. Perhaps the youth's grandfather— they bore some resemblance. I killed him before he could sink his teeth into my arm, the blackness of his death spraying me with dark slop the rain couldn't wash away.

A soggy thump sounded nearby. Joey had fallen to the ground in a heap. Had he been forced to decapitate a child? That would cause damage, I knew. "Joey?" I struggled to walk toward him—the driving rain continued to fall as I dropped to my knees beside his body.

He shook in my arms as I wrapped him in the tightest embrace I could. "I don't want to be a vampire anymore," he wept.

"Joey, hush, now. We have to get you home," I soothed. He'd been so young when turned. Barely twenty-two, he'd never been exposed to things of this nature. Death hadn't touched him at that age. While he didn't mind killing criminals as a vampire, I knew he would suffer at the taking of an apparent innocent.

"Joey, he dusted. He wasn't human any longer. He'd have killed you, if you hadn't done what you did." She knelt on his other side, brushing wet hair away from his face with gentle fingers. "Let Adam help you up, and we'll get you home."

Ripped clothing, spawn sludge, mud, blood, even, covered us as we drove home. I held Joey in the back seat of the SUV, while Lion drove and she sat in the passenger seat.

Joey was content to huddle against me. At least the tears had stopped. Vampires can cry—their tears are nearly clear, as they are blood serum and not blood, as so many might think. *We'll get you in the shower when we get back*, I sent to him.

You need it, too. Joey sat up and wiped his forehead with fingers that only shook slightly. *Thanks, Adam. I was tired, and the kid—couldn't have been more than twelve.*

Tough job, I agreed. *But he wasn't human, just as she said. You did well, son. Don't ever think otherwise.*

Yeah. He was too weary to argue.

"It's a ploy, kid," Lion tossed over his shoulder. "They send in those we might hesitate to kill, and the hesitation is what will kill *you*."

"They do this?" Joey croaked. "Intentionally?"

"Yeah. Don't let it worry you. It only looked like a child. That wasn't a child any longer."

"This is nuts." Joey shook his head and stared through the vehicle window as mountains and desert flew past us. We were headed toward the new safe house, as quickly as safety and the speed limits would allow.

If I hadn't been so tired, I might have wondered at what waited for us when we pulled into the driveway. I recognized him—Rodney, a vampire and one of Joey's on-again, off-again lovers, stood next to the garage door. Instead, I shook Joey, who'd gone into an almost-doze.

"Joey, Rodney's here. Were you expecting him?" I asked.

"Huh? Rodney?" Joey peered through my window, attempting to make out the form of his lover.

"He's here," I repeated. "Is he supposed to be?" I imagined I'd be forced to place compulsion, but it looked as if Joey had invited Rodney earlier. I couldn't imagine that he'd have found us any other way.

"Wait," she said as Joey tumbled out of the SUV before I could stop him. The horror unfolded in slow motion as I opened my door the same time she opened hers, and both of us rushed forward.

Too late. We were too late. Rodney's claws nearly swiped Joey's head from his shoulders before I could reach him. I might have screamed. I intended to, anyway. My claws were out, but she'd gotten there before me.

Rodney's head rolled down the driveway while his body dropped where he'd stood. I didn't think to wonder at the shining blade that appeared in her hand—her sword was in the back of the SUV.

Then, stunned and falling to my knees, I watched as she dropped beside Joey, placed her forehead against his and a hand against the wound in his neck. Unable to speak or plead for Joey's life, I gaped as she began to glow softly.

Merrill knelt beside me and placed a comforting hand on my shoulder. "If there's any way, she'll save him," he whispered reverently.

"Are they dead?" I asked when she fell over half an hour later.

"No." Dragon knelt on my other side. "She's just drained. She gave most of the life force she had left to our young man. If we're lucky, she'll wake tomorrow. In the meantime, we need to give Joey blood, get him clean and in bed."

"I'll take care of Kiarra," Merrill offered.

"You do that," Dragon agreed.

At that moment, I couldn't begin to describe the feelings of jealousy that swept over me. No, I couldn't approach her—something prevented it. I didn't want Merrill to touch her, however, so I growled at him.

"Hold on," Dragon blinked dark, enigmatic eyes before nodding in my direction. "Griffin, take Merrill inside. It's time we took care of this nonsense."

"What nonsense?" I asked, beginning to worry as Dragon settled on the concrete in front of me, sitting cross-legged on the rain-soaked surface. He and I were still covered in sludge and mud, although his sludge was mixed with a bit of his blood.

"Come," he motioned for me to lean forward. I leaned backward instead.

"Come." His hand gripped my neck and he pulled my head forward until my forehead rested against his.

Now, he spoke in my mind, *we'll get rid of that poison your sire has planted.*

What? I'd sent mindspeech before I could stop myself. *How?* was my second question, although it failed to convey the true question—how was he mindspeaking me?

Here. Not only could I hear him, a vision appeared in my mind. A glowing, purple knot throbbed inside my brain. *This is what I see,* he sent. *I'm about to destroy it,* he added. *Say now if you want that thing to remain inside you.*

I don't, I responded immediately.

Good.

A surgeon couldn't have excised it more neatly. With a surge of power, he'd destroyed it, leaving my mind clear. I blinked as Dragon drew away.

I now recalled the cell phone conversation I'd had with Xavier. He'd ordered me to refuse her—Kiarra. *If she appears,* he'd said, *do not touch her. She is not for you, understand?* Then, he'd told me that she'd betrayed me. Instructed me not to touch her. Told me that he'd provide further instructions later. And then, he'd told me to forget that he'd placed compulsion.

I had forgotten. Until now.

"It's time to take care of her." Dragon rose gracefully and extended a hand.

"Yes." I was weary, but not too weary for this. I accepted the hand and stood, before striding swiftly to her side. Lifting her unconscious body in my arms, I stalked into the house, daring anyone to stop me.

~

"My love." I brushed fingers down her cheek. I held her against me as we soaked in a second bath—the first one had been used and then emptied, to remove the filth from us. Our second bath was more leisurely—I checked her carefully and murmured over every bruise and scratch on her skin before kissing it.

I'd razored clothing off both of us, and it had gone straight into the rubbish bin; no part of it had been salvageable. "I'll buy you anything you want to wear, sweetheart," I murmured against her ear before placing another, careful kiss.

Lion explained that she'd used every bit of energy she had left to save Joey's life. I'd seen Joey in the kitchen, drinking a second bag of blood when I carried Kiarra through on my way to the bedroom. Lion had followed me to the door, giving me needed information. He'd closed the door to my bedroom after I carried Kiarra through. My bedroom. My bathroom. My tub. My woman.

I kissed her neck fiercely. *Mine.*

Don't get carried away, Lion's voice filtered into my head. *You need permission before you take her blood.*

Bugger off, I responded. *I won't bite unless she says so.*

Good. I won't have to beat you into the ground, then. Get her in bed. We may have to move, soon.

Got it. I lifted one of Kiarra's hands and kissed it before rising with her in my arms.

~

"Where the hell are we?" I looked about the dimly lit kitchen I'd wandered into after waking. Through a tall window nearby, I blinked at the New York City skyline beyond.

"We're at Merrill's brownstone in New York," Joey said sleepily beside me. I'd wakened to an empty bed in a strange room. My carry-all was on the foot of the bed, so I'd dressed quickly and wandered down a long hall until I reached the kitchen.

"You've been here before?" I turned to him—he still wore pajama bottoms.

"I was raised here for two years, before Timerius walked into the sun and my excuse for being here was blown. The Council took over after that."

"And Master Joey was not pleased when that happened." A tall man in his sixties, with brown hair going gray, walked into the kitchen, carrying a glass of wine. "I'm Franklin," he introduced himself.

"I liked it here. Merrill let me do research and build anything I wanted, and I didn't have to worry about money," Joey sighed.

"Joseph had a difficult time cleaning up after himself," Franklin smiled as he sipped from his wineglass. "I believe Father had to place compulsion."

"I did." Merrill walked into the room, followed by Dragon, Lion and Griffin.

"Where's Kiarra?" I demanded.

"In another bedroom. Pheligar came and tended to her. We didn't want to disturb you," Dragon said. "It's just as well; if Kiarra gets hurt, you don't want to deal with Pheligar or Karzac."

"Karzac?"

"Dragon's healer," Lion explained. "Can be a bit grumpy when people do stupid things."

"You have a healer?"

"All of us have healers. Except Kiarra. She keeps refusing. It's a long story," Lion waved a huge hand.

"All of you?" Yes, I was curious.

"Seven of us. Ask Kiarra what that means," Lion said. "Right now, we're hungry. We're going to wake her and go out to eat."

"Adam, I have blood in a fridge inside my room," Joey offered. "Then we can go with them."

"I want to see Kiarra first."

"Then let's go." Joey pulled me from the kitchen.

~

"Sweetheart, the others want to go eat," I said, brushing hair behind an ear. The bed she lay on was huge, and it made her look small.

"Adam?" she croaked, waking with a frown. "You're touching me?"

"I'm touching you. Dragon removed the compulsion Xavier placed," I added. I didn't tell her that I wanted to kill him for that. I couldn't. He was my sire, and that was frowned on by the Council.

"I don't know whether to kiss him or kick his ass for that. Dragon, I mean."

"If I weren't so jealous, I'd say kiss him. Maybe a handshake. Possibly a hug."

"Where are my clothes? I feel so tired," she muttered, accepting my help to sit up.

"Lion says you emptied yourself to save me. Thank you," Joey offered shyly.

"Don't thank me yet," she sighed, raking fingers through strands of platinum hair. "We'll have a reckoning with Pheligar before this is over," she added.

She's not supposed to interfere. Not like that, Joey sent. *Lion says there are only two reasons for her to interfere as much as she did, but he didn't explain.*

"Joey, I need to teach you how to shield your mindspeech," Kiarra attempted to slide off the bed. I stilled for a moment before lifting her off easily and setting her feet on the floor.

"You hear our mindspeech?"

"Not all of it, I'm sure." Her cheeks turned bright pink.

I laughed. Yes, that should have upset me, but it didn't. I laughed so hard I had to sit on the edge of the bed and attempt to control it.

"It's not that funny," she grumbled and stalked toward the bathroom.

"It kind of is," Joey disagreed before chuckling. "Come on, let's eat first, so we don't eat our friends."

~

Does it bother you—about Rodney? I asked Joey as we walked down the hall toward Joey's bedroom. Merrill's suite was at the top floor of the brownstone and more than luxurious, I discovered.

It bothers me, he sighed with his sending. *I think somebody set him up.*

I think so, too, but I have no idea who or why.

I know Rodney cared about me, and he almost killed me anyway, Joey said.

Do you know who made him? Look what Xavier did to me. I treated Anna—Kiarra—horribly.

I don't know his maker, and I know how much you care about her. I had no idea compulsion could do that kind of bullshit.

Your maker can force you to do anything, Joey. It's a good thing you dumped my old phone and laptop, I ruffled his hair affectionately. *Even though I didn't appreciate it at the moment.*

You were sort of nasty, all right. We stopped at the end of the hall, where Joey put his hand on the doorknob. *At least it's neater than it used to be,* he grinned before leading me inside.

"Sweetheart, I have restaurants in London," I murmured against her ear as we were led into a private room by the restaurant hostess.

"Do they serve vegetarian?" she asked as I pulled a chair out for her at a round table large enough to hold all of us.

"If they don't, they will soon," I said, taking the seat beside her.

Should I ask why a vampire owns restaurants? she asked.

"I'll explain that later, and thank you for letting me know you have mindspeech," I muttered. Yes, that stung, although I attempted to hide it.

"I didn't want to worry you," she said. "Admit it, you would have run."

"Perhaps. Joey and I have kept that secret for years."

"Adam, you won't be in trouble with me because of it," she replied while unfolding her napkin and dropping it on her lap.

"I know." I leaned back in my seat with a sigh and a slight shake of my head. Too much had happened recently, and I had no idea if I'd ever figure it all out. "Thank you for Joey's life," I whispered.

"I care about him," she turned sky-blue eyes in my direction.

"Do you know how long I've loved you?" I brushed lips against her hair. "If you don't, I'll tell you later."

"A-hem," Griffin cleared his throat. Merrill sat beside him, stone-faced and silent. I leaned away from Kiarra and forced my face into the vampire mask.

"I think I'll have the lamb. And the lobster," Lion lowered his menu and gave me a wide grin. *Don't let the old vamps get to you,* he sent.

I'll remember you said that, I replied. *Vamps—plural?* I sent after mulling his sending for a moment.

Later, he told me. *And I'll teach you how to shield your thoughts.*

Probably a good idea, I responded with sarcasm. *How did we get to New York?* I thought to ask. Nobody had explained that miracle as yet.

We can duplicate anything that's natural or that already exists on the planet, Lion informed me. *There are Elemaiya here. That means we can gate in and out, or hop from one place to another. As long as it doesn't look like a stretch to the enemy, it won't raise his suspicions. He's looking for any use of our power, so we have to be creative and only employ what's seemingly natural.*

Why do you have to hide your power from the enemy?

Once he knows we're here and looking for him, he can destroy everything.

What do you mean by that?

I mean he holds enough power on his own to blow the planet to bits. He may suspect we're here, but he isn't sure, yet. This is a bigger game than you know, and the stakes are being raised. Maybe I'll be allowed to explain it to you, sometime.

You know vampires don't frighten easily. At least in my line of work. You just frightened me.

I don't think you're frightened enough. Not yet, anyway.

"Lion, stop scaring him. We're here for dinner," Kiarra said aloud.

I said nothing when Merrill ordered a filet and ate the entire thing, with vegetables and two glasses of wine. Joey and I had red wine, but only sipped as little as possible while we talked over dinner.

"I think we're being tracked anyway, no matter that Chessman's cell and laptop have been destroyed," Griffin said after our waiter served another round of drinks and left us.

"What's the latest from Daniel in Corpus?" Kiarra asked Dragon.

"He has the Pack sorted, now. Shirley Walker is the new Packmaster. A few rogues are still in the area, though, and the Pack is tracking them at the Grand Master's orders. Daniel took your advice, Kiarra. He's Shirley's Second."

"I knew he'd been a good pick," she said.

"Sweetheart, want dessert?" I asked. She'd ordered vegetable lasagna, and ate half of a generous portion.

"There's no room for it," she shook her head at me. "Although the tiramisu sounds good."

"We'll get it to go," Merrill offered. "You'll have it later."

"That sounds fine," she shrugged.

"What will they do—if they find us again?" Joey asked. He didn't hide the shiver that accompanied his words, or the worried timbre of his voice. I had to remind myself that he'd almost died at the hands of a lover. If Kiarra hadn't intervened, he would have perished. I was still amazed that she'd been able to keep him alive.

"Child, stop worrying," Merrill said. "Things will work out."

Joey, I think Kiarra likes you a lot. I believe she took a risk to save you, too. Besides, we took down an army of spawn, plus a few vampires and werewolves. We won't go down without a fight, son.

Adam, stay away from Xavier, all right? Joey shivered again. His near-death was sinking in, now.

"Joey, want to sit beside Adam?" Kiarra asked. She was prepared to move to give him her seat; knew he was upset.

"I'll move," Dragon offered. He sat beside me, but elected to switch seats with Joey.

"Put him between us," Kiarra suggested. I took Dragon's seat, allowing Joey to sit on my chair. I have no idea what she said to him in mindspeech, but she rubbed his back while he leaned his head on her shoulder.

Joey reached out for my hand. I grasped his without blinking and held it.

~

"He'll be all right, once he goes into the rejuvenating sleep," I said later. Kiarra and I had spent the bulk of the night with Joey. He'd taken a spot in the middle of the sofa inside her bedroom, and she and I reassured him. Eventually he removed his shoes and climbed into her bed. She offered to bring his laptop, and he accepted. We'd left him playing computer games in bed.

"He always had difficulty dealing with vampirism," Merrill said as we walked into the kitchen. He and Griffin sat at a huge, granite-topped island, having another glass of wine.

"Griffin, when did you plan to tell me you'd given Merrill blood?" Kiarra sighed, taking a barstool on the opposite side.

"It's not a requirement, if all the stipulations are met," Griffin replied warily.

"I know that. I still don't understand why you didn't offer the information."

"You know, now," he pointed out.

"Yes. Now I know," she agreed.

"What's this?" I had no idea what they were talking about.

"I'll explain later," she said. "Right now, I have a headache."

"I'll get something for you," Merrill rose from his seat. Yes, that triggered my jealousy. Kiarra placed her hand over mine. "I'll just have a glass of wine, if you don't mind," she said, giving Merrill a terse nod.

Merrill poured wine into an expensive glass and handed it to Kiarra. He made sure his hand touched hers in the exchange, too. I didn't like the contact at all.

"Adam, we may have to take care of that," she said, sipping the wine. "Merrill isn't cheating you out of anything. Trust me."

"Thank you for that," Merrill nodded in her direction. "That means much to me."

Kiarra rubbed my back while she drank her wine, as much to keep me from growling at Merrill as it was to let me know she cared.

Fortunately, I found the humor in the situation eventually and offered her a smile.

~

"Adam, I have to talk with the others." She attempted to get away from me. I wanted her in bed with me for the short time remaining before sunrise.

"It's only twenty minutes, my heart. Come with me," I coaxed, pulling her down the hall to the bedroom I'd been given. "Besides, you need rest. Tell me that isn't true."

"I'm exhausted, Adam. I don't feel up to," I placed a hand over her mouth before she could tell me she was too tired for sex. She was too tired for petting, too. "I just want to hold you until I fall asleep," I said.

"Fine. Twenty minutes."

"I get to undress you," I murmured against her neck once the bedroom door was shut behind us.

"I'll just have to get dressed again," she protested.

"Humor me, all right?" I begged.

"Fine."

"Lie down, first."

"Adam."

"No, let me do this." Gripping her hand in mine—the one attempting to fend me off, I kissed it and laid it on the bed. "Stay still. Don't be afraid."

"Adam," she protested a second time.

"Shh, shh, shh," I placed a finger at her lips. "No talking. No moving. You're tired, remember?"

"I am tired."

"Then let me do this." Forming about an inch of claw on my right index finger, I employed a knuckle to graze her skin while allowing my claw to cut through her clothing. It was easy—easier than sliding a sharp, hot knife through soft butter. Taking my time, I paid attention to keeping my slices straight.

She watched me with a worried frown as I laid the pieces of her blouse flat on the bed around her. "Now, for this," I said, clipping the front of her bra easily with my claw. Gently I laid both halves on the bed.

"Pants," I breathed, sliding my finger against her skin and ripping the denim with the claw. "Both sides," I added, doing the other side exactly the same.

"Legs." I carefully moved down both sides of her legs, the fabric hissing as I sliced through it.

"Adam, I really like my shoes," she said.

"Then we'll remove those," I retracted my claw after laying the denim of her jeans flat on the bed, "in a more conventional manner." Gently, I removed both shoes, then her socks. "You have nice feet," I remarked, before kissing them.

"See, I didn't hurt you." I lay down beside her and offered her a smile.

"Is this your version of foreplay?" she asked innocently.

"You're not so hot you want to climb all over me?" I responded just as innocently.

"Yes, but you only have five minutes before you're out, and you won't wake until the sun goes down. Is this your way of making me so frustrated I'll jump you the minute you're awake again?"

"Why ever would you think that?" I asked, faking a Southern U.S. accent. "If I kiss you here," I kissed the skin just above her panties (which I hadn't removed), "then slide them down just a bit for another kiss," I did as described, making her gasp, "then you'll be screaming at me in frustration when I fall asleep, and I'll never hear a thing."

I barely had time to lie back again before the rejuvenating sleep descended.

"I have something to present to all of you," Xavier began. "After you see this, I believe you may agree with me. And, as Charles has refused to offer assistance, I have my own technology expert here to assist me." Xavier nodded to the young vampire, who tapped a key on the computer screen sitting before the U-shaped table where the Vampire Council sat.

"What is this we're about to see?" Ilaisaane asked eagerly.

"A turn we should consider," Xavier replied. "You'll see for yourself just how useful she might be to us."

~

"He has to die." Saxom sipped blood from a crystal goblet as he and Xavier lounged before a fire in Xavier's great room.

"I warned you," Xavier replied. "He hasn't responded to any of my messages. Likely, he's in thrall to them already. I'd ask Wlodek to declare him rogue, but he's already angry that I overrode his instructions and didn't show the entire video."

"Did you see how hungry several on the Council became when they saw her? I cannot believe Wlodek tabled their decision concerning her capture until the next meeting. She is mine," Saxom snapped. "I do not wish to wait for a Council decision to bring her here. Your child will die for putting his hands on her. If you don't kill him, I'll see to it myself. I have information that places him in New York."

"Then I will send mine after Adam and the others. They will bring her to us. I'll be happy to perform the turn and then hand her to you."

Saxom chuckled before nodding to Xavier. "If it's necessary," he replied.

~

"Sweetheart?"

Kiarra brushed past me, her eyes downcast. I stood in Merrill's massive kitchen shortly after sundown, where the others were finishing a meal cooked by Franklin.

"Let her go," Dragon placed a hand on my shoulder when I turned to follow her down the hall.

"What happened?" I demanded.

"The real Anna Madden's funeral happened today," Lion said, rising from his seat at the island. "Kee saw Rita and her two kids there. Rita took it really hard."

"So she's upset over that," I sighed. I was thankful it wasn't anything I'd done.

"Things aren't going so well for Rita. Manuelo is gone, and her job was just eliminated," Dragon pointed out. "She has children to feed."

"There's an article on the news, too, about the company that owns Hartshorne Oil in Corpus Christi." Joey set his laptop on the island. "The company plans to sell that one, so it'll remain closed for a while. They're distancing themselves from the Roy Cheek scandal. See?" Joey turned the laptop so I could read the article.

"Their drilling platforms are still operating, though," I nodded as I read through the article quickly.

"Those are tied to their other refineries in Houston and New Orleans," Joey said. "I guess the whole operation was turned over to them. Roy caused a bunch of problems for the company—their stock took a nosedive."

"It says here that they're still searching for Bill Gordon's body. No mention of the other two."

"The other two aren't relevant to the scandal," Lion observed. "They're just collateral damage."

"What are they saying about the events in Vegas?" I asked.

"They're blaming it on gangs, now," Dragon huffed. "Tourism has dipped dramatically."

"Gangs?" I shook my head. "People are torn apart and half-eaten, and they're saying gangs are responsible?"

"They're looking for a plausible excuse, when the truth is outside their experience," Merrill said.

"It's certainly that," I agreed.

"I think they're coming," Griffin stood and announced. Jerking my head up, I stared at him. His eyes had gone strange, and his voice was different.

"Battle stations," Lion growled low. "Come on, vampire. I believe some of these may be after you."

CHAPTER 9

"I have safeguards in place," Merrill said, tapping a key on his cell phone. We stood in the entry, leading into his spacious suite. The elevator lobby in the six-story building was right outside the heavy, double doors we faced. Merrill's suite took up the entire floor, and I was surprised the elevators didn't open directly into his suite.

"Put as many walls between you and the enemy as possible," Kiarra said. She'd stepped to my side while I considered what we might face. I watched as hidden steel doors emerged from camouflaged alcoves to cover the thick, carved wood already there.

A video screen lowered from the ceiling, revealing images of the lobby and elevator outside the doors. "Like it?" Joey breathed. He'd taken a position on my other side. "I designed it," he explained.

"You did good," Kiarra offered him a tight smile.

"What's coming?" I asked. Could spawn get past steel? Dragon's blades were strapped on, but he didn't appear overly concerned.

"Vampires," Griffin said.

Our eyes were glued to the monitor as we watched eight vampires emerge from the elevator. "Ready?" Merrill asked Griffin.

"Now," Griffin muttered.

Merrill tapped another button on his cell phone. What happened next I might not have imagined, but it made sense. For now, I was happy the technology existed.

The elevator lobby became an inferno.

Flames shot from numerous gas jets hidden between carefully placed marble tiles lining the small lobby. I wanted to cringe at the screams—vampires burn easily, but I'd never seen it happen like this. It took perhaps a minute. Maybe less.

It felt so much longer than that.

The jets shut off, the smoke cleared on the monitor and I gazed upon the blackened ash littering the floor outside the elevator. Blinking to clear my vision, I marveled that there wasn't more damage to the walls outside.

"Designed for that purpose," Lion sighed.

"What now?" I thought to ask. I stood, immobile, still too stunned to move.

"More are coming, in case these were unsuccessful," Dragon growled. "We're going to them, first."

New York City was a place I'd been many times. Had killed many rogues, there. Had even killed a few in New Jersey. I was hunting vampires again, only for a different reason. I'd become a target.

I still couldn't determine the reason for that, which meant Lion's words tumbled through my brain like coins in a dryer, pinging regularly and irritating me in ways I couldn't eliminate or ignore.

"Adam, we'll explain later," Kiarra sighed as we squeezed into the back seat of Merrill's Escalade with Lion. She sat between us; I placed a proprietary arm about her as Merrill started the engine and drove out of the underground parking garage swiftly.

Dragon sat in the passenger seat; Griffin had elected to stay with Franklin and Joey in Merrill's suite. The tires squealed as Merrill pulled onto the street—we were in a hurry, it seemed. I had no idea where we were going.

I noticed that DeKalb Avenue was in need of repairs as we drove down it, past Fort Greene Park. The sidewalks were cluttered with advertisements, street signs and benches for bus passengers. Our destination was the basement of a gray building on a street corner. Absently, I watched the traffic light turn from red to green as Merrill turned the steering wheel to go left and park (illegally) across the street.

"We won't be long," Dragon hissed as he and Merrill leapt from the vehicle. Kiarra grabbed my hand and pulled me out almost as quickly.

Graffiti covered the walls of the building and a light rain fell as I found myself running beside Kiarra. All of us followed Merrill and Dragon, whose rapid footfalls were nearly silent as they slipped down a flight of steps.

The metal door was no match for Merrill's strength; he punched right through it to get into the lower level. I barely had time to notice the spray-painted designs of a street artist on a wall beside the door before I was inside a concrete bunker.

Immediately, I realized the purpose of our haste; these vampires—ten of them—were preparing to leave. They'd gotten warning somehow, and were about to scatter. Merrill relieved the first one of his head before he had time to shout a warning.

Dragon's blades flew as he fought another vampire. A vampire's claws will generally slice through thin steel. Dragon's swords clanged against the claws, but remained intact and sound as Dragon feinted with one blade and swept the vampire's head from his shoulders with the other.

"Adam," Kiarra shouted, as two vampires charged me. My claws were out immediately, and I fought both while she fought a third who joined the fray. Lion had turned, his beast's claws more than a match for the vampire who thought to attack him.

Everything was going well. These rogues fought against powerful, seasoned warriors. I felt proud to be fighting with them.

You know what they say about pride.

"Lion," Kiarra screamed. I jerked at the sound, only half-decapitating the vampire I fought.

There are only three misters. All of them work for the Council.

That misconception almost cost us two lives.

"She was not to be touched," Saxom shouted, before raking claws across Xavier's desk, leaving deep, pale grooves in the dark, ancient wood. "Take her. Kill Adam. Leave the others dead or alive. That was my command to you."

Xavier cowered before Saxom, which was unusual for him. He was always in control. Always.

Saxom was older. Much, much older. Xavier held no notion just how old Saxom was. "Those were my instructions to the others," Xavier's voice shook. It embarrassed him. He was vampire. He struggled to calm his emotions and his demeanor.

"You failed," Saxom hissed. "I cannot see her condition. If she dies," he raked his claws across Xavier's desk a second time.

"I will not fail again," Xavier growled.

A gut wound. A death sentence. She was the only one—in my knowledge—who might save both of them, and she was one of the victims.

The mister had reformed behind Lion, just as Kiarra screamed. He'd turned to face the new threat, but not swiftly enough. She'd leapt to Lion's side, taking the second, heavier blow after Lion took the first across his chest.

I'd seen intestines before; these were spilled and steaming across cold concrete in the filthy underground portion of a New York building. Keening came from two throats—Merrill's and mine. I barely noticed as Dragon spoke one word.

Pheligar.

"Adam?" Joey held out a unit of blood. I blinked at him in confusion.

"Where are we?" My voice was dry. Cracked.

"Uh, Dragon says we're off-world. That's all he'd tell me." Joey lifted my hand and placed the unit of blood there. "Drink. You need it."

"How?" I said, unconsciously clipping the top off the bag so I could drink.

"He said they've been put back together and healed. They're sleeping. He's grim, Adam. Like this wasn't supposed to happen. I overheard Griffin say *not in the cards.* That's what he said just before Pheligar came to get me."

"I can't get the images out of my head." I lifted the bag and emptied it in four swallows. I couldn't. She'd been bloody. Broken. I wanted to vomit. I forced myself not to do so.

"This is so horrible," Joey sat beside me. He sought comfort. I had little to give. I put an arm around him anyway. "I thought Merrill was going to lose it. He never does that."

"Joey, hush," I said softly. "It'll be daylight, soon."

I blinked when the broad-shouldered, sandy-haired man appeared before me. "There's a room upstairs where you'll be safe," he offered. "Tiger and I moved beds in there. It's comfortable enough. Come with me, I'll show you."

Numbly I followed him, the wheels turning slowly in my mind. Yes, I'd seen him before. Once. That was of little consequence, now.

The room had been hollowed from solid rock. Two inner walls were still rock, with no windows. It was a safe haven for vampires. Two beds waited, made up and ready. I sent Joey to the farthest one, leaving the one closest to the door for me. They'd have to kill me before they got to him.

That thought forced me to stop short. I hadn't protected her. They should have had to go through me to get to her. Instead, she'd risked her life to save Lion's.

"Nobody here will harm you. You're safe," the sandy-haired man said softly. "Go to bed. You need the rest."

Without argument, I settled on the bed as the door closed behind him. I'd never hated the rejuvenation sleep so much in my life when the sun rose and my eyes shut for the day.

~

"She is still sleeping. You will not disturb her."

"Karzac," Dragon jerked his head toward the man I didn't recognize. I'd found my way back to the room where I'd been left by Pheligar the night before—on his way to saving Kiarra and Lion.

"I am Dragon's healer," Karzac grumbled. He and Dragon had a cup of tea in front of them at the massive kitchen island where they sat.

"Refizani," Dragon added before sipping his tea.

"What's Refizani?" Joey asked, taking a barstool beside me. He'd followed the sound of voices, finding us in the huge kitchen. Glass walls lined the front, overlooking an ocean far below. Water washed the shore and moonlight—from two moons—glittered on the dark surface.

"She likes the water," Karzac sighed. "This was too close for my liking. Refizani, young one," Karzac turned to Joey, "is what I am. I am from Refizan, and a physician before I became Dragon's healer."

"Who was the man who came last night?" Joey asked.

"Lynx."

"Does he have a healer?"

"He does. Her name is Raheela. She is an elf."

"There are elves? For real?"

"You should see the elf king. He can curse better than anyone I've ever met. I believe he may have cursed at Lynx for taking her as his healer." Dragon set his cup on the island with a shake of his head.

"He did. Accused me of being a filthy, pig-fucking rapist," Lynx appeared, a wide grin on his face. "That's the condensed version. I hear Kee's doing better."

"Better, certainly. Needs rest. Exhausted already, before that filth cut her open," Karzac declared.

"What about Lion?" Joey asked.

"Never in as much danger as Kiarra. She drew attention away from him when she went to his aid. His chest wound is healed and he is resting with his mate, who is also his healer. Marlianna will see to him properly."

"When can I see her?" I asked. I wanted to demand to see her, but preferred not to fight everyone present for that privilege. Especially since I was no longer on Earth and had no idea how to get back there.

"You may see her, now. You may not wake her," Karzac grumped.

Kiarra's bedroom wasn't far from the one Joey and I shared, as it turned out. It was much larger, however. Karzac frowned as I sat on the bed, but she didn't wake. I wanted to touch her, but didn't—she slept peacefully on pale-blue sheets, her body covered by a handmade quilt sewn in a scallop shell pattern.

She wakes at times from the healing sleep, which should not be, Karzac's voice in my mind startled me. *If you touch her, she will certainly wake.*

Healing sleep? I returned, shifting my gaze in his direction and hoping he'd receive my mindspeech.

Those explanations must wait. Come, we will leave her alone.

"I know you feel lost," Dragon took a seat next to me at the kitchen island. "This is Bearcat." He introduced a shorter, compact and quite muscular man to Joey and me. "He has offered to give you as much information as he can and answer questions."

I stared at Joey as he stared at Bearcat. I always knew when Joey fell in lust with anyone. This was certainly lust—at the very least. Bearcat was perhaps five-eight, had dark, curly brown hair, an easy smile and blue eyes. I figure Joey was already calculating how to get Bearcat's shirt off—the man was certainly muscular for his height.

"I'm a healer—Tiger's healer, actually," Bearcat explained as Dragon disappeared. I was beginning to wonder just how he and the others did that—appearing and disappearing at will. I asked that question first.

"It's called folding space. We can't do it when the Ra'Ak are present

—the power expended alerts them to our presence." Bearcat continued to smile—at Joey. "It requires a great deal of power."

"You have it, too?" Joey asked. I expected him to start drooling on Bearcat momentarily.

"Yes. The Saa Thalarr are more powerful, and can bend time as well as fold space. Healers can't bend time. If they want to, they have to ask permission from the Liaison."

"Liaison?"

"Pheligar. I hear you've met him."

"You could say that," I breathed uncomfortably. "He offered to separate my particles, whatever that means."

"He can be somewhat crusty and abrupt," Bearcat explained. "We don't know how old he is, either," he whispered. "We're afraid to ask."

"Does he have mindspeech? Do all of you have mindspeech?" Joey vibrated with excitement. If Bearcat had mindspeech, I could only imagine the messages that might pass between them.

"All of us have mindspeech," Bearcat's smile became a huge grin. "I don't suggest contacting Pheligar unless you're dying, though. Kiarra, Dragon and Lion are the only ones he answers willingly. The rest of us," Bearcat shrugged.

"I believe it's time you explained what Saa Thalarr means," I brought his attention back to me. It wasn't time to set up a date with Joey via mindspeech. It was time for answers.

～

"It is not time," Saxom snapped. "When it becomes necessary, I will tell you."

"I grow restless from inaction," Xenides complained. "Give the word and your enemies will die. You will have the seat at the center of that table."

"My plan is in place. You must stay hidden as long as possible. I intend to take what is mine, with Xavier's assistance. He has several under his command, and I prefer to place them at risk and keep you safe. If he fails me again, I'll allow you to challenge him. The outcome will not be to his liking."

"As you will it," Xenides bowed.

"You mean these things kill entire planets?" Joey gaped.

"They use them as feeding and breeding grounds, then leave them empty," Bearcat agreed. "But they can destroy planets, too—we've seen it happen before. That's why we fly under the radar, as your kind say, so they won't know we're there to stop them."

"What's to stop them anyway, if you challenge them?" I asked.

"The rules."

"There are rules?"

"Yes. But we have to face them to invoke the rules."

"That's weird," Joey muttered.

"Perhaps a flaw, when the rules were first devised. Before, there weren't any, and the Saa Thalarr were slaughtering them by the hundreds. The Ra'Ak Prince asked for rules. This is what we got."

"Who made the rules?" I asked.

"Someone so high in the Hierarchy, I can't even name them," Bearcat sighed.

"Hierarchy?"

"Uh, I think I should leave that to Kiarra to explain." Bearcat floundered, as if he'd let something slip that he shouldn't have. "I really don't know who it was, and she may not know, either."

"What is a Ra'Ak? Really?" Joey asked.

"You might think of them as shapeshifters, of the worst possible kind," Bearcat replied. "They become giant serpents when they turn, and nobody's safe after that."

"I hate snakes."

"You won't like these, either. They generally don't like each other. They tolerate one another, that's it."

"What language is that—Saa Thalarr?" Joey asked. It was a good question, and one I'd considered asking.

"It's Neaborian, which is a dead language. Neaboria is the first world the rogue Ra'Ak attacked and destroyed. It's completely empty and deserted, now. Saa Thalarr, in that language, means hope and vengeance."

"So the Saa Thalarr protect the planets under attack by the Ra'Ak?"

"Not all of them, no," Bearcat sounded uncomfortable again. "Another question for Kiarra," he said, brushing further queries on the subject aside.

"What do you do if the Saa Thalarr loses?" I asked.

"Plan a funeral. For the Saa Thalarr and the world involved. Every challenge is to the death."

"Bear, stop scaring them," Kiarra croaked behind me.

"Kee, you should still be in bed." I watched in amazement as Bearcat immediately went into caregiver mode. He was at her side quickly, taking her arm and leading her toward a barstool. "Want something to eat or drink?"

"Both would be nice."

"Sweetheart, how are you feeling?" I was right behind Bearcat, gently shooing him away before taking over and lifting her onto a barstool.

"Better. Having my guts scattered wasn't fun," she admitted.

"I know. At least they're where they should be now," I soothed. "Thank goodness."

"Thank Pheligar. He's the one who managed that. Larentii are the most talented healers. With Karzac's help, of course."

"My love, look at me," I said, tipping her head up with a finger.

"Adam?" she said. That's all she had time for—I leaned in to kiss her gently.

"Protein drink," Bearcat placed a glass of pale liquid in front of her as I stepped aside. "Fruit and cheese," he set a plate of food next to the drink. "Protein drink first. You know the drill."

"They all become unbearable if one of us is injured," Kiarra grumped, lifting the drink with shaking hands.

"Let me help." I took the glass away and held it to her lips.

Gripping my arm to steady herself, she drank. I rubbed her back with my free hand, encouraging her to drink as much as she could.

"Joey," Bearcat called softly. "Let's leave them alone."

"They have a M'Fiyah," Kiarra murmured when I took the glass away. She'd consumed nearly half of it, and I was content with that.

"M'Fiyah?" I wasn't sure I'd pronounced it correctly.

"Mate recognition. It's immediate with our kind."

"My heart, eat some of this and I'll carry you back to bed. We can talk there, if you want," I tapped the plate of fruit and cheese.

"I'm so tired, Adam." She leaned her head against my chest.

"I know."

"Has anyone told you what's happening on Earth?"

"No, and I haven't asked."

"Just as well. We can't do anything about it right now anyway. Lion will be ready to go back before I will."

"Stop worrying about that. Eat, then back to bed. Too bad my mother isn't here; she'd be fretting and watching every bite you took. If anyone could will someone better, it was her."

"I know you still miss them," she sighed, closing her eyes.

"That's neither here nor there," I said. "Eat, then bed. Don't make me tell you again," I teased.

She ate slowly. Deliberately. As if she were forcing herself. Still, she didn't eat much. "Is that all, sweetheart?" I asked when she sighed and leaned against me again.

"It's all I can handle, or I'll be sick."

"All right." Lifting her easily, I carried her toward the wood and iron steps leading to the top floor of her home. It was her home; Bearcat had confirmed that much. The windows were so tall in the kitchen that the view continued to the second floor balcony. I appreciated the design of it greatly.

"Who built your house?" I asked as we reached the second level.

"I did." Her eyes were closed, so I imagined that she'd had it built. "We'll argue about that later," she mumbled. "I'm too tired to do it now."

"Just let me know, so I can prepare myself," I whispered before kissing her forehead. "I wish I had body heat, to keep you warm," I sighed, placing her in bed and climbing in beside her. "I apologize for that."

"S'okay," she mumbled, curling against my side. "Sleep now."

"Yes, sleep now, my heart," I whispered, trailing my fingers through silky, platinum hair. "I'm right here."

~

"She's all right." Griffin poured a glass of wine for Merrill. "Just weak. Larentii are the best healers I've ever seen. Pheligar will heal her before he'll touch any of the others."

"Thank the gods," Merrill sighed and lifted the glass. "Are you sure you won't transport me to England? I want to remove a few heads for this."

"I won't take you. Interference, you know," Griffin countered.

"Why do I get the feeling there's something else going on, here?" Merrill asked, holding up his glass and studying the red wine within it.

"I can't explain that, now. Perhaps later."

"Looks good," Merrill swirled the liquid carefully.

"I told you it was good. You haven't even tasted it, yet."

"Are you prepared for my anger if I get drunk?"

"I think I can handle it."

"Don't say I didn't warn you, brother."

~

Joey's Journal

"Griffin and Merrill are having a sparring match," Bearcat informed me. Yes, we were in bed. I think it was a record—I'd never gone to bed with anyone so fast in my life. He didn't disappoint, either.

"A sparring match?" I had no idea what he meant, and was too exhausted after marathon sex to figure it out.

"Griffin was vampire once," Bearcat leaned in for a kiss. "The claws are out now. Merrill has some anger issues, I think, and he's working them out. Don't worry, they won't hurt each other. Much."

"Are you sure?" I made an attempt to sit up in bed.

"I'm sure." He pushed me back down with a smile. I had no idea how he could be aroused again after such a short time, but he was. I intended to enjoy every minute of it.

I woke to find myself the only inhabitant of the bed. I'd slept through the day and Kiarra had gotten up without me. I cursed being vampire before rolling off the bed and searching for my shoes.

The sounds of an argument reached me before I made my way downstairs. Kiarra was having a disagreement with Pheligar, from the sound of it.

"You have refused consistently, but you interfered with one who is not an intended mate. Either make him your healer or I will carry him back in time." Pheligar sounded stern and unrelenting as I stepped softly down the stairs. "Bearcat has already offered blood—he and Joey have a M'Fiyah. Choose, Kiarra, or I will choose for you."

"Fuck." She sounded defeated. "You'd really take him back, knowing he has a M'Fiyah with Bearcat?"

"Bearcat was not the one to rescue him. You did that."

"Yeah. I did that, all right."

"You're not regretting that, are you?" I had to know. Joey was like an adopted child. One that I cared for.

"I'm not regretting saving his life," Kiarra huffed as I walked into her kitchen. "Blue asshole here wants to make a big deal out of it."

I wasn't about to agree with her—not in front of the being who could turn me into atoms on a whim.

"I am merely pointing out facts," Pheligar snapped. "I have not resorted to derogatory terms to do so. I can, if that is your wish."

"I don't need a healer," she pouted.

"Kiarra, you must leave that in the past. I realize it still troubles you. Get rid of it. You know this one will be good for you."

"You want Joey to be her healer?" I blinked up at Pheligar.

"That is exactly what I want. I believe he will work very well in that role. As Bearcat is also a healer, it will allow them to be together."

"They're together?" My voice sounded higher than I liked.

"Several times," Pheligar crossed arms over his chest, as if asking me to refute his statement. Wisely, I suppressed the urge.

"Never ask a Larentii a question unless you want the unvarnished truth," Kiarra muttered. "If they choose to answer, anyway."

"Either offer him your blood or allow Bearcat to give it," Pheligar said. "Or I bend time. Choose, Kiarra."

"Fine. If Bearcat wants to do it; I don't think I'm up for a blood donation at the moment."

"I know you are not," Pheligar's voice gentled. "I would suggest waiting, if you wished to offer. You must tell Joey; the final decision will be his, of course."

"Of course." Kiarra rubbed her forehead.

"I will heal the headache." Pheligar lifted her one-handed and placed large, blue fingers on her forehead. My jealousy roared to life.

"That will not do," Karzac appeared beside me. Before I knew it, I was flat on my back, staring up at Karzac, who held me down with one hand. Past him, I gazed at Pheligar, who still held Kiarra in his arms. My jealousy had fled. Karzac took his hand away from my forehead.

"Jealousy is not tolerated," he huffed and walked away.

I wanted to ask how a healer had manhandled me so easily. I decided that I didn't want to know the answer. "You will no longer feel that emotion," Pheligar settled Kiarra on her feet nearby. "Karzac holds the power to remove it, as do I and some of the others. It is a useless and often harmful nuisance."

How? I wanted to shout. They'd done something to me and I couldn't prevent it. "Adam, you'll have to make a choice eventually," Kiarra dropped to the floor beside me. "If you refuse, you can have your jealousy back, no questions asked. For now, you're safer without it."

"Far safer," Pheligar agreed. "Tomorrow, Kiarra, you will tell Joey, and he will decide. I will return for that conversation." Pheligar disappeared.

"Where is Joey now?" I sat up and frowned at Kiarra.

"He's still in bed with Bearcat. On Tiger's planet."

"He's not here?"

"Adam, he's fine. Stop worrying."

"What about you? Are you fine?"

"As fine as I can be after losing an argument with Pheligar."

"Does that happen often?"

"More often than I like. The others don't get to argue with him. He won't even listen."

"Sounds like a few vampires I know."

"I think everybody has someone like Pheligar in their lives. It's a law of physics or nature—take your pick."

"Are you teasing me?"

"Yeah. I guess." She raked her hair back and shook her head. "Why do you ask?"

"I thought your kind couldn't lie." I did the teasing, this time.

"We can't deliberately lie. We can tease, tell jokes and employ sarcasm, so be prepared."

"Why does it bother you so much to have a healer?" If I'd had any sense, I'd never have asked the question.

"I don't talk about that," Kiarra responded coldly before disappearing. It wouldn't have been so bad, but I'd been left alone— still with no knowledge of where I was or how to get home again.

CHAPTER 10

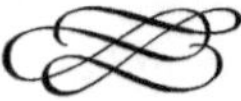

*D*ragon brought her back shortly before daybreak. I'll admit that I was angry by that time, so we didn't speak. She brushed past me on my way to the stairs and her bedroom.

I watched her go with a scowl on my face.

"Vampire, she was raped by her healer. Now do you understand?" Dragon turned dark, glittering eyes in my direction. He was angry and didn't bother to hide it. After watching him kill vampires with ease, I knew not to argue. "That's why she wakes from the healing sleep. The rest of us can't. She can, because that's when she was attacked—after she was injured and he placed her in a healing sleep. Go to bed, leech. It's almost daybreak."

He disappeared, leaving me gaping like a fool at the space he'd occupied seconds earlier. I'd been insulted, but felt it was deserved—up to a point. I'd asked a sensitive question, never realizing the damage it might cause. I had a ready argument, however. I realized as much as I climbed the steps to the second level.

Joey's gay, my heart, I sent. *He loves you and will never bring you harm.*

I received no reply.

Nobody spoke to me when I made my way into the kitchen after nightfall. Dragon, Lynx and Lion had come. Pheligar was also present. Kiarra sat on a barstool, arms crossed tightly and head bowed, as if she were under siege. In a way, I suppose she was.

"Bearcat says they're on the way," Dragon announced, his leather pants creaking softly as he took a seat at the island. Kiarra sat on the opposite side, alone and unresponsive. She'd let her hair fall across her face so I couldn't read her expression. It didn't take a genius to know she was upset—not just with me, but with all present.

"Adam?" Joey sounded terrified when he appeared with Bearcat. Kiarra's head jerked up. "Adam, he's going to take me back and let me die." Joey wiped tears away.

"You didn't." Kiarra accused, glaring at Pheligar.

"I merely offered the truth," Pheligar huffed in indignation. "Surely you recognize the value of it. I informed him that you didn't want this and taking him back was the only alternative."

"I said all right, you bastard," Kiarra slid off the barstool and stalked toward the tall, blue-skinned Larentii. "The choice belongs to him, now. That's where we left this." Kiarra stopped before Pheligar, her hair crackling with energy. "You did this to upset him. And me. Admit it," she jabbed a finger into his chest. She had to raise her arm to do it.

Pheligar didn't flinch.

"What's going on?" Joey wiped away fresh tears; he was clearly upset. I pulled him toward me and rubbed his back.

"You're going to be Kiarra's healer, Joey. I was there when she said she wanted you. Pheligar is just being an asshole. I hear he does that a lot."

I wasn't the one who had to be truthful. Pheligar and Kiarra were both telling the truth—just different versions of it. Before and after versions, if you will. Somebody had to play peacemaker and keep the situation from deteriorating.

"Kiarra's just afraid, Joey. Nobody's bitten her before. I know Bearcat may have offered, but to be her healer, I think you need that connection."

"What?" Kiarra and Pheligar said in unison while turning in my direction. Kiarra wore a look of confusion—Pheligar appeared smugly satisfied.

"Yes. I believe you need her blood. I heard Griffin gave Merrill blood, and they get along pretty well."

"But, uh," Joey began. Yes, he knew what would happen. I was looking forward to it.

"But," Kiarra echoed Joey.

"Sweetheart, he won't hurt you. Every vampire is taught how to deliver the bite."

"He's right," Dragon sighed. "You didn't give blood to the last one—you inherited him. Griffin's first healer was killed, so he inherited him before that—from Lisster, when he retired. You got him after Griffin asked Amara to be his healer. He had no blood connection to you."

"But," she repeated, shaking her head, her face going pale.

"I won't hurt you, I promise," Joey begged. "Please." He held a hand toward her.

"Joey," Kiarra stepped forward and I could see she was trembling. "Your life is safe. If it weren't—if I didn't care about you, I'd have let you die on cold concrete. There are so many things you don't know," she sighed before offering him a hug and pulling away.

"Joseph David Showalter, do you want to be my healer?" she asked.

"Yeah. I do," he nodded enthusiastically.

"Then you'll be my healer," her voice trembled on the words. "My blood is a gift to you, Joey. You will take no harm from it. There are no bindings or conditions, it is freely given."

I watched as a tear slipped down her cheek. *Stay here*, Lion's huge hand gripped my shoulder.

"I won't hurt you," Joey repeated, gripping the back of her neck. Leaning in, he placed a soft kiss against the artery in her neck. I tensed. Lion's grip tightened. I heard the gasp as Joey's fangs penetrated soft skin. He drank. I held my breath.

"Enough," Pheligar said quietly. Joey withdrew, licked the wound clean and turned in my direction.

Kiarra dropped to the floor in a faint behind him.

~

"He'll sleep for twelve hours or so," Lion said. Joey took three steps toward me before he'd gone down. I caught him on my way to Kiarra. Pheligar got to her first. There was no jealousy as he lifted her off the floor—merely irritation, as I wanted to see to her.

I was the experienced vampire. I knew the effects of the bite. Pheligar should have let me take care of her, instead of disappearing with her in his arms.

I carried Joey upstairs instead, feeling numb as I made my way up the steps. "The blood will change him," Lion continued. "He'll be able to walk in daylight."

"What?" I stopped abruptly, Joey's legs swinging with the cease in momentum.

"Changes happen. He won't be forced to consume blood if he doesn't want it. Bearcat and Karzac will teach him what he needs to know, in order to serve as Kee's healer."

"You mean to tell me that there really is something that can cure vampirism?" I began walking again.

"You heard her give permission," Lion said, reaching for the doorknob to my bedroom. "Without that, you'll die if you take our blood. It's the way we're made. Our blood isn't a cure for vampirism, unless we want it to be a cure for vampirism. Got it?"

"Absolutely."

"No, you don't. Somebody will explain it better, later. We have to put Joey to bed, first."

"What about Kiarra?"

"Who knows where Pheligar took her? He never tells us anything. They could be on the Larentii homeworld, for all I know."

"Then I want to go there. I want to see her."

"Nobody goes to the Larentii homeworld. Nobody knows where it is. You have to be escorted there—by a Larentii."

"I'll take care of Joey," Bearcat said. He'd followed silently behind Lion and me, concerned, no doubt, about Joey. "You can hold your debate downstairs if you want. I'll stay with him."

"Thank you," I nodded after settling Joey on the bed. Bearcat immediately covered Joey up and fussed about removing his shoes and making him comfortable.

"Come on," Lion led me out of the bedroom. "You can fret downstairs, and sleep in Kiarra's bed if Pheligar doesn't bring her back before morning."

"I'm worried he'll harm her."

"What?" Lion turned on the steps and stared at me.

"Isn't that possible?" I'd seen the way he'd manipulated her earlier.

"No." Lion began walking down the stairs again. "You don't know anything about the Larentii, so you can't be blamed for being ignorant. Did you see how fast he came when Dragon called? He already knew she was hurt," Lion said.

"He came for you, too," I pointed out.

"You don't know enough about him to realize how angry—and frightened he was. Joey's turning was inevitable. We all knew it. It was just getting her to realize and accept it."

"Are you calling that show of manipulation tough love?" I grumbled.

"Pheligar has strange ways. All Larentii do. Don't overlay your ideas and customs onto his race—they won't match. Karzac hasn't minded filling in as Kiarra's healer—when she'll allow someone to touch her. She needs that connection with Joey. Who knew you'd give her the solution we were all seeking—her giving him blood? I thought Pheligar was going to have to shame her into it."

"Is that where the fiasco was leading?" I asked, blinking in confusion at Lion.

"Yes, if you want the simple truth. From now on, if Kiarra is hurt enough to need a healer, Joey will feel it. He'll know before the rest of us. Marlianna took my blood, and she knows immediately when I'm injured."

"This is confusing." I walked toward the glass wall enclosing the kitchen and stared through it to the moonlit ocean beyond.

"Look, Joey didn't take much blood—it doesn't take more than a cupful to effect the change. She'll be fine in a couple of days. We have to go back, then, and sort this out. Things have been happening, and we need to be there."

"What do you suggest I do in the meantime?"

"You have two days. Use them to your advantage, vampire." Lion's hand fell heavy on my shoulder. "She's fragile, now. Pheligar knows that. Now, you do, too. Take care of our girl." He disappeared, leaving me with my thoughts.

"What do I do?" Pheligar held Kiarra in his arms while Nefrigar checked her carefully. Pheligar had gone straight to the Larentii Archives to see his brother.

"You might have accomplished your goal another way," Nefrigar sighed and pulled away. "Her heart rate is now normal; I slowed it. My suggestion? Tread carefully from now on."

"I cannot show preferential treatment."

"You say that to me? Who should you show preferential treatment to? You built this conundrum for yourself, brother. Perhaps you should dismantle it and allow things to go as they will."

"I cannot." Pheligar shook his head.

"Then take her back and be done with it. You cannot remain in this position of continuous vacillation. It upsets both of you. You ask my advice? I give it to you. You choose not to heed it."

"I will consider your words."

"Do so. It never does harm to treat anyone with consideration, even when they test your patience. Remember that."

"I will try."

With nothing else to do, I settled onto Kiarra's bed with a book I borrowed from her library. Yes, she has a library, but I had to follow my nose to find it. Ink on paper has a distinctive scent.

The book was a mystery by a favorite author—Sarah Fox. There was never a photograph on the dust jackets, just a short blurb explaining that the author lived in the Southern U.S.

"I had to bend time to get that one; it hasn't been released yet," Kiarra walked into the bedroom just as I opened the book.

"You can travel into the future?" I patted the bed beside me.

"Only a short way—we're not allowed to go very far in that direction."

"When did you arrive?" I worried that I'd been buried in her library while she searched for me.

"Just a few minutes ago. I checked on Joey. Bearcat's keeping an eye on him. Why didn't you tell me what happens with the bite?"

"I thought you knew everything," I hedged, setting the book aside and watching her carefully.

"I only know things when I *Look* for them specifically," she said.

"Was the experience a good one? Usually it is."

"I'd prefer it to be from someone else," she muttered, dropping her eyes.

"Do you know how they teach young vampires the bite lesson?" I asked. "Come on, sit here on the bed with me," I coaxed.

Reluctantly, she walked around the bed and settled on it, leaving two feet of distance between us on the large bed. Her shoes were removed and tossed onto the floor with barely a thought.

"How do they teach young vampires to bite?" She blinked curious blue eyes in my direction.

"First, your sire brings another vampire to you. As there are so few females among the vampire race as to be non-existent, the outsider is generally male. Your sire explains that you must place compulsion, and inform your donor that they will not be harmed. The outsider illustrates your sire's instruction, by holding your neck firmly in one hand and placing compulsion. Young vampires are susceptible to an older vampire's compulsion."

"Right. That explains a lot," she murmured, turning her head away. Her bedroom had no windows, either—all the windows were at the front of her home. I resolved to ask her about that later.

"It's easier to protect during hurricane season," she said, answering my unspoken question.

"I see. Now, after compulsion is laid and reassurances made, the young vampire is bitten by the older one. The climax is always given during that initial bite. The one drinking should make the bite as gentle as possible, although I have heard stories from others, telling me that didn't always happen. The climax is supposed to make up for any pain caused."

"Was it that way for you?"

"Xavier invited a crusty old bastard named Cecil to his manor. He could have been more courteous during the bite," I grumbled. "After that, you have to prove that the lesson was learned by biting another, experienced vampire. I bit Xavier—he insisted on it. He didn't complain, but he didn't praise, either. He never has."

"Have you bitten any vampires since then?"

"No vampires. Only humans, before bagged blood became available."

"I see."

"Sweetheart, I don't consider them cattle. Some vampires do—I don't. I recall being human, although Xavier has made considerable attempts to drive it from me. Did Joey hurt you?" I moved closer, reaching out with a hand to touch her throat. No marks were left behind—vampires healed their bites to hide their existence.

"No. It just—scared me."

"That's not how it should be," I leaned closer. "It's supposed to be pleasurable. A gift, in exchange for the blood taken."

"Your donors have always been under compulsion," she pointed out as I attempted to pull her into my arms. "They're not afraid when you bite them. Compulsion doesn't work with me, remember?"

"I know." Gently, I lowered her head onto the pillow. "I know," I breathed against her mouth. "My girl was scared. Mistreated." I kissed her again.

"Adam," she struggled against me.

"Shhh, sweetheart, it's all right." I stroked hair back from her forehead. "You taste like sunlight," I whispered reverently, kissing her again. "I promise I won't hurt you. Let me know if I scare you. We'll take it slow."

I didn't want to take it slow. I wanted her. Immediately. I couldn't do it that way. Perhaps in the future, when she might want me as badly as I wanted her. This was like soothing a virgin or a frightened mare. I realized she was practically both those things.

Had I thought to have sex when she returned? We were well on our way. My tongue probed her mouth gently as I ripped through her clothing with a claw barely formed on a finger.

"These are perfect," I nuzzled and nipped her breasts before kissing my way to her throat. "All of it, perfect," I declared.

Yes, I allowed my lust, which I'd kept in check for nearly a hundred years, to surface, and my fangs descended. The words came swiftly, tumbling from her lips as I pierced her throat and drank.

"Aaadam," Joey sang. "Time to wake up. Are you hungry? Lion's cooking steaks."

"What?" My eyes opened slowly and I blinked to bring Kiarra's bedroom ceiling into focus. "Where's Kiarra?"

"Walking on the beach. Adam, you dog." Joey slapped my shoulder with a wide grin. "Lion says you should apologize, but you need to come with me, first. It's daylight, and we're both awake!"

"Is that true?" I flung the quilt back and sat up in bed, still fully clothed. Kiarra's blood had been both sweet and potent, rendering me unconscious in seconds. *Just as it had Joey*, I reminded myself.

I hope you intend to honor your commitment to her, Dragon sent as Joey and I walked into the kitchen minutes later. Daylight streamed through the tall windows and I blinked in the brightness of it. I hadn't seen daylight in a very long time.

"What are you talking about?" I focused on Dragon, who sat at the island, polishing one of his blades.

"We're allowed to form a blood-bond, but only with those who are our mates, healers or have made a great sacrifice in our defense. Our blood-bonded must be above reproach and fully committed to us in some way. Our blood makes them immortal, if they aren't already. Blood bonds are generally for mates and healers only. Griffin received a great deal of assistance from Merrill in the past; therefore, Griffin has a blood bond with him."

"What he's saying," Lion thumped a plate of steaks on the island, "is that you better be ready to stay with Kiarra—as a mate. Otherwise, both of you are in trouble. You for taking her blood without permission first, and her for giving you permission during the act. Got that?"

"How does she feel about this?" I asked.

"At least he knew to ask about her first, instead of looking to protect his own ass," Lion turned to Dragon. The blade Dragon wiped carefully gleamed in the afternoon light as he examined it with a practiced eye. I swallowed nervously, only realizing then that I could perform that simple act. These two sought to protect Kiarra. I was an outsider, and may have gotten her in trouble.

"Lunch," Lion indicated the plate of steaks. "Bearcat's bringing the vegetables. Grab a plate and sit down. You'll be able to eat this, now."

"I've done nothing but eat since I woke up," Joey whispered beside me. "Come on, Adam, it's like heaven."

I'll admit—the food did smell good for the first time since I'd been turned vampire. I sat down, Lion placed a thick steak on my plate, Bearcat added a baked potato and asparagus and I dug in.

"I could serve this in my restaurants," I muttered, swallowing a half-chewed chunk of steak.

"That's just because you haven't eaten real food in a while," Lion said, cutting into his steak and brandishing the fork in my direction. "I figure your chefs can do better than this."

"I don't care. This is the best food I can remember," I said, cutting off another bite.

"Appreciates food—I like that," Lion nodded to Dragon.

"He's decent in a fight," Dragon agreed, laying his blade aside and cutting into his steak. Joey sat beside me, his mouth continuously too full to speak. Bearcat smiled at him often and shook his head while eating.

The thought hit me like a thunderbolt, then, and I dropped my fork. "Will I," I began.

"You still have your claws, fangs and red eyes, in addition to the vampire speed," Kiarra sighed. She'd appeared near Lion. Not me—Lion. "The biggest difference is that you can obviously eat," she didn't look at me, "and sit in daylight while doing it."

"Kee, your plate is on the barbecue," Bearcat said. "I'll get it."

"No, I will." She sat beside Lion, who shrugged away my pointed glance and made the plate appear in front of her.

"It's called *Pulling*," Joey explained." Bearcat taught me how to do it, too."

"Here," Lion did the same, *Pulling* in an unopened protein drink. "You need this," he pushed the drink toward Kiarra.

With a sigh, she opened it and drank.

"Pheligar is bad enough. Thorsten will be worse if he shows up."

Kiarra still hadn't allowed me to touch her. We stood on the deck outside the kitchen, not far from the barbecue where Lion had cooked steaks. She leaned against the heavy, wood railing, staring at the ocean beyond.

"I want to stay with you. I'm sorry, sweetheart, but ever since I saw you the first time, I haven't been completely rational," I admitted. "So that's nearly a century of irrational behavior."

"What?" She whirled toward me.

"I saw you, Lynx and another woman in the 1920s," I said. "I fell in love with you, then. Haven't been with a woman since."

"What?" Her pretty bottom lip was gripped tightly in her teeth.

"I saw you. I barely remember Louis Armstrong, that night. All I could do was stare at you the whole time."

"But what about—all right, I guess it doesn't matter." She turned away from me again.

"What about Anna Kay, you mean?" I asked, moving toward her carefully. "That was never Anna Kay. That was always you. Admit that, at least." My arms went around her. She shivered; I tightened my embrace.

"Kee," Lion poked his head out the door leading to the kitchen. "Thorsten's here."

"Fuck," she sighed, moving away from my embrace. "Adam, stay here. I'll handle this."

I felt lost as she walked away from me. Lost *and* guilty.

"Thorsten. One of The Powers That Be. He supervises the Liaison and the Saa Thalarr," Lion said, pouring me a drink from the bottle he'd purchased at a bar.

"What exactly is that—The Powers That Be?"

"We can't say what they really are, but to you, they'd be a demi-god or something similar."

"How much trouble did I cause?" I tossed back the glass of whiskey. I tasted it, too; felt the burn as I swallowed that I'd almost forgotten from my early, human life.

"Enough." Lion drank his whiskey and poured more. I held out my glass and he obliged my silent request, the liquid smooth and quiet as it slid into my glass.

"I haven't been drunk in a very long time," I said.

"This is a good time for it," Lion said.

"This is good whiskey," I countered.

"They serve good whiskey on Wyyld," Lion agreed.

"Wild?"

"Wyyld."

"Got it."

"No, you don't. W-y-y-l-d. That's how it's spelled—in English."

"I am English," I covered a half-drunk burp.

"I could never tell by the accent," Lion muttered.

"Is that sas-casm? Sar-casm?" I corrected myself.

"Most assuredly." Lion spoke in a British accent. I blinked at him in confusion.

"We have to fit in, wherever we go. That means languages, dialects and accents. If we stand out, we die."

"But what about," I waved a hand in the air, searching for words to describe the events on Earth.

"Completely out of the ordinary." He poured more whiskey for both of us. "In fact, we usually go in alone or accompanied by our healers. This one, well, this one is really strange. It's strange, too, that so many of us were available to go at the same time. Usually, we're scattered across the universe."

"How many?" I drank this glass slower than the others.

"Seven, plus our healers. We're the smallest race—in numbers—in existence."

"Bugger me," I sighed after emptying my glass.

"No, thanks."

I laughed.

I did appreciate the food and daylight portion of my new existence. I didn't appreciate the hangover I had.

"It's your own fault," Karzac chided as he held my head in his hands. In seconds, there was blessed relief.

"Partly Lion's fault," I said automatically.

"And that's why I'm here, instead of leaving you to suffer."

"How's Joey?"

"Learning quickly. Appears to have a talent for healing."

"Where's Kiarra?" That's the question I really wanted to be answered.

"Running on the beach. Come with me—it's time you saw."

"Saw what?" I blinked at Karzac in confusion.

"Come."

I still hadn't grasped the concept of folding space, although I appreciated it greatly. Karzac folded me to the beach below Kiarra's home. I must have gaped, because Karzac asked me to close my mouth. He may have added something about letting insects in if I didn't, but I ignored him.

"This is her fighting animal. You've only seen the smaller version before."

Nine feet tall at the withers. I couldn't speak. Couldn't breathe. Blindingly white, she glowed in the sunlight, her reflection as she ran echoed in the water washing onto the shore. That's not what drew my attention, however.

"If that touches evil, the evil dies," Karzac sounded smug.

Three feet in length and wickedly sharp, her horn would skewer almost anything. "Why couldn't I see it before?" I breathed.

"You're lucky to be seeing it now. Do you understand how close you came to dying?" Karzac turned to offer me a scowl. "If she hadn't done as she did, you'd be nothing more than a pile of ash and a memory."

"I made a mistake," I admitted. "Do all of you take pleasure in punishing me for it? She won't talk to me, and the rest of you keep telling me how fortunate I am to be alive."

"We cannot lie. Do you wish us to?"

"Hell, no. Why would I want that?" Before he could answer, I began to run. Yes, I can run very fast as a vampire. I ran after Kiarra.

"We've been assigned a test," Kiarra said as we sat in the kitchen later, having juice and a sandwich. Mine was roast-beef; hers was cheese. "But I have to take you somewhere, first."

"Where is that? What's the test?" I bit into the sandwich, which was quite excellent. I appreciated the crunch of the lettuce and the texture of the meat and cheese as I chewed.

"I can't tell you. You'll know it when you see it," she sighed. "If you'd just waited until I could present all the pros and cons, giving you the option of making an informed decision, we wouldn't be in this uncomfortable spot."

"I smelled your blood, sweetheart. I think that's what did it."

"Adam." A hand went over her face.

"When?" I asked.

"Tonight. We're going out for dinner, first." Her hand dropped to the island and she shook her head before turning away.

"I'll settle for dinner," I agreed amiably. "Any chance I can get you in bed before then?" We still hadn't had sex, and that irritated me.

"Wait until after the test," she replied. "I'm going out for a while. Please stay here." She walked through the kitchen door and onto the deck before disappearing.

"Five pounds of gold says he doesn't." Dragon dropped a heavy canvas bag onto Lion and Marlianna's kitchen table.

"I'll see that bet," Lion agreed. "I think he will. Want some tea?"

"Falchani black?"

"You got it."

The sun had fallen below the horizon when Kiarra returned. I'd fussed, fumed and cursed during her absence. I hated this. Generally, unless my dealings involved older vampires, I was in charge.

I considered, too, what my current circumstances might mean to my position as Chief Enforcer. Would it matter? Did I even want to keep it? Was I still obligated to answer to Xavier? I'd wasted time and hadn't asked Kiarra so many relevant questions. Was this what she meant by pros and cons?

"We have to leave soon," Kiarra said. "You can shower, or I can get you clean using power. What do you prefer?"

"Will you?" I began.

"I'm not showering with you."

"Then do what you have to do to get me clean," I insisted stubbornly.

"Fine." I was bathed in light for a moment before my vision cleared. I stared, first at her, then at me. She'd changed our clothing, too.

A tight, embroidered blue-velvet bodice over a darker blue silk skirt complimented her eyes perfectly. The neckline was low, revealing pale skin. Her hair was caught up in combs atop her head and I sighed in appreciation before studying the clothing I wore.

A black, embroidered waistcoat over wool pants and boots. We looked ready for a costume ball.

"That's not it," she shook her head at me. "It's time." She folded space.

And bent time.

"This is," I breathed, stunned nearly speechless. It was. The restaurant where I was supposed to meet my brother and his new wife for dinner. I'd refused, choosing to tend to my horses, instead.

"Yeah. It's that, all right."

We stood across the street, staring at the door—and the doorman just outside—for several moments. Somehow, I knew my brother Justin waited inside for my arrival, although I'd sent a note claiming I couldn't come. I'd listed other obligations as my excuse.

"Taken care of," Kiarra whispered. The sights and scents of London in 1790 permeated my senses. Horses clopped by, carriages clattering in their wake over cobblestone streets. Pipe tobacco smoke drifted past as a gentleman, carrying a silver-topped cane, walked by.

"I don't believe this. Is it real?" I asked. I wanted it to be real. Hoped it was real.

"It's real, Adam. Your brother is waiting." She took my arm.

In a daze, I walked her across the street. The doorman, whose name I'd never bothered to learn, recognized me immediately. Tipping his hat, he opened the door for us. "This is a dream," I muttered as someone came to take my hat and coat.

"This is a test," Kiarra responded as we were led to the table my brother had reserved. There, I received another shock.

It wasn't only Justin and Catherine who waited for us. My parents had come as well. For a moment, I forgot to breathe.

CHAPTER 11

"Mother." I wanted to weep as I leaned in to kiss her cheek. "Father," I clapped him on the back. "Justin," I did the same for him, before kissing Catherine's hand.

"Adam, aren't you forgetting something?" my mother asked, cutting her eyes toward Kiarra, who waited patiently behind me while I greeted my family.

"Mother, this is Kiarra," I pulled her forward. She reluctantly allowed me to present her to my family.

"You've never brought a woman to a family dinner before, old man," Justin teased.

"There has never been one I wanted to bring until now," I said. "I'm asking her to marry me."

"Oh." My mother fanned herself and dropped to her chair. "I never thought this day would come."

"Son?" my father asked, giving me a look. I knew what that look meant—was she of good breeding? Was her family financially sound? I longed to tell him how things were in the twenty-first century. I didn't. I merely gave him a nod, telling him in the way we had of understanding one another, that all was well.

"She's so beautiful, Adam. I can see why you chose her," Catherine's smile was tight. Catherine had a bit of an image problem, after all, but Kiarra would put every woman in the place to shame.

"He hasn't asked me yet, and I haven't answered yet," Kiarra spoke for the first time.

"A spitfire, Adam? I never suspected," Justin teased me again.

"I could write several volumes concerning what you don't suspect," I teased back. Yes, I felt giddy, seeing my family again. Talking to them again. I didn't want to wake from this dream, if dream it was.

"You'd stoop to write?" my mother chuckled. "Justin writes. I've never known you to slow down long enough to voluntarily put pen to paper, unless it's an excuse not to attend a function."

"He failed in his art lessons," my father informed Kiarra with a smile. "His tutor asked him once to draw a tree. He drew a straight trunk, then placed the word *leaf* where every leaf should be. He has always excelled in innovation, and failed miserably at anything having to do with fine arts."

"That isn't true," I shook my head. "I am quite good at architectural drawing."

"That you are, my boy," he laughed. "I think you'd have gone in that direction, had I not asked you to oversee the Oriental shipping contracts."

"True," I agreed. "What is on the menu tonight?"

"Roast duck," Justin said immediately. It had been my favorite.

"I'll have that," I said.

I never wanted the evening to end. My mother was quite taken with Kiarra, I could tell, although she spoke little. Justin teased her lightly, telling her what an awful bachelor I'd been, preferring horses to balls and garden parties.

Kiarra smiled and said she understood that perfectly well. I kissed my mother again when she and my father rose to leave. I had no idea they'd planned to come to London and stay at the town house for a few days. Justin had planned the dinner as a surprise, and I'd refused to attend the first time.

"Shall we exchange correspondence?" My mother asked Kiarra.

"Of course," she smiled and agreed. I didn't point out that her kind couldn't lie. Half an hour later, Justin made his excuses. I signed for dinner as I watched him and Catherine walk away.

"Now what?" I turned to Kiarra.

"I want to see your horses," she said softly.

"I can arrange that."

I did. Hiring a cab, I paid with money I'd found in a pocket of my borrowed clothing.

"Mind your dress, mum," the cabbie warned as he helped Kiarra from the coach.

"I will, thank you," she said, allowing him to take her hand.

Once the cab drove away, I led her into the stable where my four were quartered.

"These two draw my carriage," I stroked the noses of my matched pair. "The other two, I ride."

"Do you hunt?"

"No," I shook my head. "That's for dandies and fops."

"Seriously?" she blinked at me in disbelief.

"I am of the merchant class. We work for a living," I replied, my voice haughty. "I did do some hunting," I admitted. "Didn't like it much. Felt bad for the animal. If you're going to kill something, make it clean and merciful if possible. I don't like scaring it half to death, first."

"Adam, this is the test," she said, her fingers linking together and gripping tightly. I watched as spots of color formed high on her cheekbones, enhancing her beauty.

"I can leave you here, and you can continue your life as if you'd never been made vampire," she said. "You know how to avoid that, and you're strong enough to fight off your attackers. You can stay with your family, here and now." She dropped her eyes, refusing to look at me.

"Do I have a choice?"

"You have the choice—of staying here, where you are known and loved. Or, going back with me, to an uncertain future. I'm involved in a long war, Adam. Every time, the challenge is to the death. I don't know if I'll live another hundred thousand years or die tomorrow. That's the uncertainty I deal with every day." She turned her gaze on me, then.

"You'll leave me here, to continue my life as it should have been." I didn't make it a question.

"If you want that, yes."

The prospect squeezed my heart. Yes, it beat again, after more than two centuries of stillness. I'd felt unfettered joy for the first time since becoming vampire, upon seeing my family again.

"You'll leave me behind, won't you." Again, not a question.

"If you make this your choice."

Either choice I made would inflict pain. Mentally, I cursed the one who'd designed this test; forcing me to choose one thing I loved over another. I had to weigh my options and do it quickly—Kiarra looked as if she were prepared to leave at any moment. That's when the visions came. Perhaps it was what they meant by *Looking*. Either way, it hit me—a flood of images I couldn't seem to stop or turn aside.

Yes, I saw myself living in London. Seeing my parents and my brother from time to time. Saw myself falling into old habits. Saw myself not aging. Being forced to move from place to place and eventually refusing to see my relatives, because I hadn't changed as they grew older and infirm.

All that time, too, I had one goal in mind. One thing I sought, throughout the centuries. I couldn't find it. Would never find it again. Finally realized what I'd done. Wherever I went, whatever I did, I'd be looking for her. *Kiarra*. I'd searched for her during my lifetime for nearly a century. I'd be trading that for immortality, without her at my side.

Yes, she warned me. I didn't care. I had to take whatever I could— whatever time we might have together. I'd go crazy if I didn't.

"I've seen them grow old and die once before—from a distance," I said. "A part of me knows that. The rest of me knows one thing," I said.

"What's that?" she blinked. I saw she was close to tears. Suspected my choice wouldn't be her.

"That I can't live without you," I said. "I've searched for you so long, and to have you now, and throw that away? What kind of fool would I be?"

The light knocked me down when it came. It rendered me unconscious as well.

"Six people have disappeared from the Aransas Wildlife Refuge since Saturday," the newscaster announced. "Some forensic evidence was found on a beach there, but the authorities haven't released any details. Meanwhile, area families are waiting—and hoping—for their loved ones' return."

"Kapirus," Kiarra flopped her head onto the pillow beside me, turning off the vid-screen with a remote.

It wasn't a television, it was a vid-screen. I knew that, now. "I got this information from Dragon earlier," she said. "He got it from Daniel, who has been sending it regularly while we've been gone."

"Love, what happened last night?" I asked, reaching for the neckline of her pajama top and pulling it gently aside.

"Thorsten's superior happened last night." She sighed as my mouth settled on the nipple I'd uncovered.

"Nice," I breathed against pale-pink skin before helping myself a second time.

"Belen?"

"No. This." I nipped gently, allowing my fangs to descend just a bit.

"He seldom appears. Thorsten goes to him and reports, instead," she gasped as I nipped again.

"These need to go." I moved downward, pulling her pajama bottoms down with me. I had a goal in mind and I wasn't going to be denied this time. I intended to taste every delicious inch of her before satisfying my growing urge.

"You called it your John Thomas last time," she reminded me before gasping again. I'd nipped her for that.

"You must learn not to talk business while we're making love," I said. "John Thomas needs sufficient room," I kissed and nipped her thigh, "and generous lubrication before making himself at home."

"I thought he was only dropping by for a visit." Her voice was breathy. Aroused.

"Oh, no. This will be his home," I placed fingers in a sensitive spot, forcing her to draw in a breath. "He just has to leave now and then, to get a bit of work done. Now," I dropped my head, "meet John Thomas' cousin." I tongued what I'd touched. She arched her body. I love that. It's as if a woman can't decide at first whether she wants more or is attempting to back away. I intended to give her the former and disallow the latter.

Simple. Direct. She tasted like heaven. *It's time, my heart*, I sent, *to show you the pleasure.* Turning my head slightly, I bit her inner thigh. She screamed as the waves of an intense climax hit. What Joey had given her was nothing compared to this. He'd held back as much as he was able.

This was full-blown, her body jerking against my face. I loved every moment of it. *Now*, I sent when her body flattened against the sheets in near-exhaustion, *let me introduce you to John Thomas.*

She lay in a tangle of sheets, sleeping. "Shhh," I soothed as she murmured at my touch. I shifted the sheet to cover a bare shoulder; considered waking her, so we could go again.

Forcing that thought away, I slid off the bed and padded toward the door. Surely there was something in the refrigerator to eat and drink. I didn't care that I was naked. Joey and Bearcat, who sat at the kitchen island when I made my way downstairs, didn't seem to mind, either, exchanging an appreciative glance as I approached.

"There are scrambled eggs in the skillet on the stove," Joey said as I sniffed the air. My nose told me the same thing. I went to find a plate. Yes, I'd had Kiarra's blood—twice. I'd forced myself not to take much. Eggs sounded good enough to ease the rumble in my stomach.

"What are you two doing here?" I asked, sitting down and stabbing a fluffy clump of eggs with a fork.

"Dragon says we're going back today," Joey said. "I can still help in an emergency—fighting or healing. I think everybody is supposed to gather here eventually, so Pheligar can take all of us at once."

"When are they coming?" I asked, spearing more eggs and stuffing them in my mouth.

"Now," Lion announced, appearing nearby. "While pants aren't required, they do serve a purpose," he grinned.

～

"I'm not wearing jeans," I said.

"Adam, you'll stand out. We don't need that. What we need is to walk that beach and look for evidence. If the Kapirus has taken up residence in a nearby swamp, we need to know that."

I watched shamelessly as she jerked a knit top over her head and pulled her hair away from the neck.

"You're not dressing," she pointed out. "I have to braid my hair." She flounced past me and into the large bathroom attached to her bedroom. "Get dressed. The others are waiting for us."

She'd tossed the pair of jeans at me the moment I'd bounded into the bedroom. I wasn't embarrassed that Dragon and the others had seen me naked, but Pheligar displayed impatience the moment he appeared, so I decided it was time to get dressed.

"I don't wear jeans," I muttered, pulling the infernal things onto my legs. Jeans are either stiff with dark dye or soft and faded from many launderings. These were somewhere in between. At least I wore underwear—the zipper looked lethal.

"I'll get you button flies next time," Kiarra muttered, brushing past me and throwing a yellow polo in my direction.

"At least it's not a T-shirt," I mumbled, pulling it over my head. "Shirts are supposed to button up." My arms went into short sleeves before the fabric settled about my torso.

"Are you going to whine or are you going to put shoes on?"

"I detest sandals."

"Adam, it's ninety-six degrees where we're going. While you didn't sweat as a vampire, you'll sweat now. All that was restored when you arbitrarily took my blood. Live with it."

"Are we grumpy?"

"Yeah. Sorry. I'm not used to herding someone else around before I take off."

"I'll herd faster," I mumbled, reaching for the sandals she'd provided. "These are quite comfortable," I said after slipping them on.

"You have nice feet," she said. "Ready?"

"Yes."

"Good."

~

"This is where they were taken?" Dragon asked Daniel.

"That's the rumor, but I can't scent anything here," Daniel shook his head. "I and several others from the Pack have been out here, and they didn't find anything, either."

We'd been dropped at the Aransas National Wildlife Refuge, near the gulf waters. Behind us lay grass-covered dunes and beyond that, marshy land where snakes, insects and alligators abounded. In the winter, the refuge was home to the last of the migratory whooping cranes. It wasn't winter, and, as Kiarra said, the temperature was in the nineties.

"If they pulled a boat up and loaded victims, the waves would wash away any evidence," Kiarra's shoulders drooped. "How did the victims get here?"

"Their vehicles were located at a parking area on the other side. They were reportedly hiking in this direction," Daniel replied. "You're right, though. If they were hauled away by boat, there'd be no evidence left behind. This might explain why they wanted Bill Gordon's boat in the beginning."

"I can't understand what's blocking the information on where they were taken and how," Lion muttered. "That shouldn't be."

"Blocking the information?" I turned to Joey for answers.

"They can *Look* to get information. It's easy, I've done it with Bearcat's help. Something is keeping them from finding this."

"That must have been what happened to me," I nodded absently. "We know for sure that the kapirus was here?"

"We're certain," Lion said. "Two scales and an earring from one of the victims was found here; it was collected by the authorities. The scales belong to the kapirus. As for the rest of the information, there's a big hole where it ought to be."

"Pheligar says he's checking on it," Bearcat rubbed Joey's shoulders affectionately. "We can't spot the enemy because they're shielded, but this is really confusing. We ought to be able to track a kapirus with no trouble."

"Confusing doesn't begin to describe this," Kiarra said, digging into wet sand at her feet and coming up with an earring covered in grit. "One victim thought to leave what she could behind. She's probably dead, now."

"Merrill, the bastard is heading for the states."

Merrill jerked his head up at Griffin's words. Franklin, who'd busied himself putting a pan of lasagna together, frowned at Griffin as well.

"Where?"

"Likely Corpus Christi. I have no idea how he's getting information, but it hasn't escaped my notice that he left England behind almost the moment Kiarra returned to Texas."

"He needs to stay far away from her," Merrill hissed, his eyes going red.

"There's nothing to stop us from using conventional means to get there, or even hopping there."

Merrill pulled his cell phone from a pocket and dialed a number. "Have the jet ready in three hours," he said before ending the call. "Franklin do you wish to come?"

"No. I'll stay here. It's Greg's birthday."

"Yes. Of course. Extend my best wishes. Griffin and I will travel tonight, after dinner."

"Stay in touch. I don't like this, Father," Franklin said, turning his attention back to the lasagna preparations.

"Neither do I, but I refuse to allow that ill-bred snake near her."

"Then be safe."

"As always, child."

"Pheligar made arrangements to buy it for me, that's how," Kiarra shook her head at me as we walked into a huge home located on Mustang Island, just south of Port Aransas. More than ten thousand square feet on three levels, it had additional guest quarters over a large garage and a walkway to the beach. "He said he only wanted to shield one space, so we'll all be here," she added.

"The Dallas Packmaster has a vacation home nearby," Daniel observed as he studied the interior of the house. "This is nearly twice as big."

"It's not a contest," Lion clapped Daniel on the back. "We needed this much room, or we'd be sitting on one another's laps."

"You're right."

"Two more coming," Dragon sighed.

"Who?" Kiarra turned to ask.

"Griffin and Merrill are on their way. They have news."

"I hope it's good news," Kiarra muttered before walking toward the expanse of glass covering the back of the house. The view of the beach was stunning, and I appreciated the play of the afternoon sun on the water.

"My heart," I stepped behind her and wrapped my arms about her shoulders, pulling her against me.

Adam, I'm worried, she sent. *This is far outside the norm. Something's wrong here, and we don't have any clues. We're going at this blind, and that's a terrible position to be in.*

We're together, I reminded her. *That counts for something, doesn't it?*

I suppose it does.

We have sex to take our minds off our troubles, you know.

Adam, I, she began before cutting off the mental conversation.

"What?" I said aloud, leaning down to kiss her neck.

"We have so much to do, and no idea where to start."

Griffin and Merrill arrived after midnight. Kiarra stayed up to greet them, therefore, so did I. I'd noticed Griffin's slight limp before, but never commented, as I had no idea if it were chronic.

"You seem better," Lion remarked as Griffin and Merrill walked through the front door.

"I feel better," Griffin agreed. "Amara says I'm pushing things, but this is important."

Injured during his last assignment, Kiarra explained through mindspeech. *His leg was nearly cut off by the tail spikes of an enemy.*

Tail spikes? I almost yelped the mental words.

Yeah. See, maybe you made the wrong choice after all.

No, I made the right choice. I just need to know what I might be facing, that's all. Tail spikes and serpents don't usually come in combinations.

Also spikes on the head. Lots of teeth. Scales are deadly, too.

Are you trying to frighten me?

If you're not, you should be.

I'm afraid I may need comfort, now.

Seriously? Where's that stiff British vampire's upper lip, or whatever?

That's not what's stiff, and I'll use any excuse to get you in bed. Come on, we've greeted our guests. Time for us, now.

Kiarra said goodnight, and I quickly herded her toward our

second-floor suite. I only kept her awake for another hour—she was tired.

～

"Russell? I don't recall summoning you." Wlodek didn't bother to look up from the papers he was reading, his dark eyes scanning reports from one of his assassins.

"You didn't summon me. I explained to Charles what the difficulty is, and he saw fit to admit me."

"Then I will speak to Charles later," Wlodek looked up, his gaze unblinking as he studied Russell. "Tell me quickly and be done with it."

"It's about Xavier. And the Seer."

"What about them? Xavier is your sire, as I recall."

"And I believe the Seer intends to see him dead." Wlodek's fingers toyed with a gold pen for a moment before stilling.

"Tell me why you believe this," Wlodek commanded, compulsion thick in his voice.

"Because I overheard the Seer saying it," Russell replied, his eyes clouded with Wlodek's command.

"Where is he now—your sire?" the question was soft. Deadly.

"On his way to the U.S. He believes he can capture the woman in the video shown at the last Council meeting. He intends to turn her."

"I did not give that command. The Council has not made that decision as yet." Wlodek resumed toying with his pen.

"The Seer gave the command."

"Where is the Seer? I will speak with him."

"With Xavier. I followed them to the airport, Honored One. Xavier's jet was ready and waiting."

"What persuaded you to follow?"

"I am concerned for my sire."

"I am concerned for your sire as well," Wlodek lifted his cell phone and dialed a number. "Is there anything else I should know?"

"The Seer wants Adam dead, too."

~

"Coffee." Lion placed a steaming mug in front of me the following morning. Merrill settled on the barstool next to mine and received a mug as well. He sipped his readily. I was more reluctant.

"Want pancakes?" Kiarra walked in, tying her hair back with a stretchy band. I'd left her sleeping in our bed moments earlier. I must have wakened her, going out the door.

"Pancakes would be great," Lion grinned. "I'll do bacon if you'll do pancakes and eggs."

"Done," she agreed. Merrill's cell phone rang as I watched her put pancake batter together.

"Wlodek?" Merrill sounded surprised. I listened shamelessly to the conversation.

"The Seer has gone rogue, and he's taken Xavier with him," Wlodek growled. "I know you warned me."

"I hear he may be planning a takeover," Merrill responded.

"Of what?"

"Your seat at the center of the Council, that's what. He wants what is here, first, before he returns to England to take what is yours."

"How do you know this?"

"You should know better than to ask that question."

"I despise that source, as you know. I do not question its veracity, however."

"Then I advise you to place your known allies on alert. You may come under attack, and I am not in the country to offer assistance."

"Where are you?"

"In Texas. I must do what I can to prevent catastrophe. I believe the Seer is allied in some way with these rogue werewolves, and those must be dealt with, in addition to the other threats we face. Have you spoken with the Grand Master?"

"Yes. Most evenings. Information has come to him from several Packmasters, listing wolves that have disappeared. He fears they are rogue or dead."

"I believe the rogues may be collecting in this area," Merrill confirmed. "Gathering and lying in wait for some prearrange signal—likely from the Seer."

"Do you need assistance to deal with this?"

"I would not refuse your offer."

"I will send Russell, Radomir, Will and Brock," Wlodek said. "Utilize those two from the area as well. Do you know where Adam is? His life is in danger. The Seer wants him dead, for some reason, and as Xavier appears to be under the Seer's command, Xavier may be instructed to destroy his child."

"Adam is here with me," Merrill said.

"Then he is safe for the moment. Will you advise him of this new development?"

"Of course."

"We must also consider the Seer's replacement, when this situation is resolved."

"Let us see this through, first, before we dwell on future events."

"I'll consider it. Keep me advised." Wlodek ended the call.

"You heard?" Merrill turned to me.

"Yes." I was seething. It failed to surprise me, however, that my own sire might attempt to take my life. It would require little coaxing from the Seer, in my estimation.

"He comes near you, he'll get a surprise," Kiarra hissed. I hadn't considered that she'd heard the conversation, too.

"You're no longer bound to obey your sire," Lion said, dropping strips of bacon into a heated skillet. "He can't command you to stand still while he murders you. Not after getting Kee's blood."

"He's not bound to obey any vampire," Kiarra angrily whisked ingredients together in a bowl. "Compulsion won't work, Adam. You're free of that, now."

"You received her blood?" Merrill asked. He sounded upset.

"Can we not discuss this?" Kiarra poured batter into a skillet while Lion turned the bacon. "We have rogues to hunt, spawn to kill, a kapirus to find and who knows what else waiting for us. A discussion about blood can wait."

"He just wants a taste. Merrill, that is," Griffin took a seat next to Merrill and lifted an eyebrow at Kiarra.

"I fail to understand why."

"Just humor me. It won't hurt to be connected to more than one or two, now will it? And since I've already given permission for blood, you won't have to do that part."

"Connected?"

"You'll feel her—if she's in trouble or gets hurt, just as Joey will," Lion explained, setting a platter of bacon on the island. "It can't hurt to have more connections. Karzac is connected to all of us, except for Kee."

"I'll get Karzac connected," Kiarra muttered, setting a platter of pancakes beside the bacon. "If somebody will get plates and forks, I'll make eggs."

"It'll only take a nip," Griffin coaxed. "Come here."

"No. I know what happens," she said. I blinked—I should have been roaring my jealousy. I didn't feel a thing.

"Then come to the back deck with us," Griffin said.

"No. I want to make sure she isn't hurt," I said.

"You think I'd hurt her?" Merrill's piercing blue eyes bored into mine.

"Stop arguing. Is this necessary?" Kiarra turned to Griffin.

"From what I can see, yes."

"Fine. Let's get it over with." She stepped around the end of the island.

"Sit here." I rose to offer her my seat. Merrill rose as well. Stepping back, I allowed him to stand next to her. He kissed her. Griffin tapped me on the shoulder when I thought to curtail prolonged contact.

Then, his head lowered, he placed a kiss on her throat. "I will never harm you," he promised softly before delivering the bite. She gasped and writhed against him. Her head was in the palm of one hand, her body gripped tightly against his with the other as he drank.

"Enough," Griffin said. Merrill reluctantly disengaged. Kiarra was already unconscious from the climax; Merrill lifted her easily and followed Griffin from the kitchen. I trailed behind them, feeling angry and confused.

~

"I'll do this," I pushed Merrill aside after he'd laid Kiarra on our bed. Griffin pulled Merrill out of the room while I patted her cheek, attempting to wake her.

~

"This is as much as I can do," Griffin hissed as Merrill's eyes went red in anger. "Don't push her. Give her time to adjust. Your day will come."

"I grow tired of waiting." Merrill stalked away, leaving Griffin standing in the hall not far from Kiarra's bedroom door.

~

"If vampires were for sale, every woman on the planet would have one," Kiarra mumbled when she opened her eyes.

"Like those climaxes, do you?" I teased gently.

"I guess I do. Not that it isn't fucking embarrassing or anything."

"There is nothing shameful about sex. It is as natural as breathing; it just doesn't occur as often."

"I don't think I could handle it as often as that," she said.

"Sex can be draining, although I've heard it's excellent exercise. Gets your heart rate up."

"I've noticed—at least when I'm conscious, I've noticed."

"Come downstairs; we haven't had breakfast yet," I pointed out. "Have to keep your strength up, you know."

We walked downstairs together, while I kept a steadying hand on her elbow. Donating blood—even a cupful, can make the donor feel tired. Joey and Bearcat served our breakfast when we got back to the island, and Joey, grinning, pushed a protein drink in Kiarra's direction.

Griffin, who once again sat beside Merrill at the island, flipped on the television hanging below a kitchen counter opposite the island. Kiarra's fork clattered to her plate and she gasped—Rita's photograph was displayed on the screen, as the journalist described how she and her brother Rick had been found murdered at a home on the western edge of Corpus Christi.

CHAPTER 12

"This is the way to get her attention," Saxom snapped at Xavier.

"We risk drawing the attention of Wlodek and the Council," Xavier growled. "I have no care that I killed the woman and her brother, but I don't wish to jeopardize my position as a trusted advisor to the Council, and I certainly have no desire to be branded a rogue and face Gavin if he comes."

"We have the attention of Wlodek and the Council," Saxom laughed. "You're a rogue already. Let me worry about Gavin Montegue and the others, if they come."

"This is a way for the enemy to draw you out," Dragon said. Kiarra sat alone on a chair, arms crossed tightly over her chest and refusing to speak to any of us. "You know what the stakes are, and what their game plan is. If we befriend anyone, they can become a target. It couldn't be helped this time. You know that."

"She has children," Kiarra muttered, refusing to look Dragon in the eye.

"I know. I hear Rita's mother has them, now."

"Is there a way to ensure their safety?"

"I have wolves patrolling the neighborhood," Daniel offered. "With Shirley's blessing. She knows you're willing to help with the rogue problem, so this is her way of saying thanks."

"I have an assignment for you, Griffin," Kiarra stood and turned in his direction.

"Anything," he agreed with a shrug.

"Let me know if that household goes blank. I want to be alone for a while."

Stay here. Dragon's hand landed heavily on my shoulder.

"What does she mean—if that household goes blank?" Joey asked.

"When—or if—I can't see it by *Looking*," Griffin explained. "I'm the most talented in that area," he shrugged. "And it's something I can do while I'm nursing an injury."

"Like the other blank spots?" I asked. I still wanted to go after Kiarra. Dragon's hand remained on my shoulder.

"Yes. The ones that shouldn't be there," Griffin agreed. "If that house or the people in it go blank, it's a good indication that the enemy may be there, with or without the kapirus and whatever is causing these blank spots."

"How was she and her brother murdered—do we know?" Joey asked. The journalist had little information to offer regarding how Rick and Rita died—only that the authorities were withholding the information.

"Throats slashed," Griffin sighed. "They want us to know a vampire did this."

"The Seer is behind this," Merrill said.

"Correct," Griffin agreed. "While he may not have done it himself, he ordered it done."

"Xavier," I growled.

"Likely," Griffin said.

Are we going to tell her? Griffin sent mindspeech.

I want to hold back—she's upset enough as it is, Lion responded.

Adam, stay out of this conversation, Dragon ordered. *We can shield our mindspeech. You haven't learned, yet.* I turned from Griffin to Lion and then Dragon. Something was going on; I just didn't know what it was. *Yet.*

❦

"Bearcat won't tell me," Joey said later. I'd waited until we were alone to ask. I had no idea why the others were keeping something from Kiarra—it made no sense. "What I do know is this, though," Joey sighed.

"What's that?"

We sat on the third-floor deck, just outside Joey and Bearcat's shared bedroom. The afternoon was bright and hot, with a breeze coming off the gulf waters and ruffling our hair as we spoke. "They don't go to every world to challenge the Ra'Ak when they attack," Joey said. He sounded uncomfortable, for some reason.

"How do they pick and choose, then?" I asked. Yes, I'd been curious ever since I'd heard that reference before.

"Planets are rated," Joey explained with a heavy sigh. "From one to six."

"What does that mean?"

"The highest rating is one, and they'll save those first. Those worlds are the ones that are peaceful and living generally in accord. The ones with a single government, no matter how many continents are involved. The ones rated two through four may have more than one government spread across the continents, but are generally at peace, and are worth saving in most cases, but the fours are studied carefully, to make sure things aren't deteriorating. Fives and sixes, well, those are considered not worth saving and they don't bother with them."

"How are we rated?" I asked. We had to fall somewhere in the three or four categories, I felt.

"Adam, we're a six," Joey said.

❦

"I'm not complaining, but what the hell are you doing here?" I demanded. I'd found Lion in the media room, sorting through a collection of videos.

"Sit down," Lion said. "I'll try to explain so it'll make sense."

"Please," I responded, my voice gruff and demanding. It angered me enough that Earth was considered past saving, but why the hell did they come?

"At times," Lion began as he took a seat nearby, settling his large frame on the leather chair and making himself comfortable, "when a world is considered by the Liaison and his superior to be not worth saving, one of us can volunteer to go anyway. But there are generally rules concerning those expeditions."

"All right, explain that," I said. I still wasn't happy, and it showed in my voice and demeanor.

"The rules are that you go alone, with no assistance from the Liaison or anyone else, and you're pretty much on your own. You win, you get out and leave things as they are, hoping the world manages to correct its course. You lose, you either die or get the hell out before the Ra'Ak takes over or destroys the planet outright."

"So why are you here, then? Why are several of you here? It makes no sense, given what you just said."

"We've told you all along that this is unusual. This is Kee's home world, so she announced she was going to try for it. Just before she left, we got word from above. And when I say above, I mean *far* above what we usually get. Somehow, this world is important, and I can't say why that is. Either way, we're here and we're doing our best to make this come out right. It's like a dance. We both suspect our enemy is out there, but we can't prove anything, yet. The enemy has an interest in this world as well, and I can't help but believe the reasons are intertwined."

"This is more than confusing," I shook my head.

"Under normal circumstances, we'd have left this one to die."

"That doesn't make me feel any better," I said. "In case you were trying."

"Try to see the humor in it," Lion suggested.

"I fail to see any part of this as humorous."

"Yeah. Same here."

"What about," I began.

"We can't talk about it. Not yet," Lion held up a hand. "You'll have to trust me with this. We let the cat out of the bag, as your kind are fond of saying, and we'll be in trouble—on several levels. Whatever you do, don't let anything slip around Kee. You're vampire; that ought to be simple enough."

"This is important?"

"Extremely."

"All right."

"Good. Ready to hunt rogue werewolves tonight?"

"Absolutely. I was almost killed by rogue wolves. I wouldn't mind a bit of payback."

"This is Kee's version of payback. They kill one of ours; we hunt theirs. Since we know on some level that this world is important to the enemy, we figure we can get away with a few things without them blowing the planet to bits. And since it's not worth saving," Lion shrugged instead of finishing his statement.

"You're not very reassuring, you know."

"Never meant to be. Can't lie, remember?"

"Bearcat wants to go, so I'm going, too," Joey said. "He was a shapeshifter before, and he likes to join the battle, sometimes."

"Still have your fangs and claws?" I asked.

"When I need them," he nodded. "The nice thing is I don't have to if I don't want to. I feel amazing, Adam. Like I awoke from a bad dream."

"You're saying being a vampire was the bad dream?"

"Kind of. I never did like it much, except for the speed and a few other perks. That whole sleep of the dead thing during daylight bothered me a lot."

"Then dress carefully," I warned. "I don't want you bitten by any of those rogues."

"Hey, I saw what happened to you. No, thanks," Joey shook his head. "Do we know how many?" he added.

"I haven't heard numbers," I said. "Ready? The others are waiting downstairs."

～

"One of Shirley's wolves disappeared in the area," Daniel informed us as we climbed from two vehicles and looked about us. Empty land surrounded the SUV, with only a narrow track to drive on. If the area isn't plowed for agriculture, included in the yard around a home or located on a Gulf Coast beach, the land tends to be covered in brush and scrub over sandy soil.

That's where we were—on a side road south of Corpus Christi, with no houses in sight. Joey was taller (but not by much), than the brush lining both sides of the dirt and gravel road. "See this," Daniel pointed toward a narrow space between the growth. The path was barely wide enough for a wolf to have traveled through it.

Darkness had fallen; Lion and Dragon didn't want to call attention to the fact that we were out in numbers, so we'd waited for nightfall. Kiarra was with us, but she'd remained silent for the duration of the trip and I chose not to press her.

She did sit beside me in the SUV, however, and I'd kept an arm about her shoulders while Lion drove. "Do we follow, or split up?" Dragon asked.

"I say split up," Daniel said. "I'll go this way," he nodded toward the trail.

"I'll back you up," Lion offered, before turning into the black Lion. I realized that this was his smaller version, like the white mare was Kiarra's smaller animal. I wasn't sure I wanted to see the large, fighting Lion. Dragon? *Forget that.*

"Two more groups, and spread out," Dragon ordered. I followed Kiarra and Merrill, who went east of the trail Daniel and Lion followed. Dragon went westward, with Joey and Bearcat following him. If our luck held, Daniel would surprise the rogues, while the rest of us converged from different angles, attacking the makeshift Pack from behind.

Four miles in, I caught the noise. Merrill did as well, but Kiarra had already stopped still in front of us. The scent of a fire and cooking meat came moments later. Somebody was camping out, that much was evident. I was surprised the wolves bothered to cook at all. They merely had to change and eat their prey raw.

We stood amid shoulder-high brush and tall grasses, while Kiarra considered a course of action. Likely, she was alerting the others as well, but I'd been shut out of the conversation.

Are you hearing her mindspeech? Merrill asked, shocking the hell out of me. He had it, too.

Through Griffin, when I received his blood, Merrill explained before I could ask. *As deaf as a wall before that,* he added.

We've been shut out of the conversation, I responded. *I suspect she knows something and she, Lion and Dragon are debating what to do.*

You're probably correct.

As unfortunate as that might be, I agreed.

I'm concerned about the reason werewolves might cook meat. Especially since these are supposedly hiding, he sent.

As am I.

Get out of there, Griffin's voice blasted into our minds at the same moment the area blew up around us.

Kiarra paced and cursed, in so many languages I failed to understand more than half of them. I was grateful she, Dragon and Lion had chosen to include the rest of us inside their personal shields. If they hadn't, we'd be dead. That's what their silent conversation had been about—the fact that they sensed danger ahead, and how they might protect the rest of us.

"We don't usually include anybody inside personal shields," Lion handed me a cup of tea. Kiarra's cursing had gone soft, so it was easier to hear Lion's words. "She did it twice—to heal you and Joey. The enemy would have been alerted by the power expenditure if she hadn't."

"What's the problem with doing that?" I asked before sipping tea. Lion had sweetened it and added milk, just as I preferred.

"It leaves us vulnerable," Lion said, gesturing for me to sit down. He took a seat on the sofa with me and drank his tea before continuing. "You could strike out at us while you're inside our shield, and we'd be in trouble," he added.

"That's frightening," I said.

"That's why we seldom do it. It takes a great deal of courage and trust to include someone in that tight bubble around us."

"What, exactly, blew up out there?" I asked. It was on the local news—the fact that a wide area of land was burning south of Corpus Christi. Many reported hearing an explosion, but nobody could assign a reason for it. Fortunately, our vehicles were parked far away, and Pheligar saw fit to move them with power, along with the rest of us.

"Things are worse than we imagined," Lion muttered. "Somebody got the undocumented immigrants in the area in a panic, and told them they would be arrested if they didn't get out of town. I figure at least forty people were at that campsite. They're all dead, now."

"They were sent to a campsite that was booby-trapped?"

"Looks that way," Merrill took a chair nearby.

"I figure they'd have been bitten by spawn if we hadn't set off the bomb somehow," Lion observed. "They were being herded, that's easy enough to see."

"How did we set it off?" I asked.

"Could have been anything. While we employ cunning whenever we act, the enemy can be just as cunning—and much more destructive. Those people were dead, no matter what we did." Dragon walked in, carrying a mug of the dark tea he liked so much. I didn't have enough courage to try it; it smelled too strong.

"And we're back to the beginning, hunting werewolves," Daniel and Griffin joined us. "I just spoke with Shirley," Daniel went on. "We have more leads, but I don't want them to turn out like this one."

"Where was Rita's body found?" Kiarra stopped pacing and cursing to ask the question.

"They said a house outside town," Daniel replied. "That's all I know."

"Then it's time we found out," she said.

Griffin rattled off an address for her. She frowned.

"That's down the street from Roy Cheek's house," Joey said. He and Bearcat had just walked in.

"Adam, how fast can you turn to mist now?" Kiarra asked.

"I haven't tried it," I said, rising to my feet. "You know I'm a mister?"

"Yes. Try it now."

I did. "Wow, Adam," Joey breathed. "I didn't even see it, it was so fast."

I became corporeal again and blinked stupidly at Kiarra. "It's my blood," she shrugged. "How about a reconnaissance mission? I think we should check both those houses."

"They won't be able to detect his mist," Griffin laughed.

"Can you take someone with you?" she asked.

"I've never been able to turn anyone else with me," I hedged.

"Try it now," Griffin nodded.

"Come here, sweetheart," I motioned for her to come to me. She did. I pulled her into my arms, offering her a quick kiss before going to mist.

"It works!" Joey crowed. "Adam, you're both mist. That's outstanding."

"We'll go tomorrow," I said, allowing us to become corporeal. "I think we need to sleep on this."

"I think that's an excellent idea," Dragon said. "How about before dawn?"

"Always a good time for an attack," Kiarra nodded.

"Kee, reconnaissance only," Lion reminded as we prepared to go the following morning. He and Dragon were dropping us off two miles away, then driving to a small restaurant on the west side of town for breakfast. We'd mist to the houses in question from our drop-off point and report our findings.

It took less than a minute to mist to the first house, where I found the barest crack to slip through. The blood was easy enough to find—it was dried on the carpet in one of the bedrooms. My nose, curiously enough, still works while I'm mist. I was grateful.

Werewolves were here, I informed Kiarra. *The smell of them is everywhere. I smell Rita, too, and her blood. I also smell my sire, and one other vampire. Too bad they're not still here,* I grumbled.

So we know they're all together in this, she returned. *Let's go to Cheek's house.*

Misting through the same crack a second time, I changed course and headed down the street toward Cheek's house. Joey had staked it out several times, as had Kiarra. The garage door was easy enough to slip past, and the back door leading into the kitchen allowed enough space between it and the jamb to slide my mist through to the interior.

They've been here, too, I said. *All the scents, plus other vampires. I don't like this at all, my heart. I smell at least six vampires and a dozen werewolves.*

Adam, let's get out of here, Kiarra said, a fair amount of panic in her sending. I sped toward the cracks I'd found in order to enter the house. We'd barely made it out again before Cheek's house exploded behind us.

"Somebody knows how to build bombs," Lion handed a menu to me when Kiarra and I walked in and sat down.

"That much is certain," I said, accepting the menu and opening it. Kiarra scooted as close against me as she could—Lion and Dragon had chosen a booth near the door, and Dragon had moved from his seat opposite Lion so Kiarra and I could sit together.

"They're either good guessers or they have an edge of some sort," Dragon pointed out.

"I'd say guessing on this," Kiarra said. "They knew we'd latch onto that information, and after we set off what we did last night," she shook her head.

"So they're laying traps, and hoping we'll fall into at least one of them," Lion nodded. "Sounds about right. I think I'll have steak and eggs."

"Shirley has someone watching both houses, now," Daniel said later, after ending a phone conversation with the Corpus Christi Packmaster. "The one where Rita was killed was an empty rental property. It's scheduled for cleanup and renovation now, but that won't happen for a few weeks," he shrugged.

"What have the authorities made of the scales they found?" Dragon asked.

"They have no clue, and forensics hasn't been able to identify what type of scales they are. We have a wolf on the force, so that's how I'm getting information—through him."

"At least they came from the same kapirus," Kiarra said. "I know by *Looking*," she held up a hand. "How are these rogue werewolves feeding themselves?" she asked, changing the subject.

"Deer and small game are in the area," Daniel said.

"Enough to feed a group? Every day?"

"Probably. They'll hunt coyotes if they're desperate, and there are plenty of those around."

"That sounds tasty," Joey made a face.

"How are the vampires feeding themselves?" I spoke my thoughts aloud.

"Good question," Merrill said. "Very good question."

"If they're following the rules, then no bodies will show up and the human won't remember being bitten after compulsion is laid," I said.

"What about the safe house?" Kiarra asked. "You left bagged blood in the fridge."

"Shall we go see?" I turned both of us to mist before anyone could object and flew toward the door.

~

The safe house refrigerator had been left open, and all the blood had been taken. We studied it for only a moment—there was no other evidence that the house had been inhabited—before misting away again.

"There's enough to feed them for several days," I said when we reached the beach house again. "They took all of it, including what was in the freezer."

"I'll let Charles know the safe house has been compromised," Merrill said. I knew what that meant—the house would be destroyed and the property sold before Charles searched for a new location to build another.

"What now?" I asked. "They have a food supply for a few days. Past that, it's donors unless they find another source of bagged blood."

"I have a suggestion," Griffin said.

"What's that?" Kiarra turned to him.

"We know they're housing part of their army on those two oil platforms. At the moment, those things are still in operation, to keep the corporate offices off their back and to make everything appear normal. I say we take the fight there, to let the enemy know we're not backing down."

"Is that what you meant when you said the crews had been fired and replaced?" I asked Kiarra.

"Yeah. But you didn't take the bait, did you?"

"No. I feel naïve now," I said. "The more I learn, the more I realize I don't know."

"But you didn't feel so naïve then, did you?" Lion grinned. "Ignorance really is bliss, sometimes."

"The ground certainly felt firmer beneath my feet," I conceded. "I'm standing on quicksand now, and slowly sinking."

"Sweetie, stop worrying. We're nearly as clueless, and we've been dealing with this for a long time," Kiarra rubbed my back.

"Did you just call me sweetie?" I lifted an eyebrow at her.

"I called you sweetie. Does that mess with your tough vampire mojo or something?"

"It might," I rumbled.

"You may call me sweetie," Merrill offered.

"Adam can stare down most vampires," Joey chuckled. "The rest of them bow and scrape, because they're afraid. I've never seen him lose a fight," he added.

"His Council records are impeccable," Merrill agreed.

"You've read them?" I turned to Merrill with a frown.

"Of course. I've read all the records on Enforcers and Assassins."

"You have access?"

"I do. Wlodek is my sire."

"Holy fuck," Joey breathed. "No wonder he takes your calls."

"He is still unaware that you are my turn," Merrill informed Joey. "I was warned to keep that information from all the Council, so I have."

"Are we going to the oil platforms?" Kiarra asked. "I worry that it may set something in motion we may not be prepared for."

"It will come anyway, regardless of what we do," Griffin advised.

"Probably true. When are we going?"

"Tonight. I'll find a fishing boat big enough for all of us, plus a few werewolves."

"I'll contact Shirley," Daniel said and pulled out his cell phone.

"How dangerous will this be?" I asked, moving the collar of Kiarra's shirt aside to kiss her shoulder. We were back in our bedroom; the decision to rest before going to the platforms later was an opportunity for me and I intended to seize it.

"Dangerous enough. You've already fought spawn, in small

numbers. This will be an army of them. Some may be older and larger, like the trolls you saw in Shreveport."

"How far apart are these platforms?" I slowly began to unbutton her blouse.

"Less than a mile. The good thing is that once we attack, the spawn from the second platform will be forced to join the others by conventional means, unless the enemy is willing to reveal himself. I doubt he's ready for that, yet."

"Meaning we may have time to eliminate one army before the second attacks? That's something, I suppose. This will anger the enemy, no doubt, if we eliminate a major portion of his fighting force," I said.

"I thought you didn't want to talk business while making love."

"We're not there, yet. This is merely the opening volley. I feel you out, determining your readiness for me to proceed. So far, the indications are quite positive."

"Indications, huh?"

"Pulse and respiration. Scent. Taste." I nipped her collarbone gently before lowering my head and scraping fangs carefully across a bared nipple.

"You're still dressed," she pointed out. I nipped harder, making her gasp.

"I am already aroused. It is my duty to see to your arousal," I knelt and breathed against the tender skin of her belly. "These must go." I undid the button of her jeans and lowered the zipper.

"And what if," she began.

"I can smell it, my heart. Therefore, it is my desire to make you wait just a bit, to make it wilder and sweeter."

"I can rip some of this out," she ran her fingers through my hair.

"Really?" My fingers gripped much shorter hair, lower down. "Tit for tat?"

"Uh, no, thanks."

"Then make no threats. I promise this will be worth your while." Backing her against a wall, I proceeded to undress her slowly, kissing my way up and down her body. If she became too breathless and aroused from my stimulation, I backed off and traveled to safer territory.

"You're driving me nuts," she said eventually, burying her fingers in my hair. "I'm not sure I can stand up much longer."

"You think I can't hold you up?" I tilted my head back and gazed up at her. I proceeded to show her that she could straddle me perfectly well, her knees hanging over my shoulders while I stood and busied myself with the scent and taste of her. She may have shrieked a time or two when she came, but it only made me smile.

∽

"I find this quite appealing." I ran a finger down the black leather vest. Like Dragon, she'd dressed in black leather for our trip to the oil platforms. The vest was sleeveless and fit like a second skin.

"It's better protection than cotton," she shrugged.

"How are we going to sneak up on them?" I asked. "They'll know we're coming."

"We're posing as night fishermen. That happens often enough. You're going to get us onto the platform, Adam, by turning us to mist."

"But," I began.

"I think you can take all of us. I think you just don't realize yet what you might do after getting my blood."

"If I can, I will," I said, still feeling skeptical. I'd only been able to become mist alone, before. After all, I hadn't gotten used to becoming mist so quickly.

"Adam, if we survive, that trick is going to be quite handy in the future."

"Generally I don't worry beforehand about surviving, but you've certainly planted the seeds in my mind," I shook my head at her. "Do you know how beautiful you are?" I pulled her against me. "Your mouth is perfect." I kissed her to illustrate my point. "Together or not, I've loved you for a very long time."

"I'm still trying to comprehend that," she mumbled against my chest. "I never knew you were there."

"I'm very good at stealth," I kissed the top of her head. "You weren't meant to know, unless I wanted it."

"Mission accomplished."

"Exactly." I kissed her again.

"I come from a family of merchants," I said. "My father was in the shipping business. I've been on boats before." Joey had trouble getting his balance while I stood comfortably on the deck of a large charter fishing boat, watching as seawater splashed up from the prow with a loud hiss.

Griffin piloted the boat while the rest of us lined the rails, watching as the first platform became larger as we sped toward it. Shirley Walker had come with us, bringing Sam Greene's widow, Kathy Jo, with her. Daniel and seven other werewolves had also joined our party.

Griffin didn't intend to join the fight—he wasn't ready for battle, according to Bearcat. That brought our total to seventeen fighters. Seventeen, to do battle with what Kiarra described as an army of spawn.

"Griffin calls them demons, in case the enemy is listening for the word spawn," Dragon moved to the rail beside me. "Most of the rest of us follow his example. Kiarra's the one who refuses to call them anything but what they are."

"The vermin that shouldn't be named?" I lifted an eyebrow.

"If that's how you wish to look at it."

"It doesn't matter what they're called. We need to make them dead," I replied.

"Agreed." Dragon slapped me on the back.

I'd always worked assignments alone, until I met Joey. I didn't mind working with him at all, once we got to know each other. I now found myself fitting comfortably into a fighting force that most couldn't comprehend—one that I couldn't have imagined in my wildest fantasies.

"Whether we live or not, we'll be fighting beside our brothers and sisters," Dragon nodded. "There will never be a doubt that they care, because they do."

"Adam?" Kiarra worked her way under my arm, wiggling between Dragon and me.

"My heart?" I smiled down at her.

"Are you ready for this? I wish this weren't so dangerous, but there's no help for it."

"I'm ready."

"All right." I rubbed her arm as she turned her gaze to the dark waters flashing past the boat. There is a sound the spray makes as a boat flies through the water. I hadn't realized how much I'd missed it as a vampire.

"You're not regretting your decision, are you?" Her eyes turned to me again.

"No. This is merely a long-forgotten memory," I said. "I'll buy a boat, I think, if we survive this."

"I'll buy it for you," she said. I smiled at the thought of it.

"When I give the word, send them," Saxom instructed Xenides by cell phone. "They'll see what attacking any of mine will get them."

"It will be as you wish, my sire."

"I trust you to accomplish this mission with extreme prejudice," Saxom added. "You know whom to spare."

"I do."

"Wait for my instructions."

"Of course."

CHAPTER 13

The first platform resembled a small city from our position. Griffin dropped anchor a quarter-mile from the platform and we studied the structure—it was well lit at night, so as not to arouse suspicion.

Built on three levels, the platform held housing for a crew, a helideck and a drilling derrick that rose higher than the rest of it. "How will we flush them out?" I asked, shaking my head at the warren of decks, platforms, modules and multiple hiding places.

"Don't worry," Lion reassured me, "once we attack, they'll converge on us like hyenas on a kill. So far, they think we're just fishermen."

"That's not comforting at all," I mumbled. "Do you suppose any of our vampire friends are there?"

"Griffin says there are blank areas, so I can't say for sure."

"Not good."

"You have Merrill and Joey with you. I imagine they'd have to be highly skilled to get past all three of you."

I've seen Joey go down already. I don't want that a second time, I sent.

Then put him between you and Merrill. I figure both his fathers might keep him on his feet and fighting.

I nodded my answer.

"It's time," Kiarra said. "Turn to mist, Adam, and set us down outside the housing area."

"All right." I let her go and pushed myself away from the rail.

"I wish we had Radomir, Russell and the others with us," Merrill shook his head at Griffin, who sat on the captain's chair, staring through the window at the platform beyond. "I know you asked me to call back and tell Wlodek to keep them in England for the moment, but we could use their help here and now."

"I feel it's necessary," Griffin's eyes went strange. "You have to trust me. I can't say exactly why they needed to stay there for now, but they do."

"Then I hope we live past tonight, brother."

"So do I."

Charles set his laptop bag inside the boot before closing it. Brock was driving them to the Council meeting in Merrill's Rolls-Royce. Wlodek was already inside the vehicle, waiting. Charles's shoulders sagged as he walked around the car and opened the door.

I never thought to be carrying so many with me before. Sixteen were inside my mist as I flew toward the platform. *There*, Kiarra sent. I agreed with her—there was space enough for all of us to materialize just outside the housing module. Barely. I didn't see anyone or anything in the area, but suspected Lion was right—the moment our feet touched any part of the platform, they'd come. They'd likely not be slow about it, either. In my limited experience, spawn were wicked fast.

It took a vampire, werewolf or some other type of supernatural being to fight them. Humans wouldn't have a chance.

This was why Merrill intervened in my assignment, I thought as I lowered my mist toward the platform. I'd been angry at the time. He—and Griffin—had known to send *me.*

Be ready, Dragon warned all of us. I wondered if the werewolves might hear his mindspeech. I should have known better than to ask. Every one of them, Daniel included, was wolf when they materialized, their teeth bared and growls rumbling as spawn erupted from every shadow and crevice about us.

~

"Now we wait to see if our army can defeat theirs," Saxom shrugged. Xavier, who sat dejectedly at a desk nearby, felt fear steal his breath.

~

They crawled down pipes and across rails faster and more surely than any spider. We formed a ring, much as we had in Nevada, to fight what came against us. I never imagined there would be so many. We'd upset an angry hive of wasps, and fought to keep them away from us when they attacked in waves.

Dragon's blades rang nearby. Werewolves snapped and growled, their nails digging for purchase against metal flooring. I heard a yelp. We were down one. Our circle tightened. I kept fighting methodically, my claws swiping heads off anything that came close. Joey fought between Merrill and me, as suggested. He was holding his own.

Bearcat, who truly was an animal resembling both large creatures, fought on my other side. I knew he wanted to be near Joey, but I was astounded at how effective he was at fighting spawn. Being labeled a healer didn't give him due credit; he was lethal.

Lion also fought in his animal form, but Kiarra and Dragon had their blades ready, cutting heads and barely blinking when the spawn dusted as they died. My concern, however, was how long the wolves would last, and if the rest of us had enough strength to fight off what seemed to be an endless mass of spawn.

"We knew there would be losses." Saxom's eyes were strange as he turned toward Xavier. "We have lost less than a third. More than acceptable. They have lost two wolves already. How much longer do you think they might continue to stand?"

"I don't know." Xavier's hands covered his face.

"Don't be so concerned. Your skin is safe," Saxom chuckled.

"Pryce Fleming, you are brought before the Council, accused of killing humans and risking our race. Do you have any defense for your actions?" Wlodek asked. "If so, present it now, before I submit this to the Council for a vote."

"They threatened me," Pryce declared.

"I can't imagine that a seven-year-old threatened you in any way," Wlodek responded, his voice dry. "I remain unconvinced. Does any member of this Council wish to question our prisoner?"

"What were you doing near that school function? Surely you could hear them from quite a distance," Susila began. "That alone should have warned you away."

Pryce snorted and refused to reply.

We'd lost three werewolves and our fighting circle was shrinking. Still, we weren't desperate.

Weren't.

I could see the back edge of the sea of spawn when something roared behind and below them. For a moment, I didn't breathe as the monster came into view, climbing up the side of the platform as easily as a monkey climbs trees. He was dripping seawater as he leapt over the railing and came down on the platform with a thump that shook everything beneath our feet.

From the other platform, Lion's voice sounded in my head. *He's almost ready to make the turn into the ultimate enemy. Stand steady and keep killing spawn—he'll wait until they're all dead before he attacks.*

Of course, I returned, not sure at all that I trusted Lion's words. This thing looked ready to jump all of us.

Twenty feet tall. How could anything survive an attack from that thing?

Stay steady, Adam, Lion said. *Keep Joey from panicking.*

All right. I went back to lifting heads from spawn shoulders. Joey, who'd appeared rattled at the giant spawn's appearance, settled back into a rhythm once he saw that Merrill and I still fought beside him.

The lines of spawn thinned. The twenty-foot monster took a step toward us. And then another. A fourth werewolf fell.

Stand tall, Joey, I sent. *We won't go down without a fight, and I reckon Bearcat will stand over you and protect you with everything he's got.*

I will, Bearcat joined the mental conversation while killing another spawn. *We're not without resources.*

We still haven't seen vampires, Merrill pointed out, slicing two heads so swiftly I barely saw movement.

You speak too soon, I said. From the edges of my vision they came, moving in between the monster and remaining spawn. Six of them.

~

"They've lost four," Saxom chortled. "And the vampires have only now joined the fight. Let's see if they can survive them and our eldest spawn together."

~

One monster was bad. Two was worse. Combine that with six vampires and we were in real trouble. The second monster, almost as large as the first, climbed over the railing as the vampires stole closer.

With claws out, eyes red and fangs showing, they headed straight for Merrill, Joey and me. I never saw Dragon and Kiarra change; I was too focused on what stalked in my direction.

Don't worry, Joey, I have a plan, I sent.

I'm glad you have one. I'm too scared to think, he replied.

I knew they'd rush us. I held my claws in the ready position—we'd finally eliminated the last of the spawn. Joey and Merrill did likewise. Bearcat, beside me, prepared for their onslaught.

I wanted to laugh—I went to mist and gathered Joey, Merrill, Bearcat and the remaining werewolves.

Lion, Dragon and Kiarra waited as six vampires flew right through my mist, confused as to how their targets had disappeared before them.

"Guilty," Montrose said.

"Guilty," Jarl intoned.

"Guilty," Oluwa agreed.

Pryce watched and listened as his fate was decided by the members of the Vampire Council.

Vampires, I discovered, are no match for a huge, fire-breathing dragon. Had their claws been able to pierce Dragon's scales, they still would have died. He was swift. Efficient. Thorough.

Ash blew across the platform when Dragon stopped breathing fire. As mist, I and the others floated above Dragon, Kiarra and Lion, who'd gone to his larger form.

Were they impressive?

I couldn't begin to describe how impressive they were. A red Dragon, whose scales gleamed in the platform's light, a blindingly white unicorn and a Lion so black he shone blue at times. The giants strode in their direction.

❧

"I abstain," Cecil muttered.

"Seven votes guilty, with one abstention. Let the records reflect the vote," Wlodek announced.

"You're all dead," Pryce sang. "You're all dead, you're all dead, you're all dead."

"Keep him quiet," Wlodek jerked his head toward Radomir, who waited against a wall of the cave. "Gavin, will you perform the execution?"

"I will consider it an honor." Gavin peeled away from the cave wall near the entrance, just as thirty rogue vampires stormed into the cave at his back and the battle began.

❧

Dragon! I heard her scream. Something was happening, but I couldn't guess what.

Oh, no, Joey sent.

What? What is it? I shouted mentally at him.

The Council is under attack, Merrill informed me. *They need our help.*

What the—we can't get there, I blustered. Below, the first monster leapt at Dragon, who jumped away and snapped at the neck, missing by inches. Lion went for the creature's back while it was turned toward Dragon, expecting another attack.

Lion raked the monster's back, forcing a terrible shriek from its mouth while Dragon's head snaked in and bit its throat.

What concerned me, however, was the second creature. Kiarra faced him down. I wanted to shout advice to her—give her warnings. I worried that her hooves would slip on the flooring. That she might be knocked down. That the monster would take the opportunity to make his kill.

Steady, Griffin warned.

He stalked her. She backed up. He took another step. She backed up again, her hindquarters coming in contact with a wall of the housing module. I worried that she was frightened.

She was looking for leverage.

I only saw the blur as she launched herself toward the creature.

Karzac was right.

When her horn touches evil, the evil dies.

I was more than grateful I was mist; the fist-sized chunks of both monsters flew harmlessly through on their way toward open water. I heard the plop and hiss as they rained into the gulf around the platform.

Some of them clanged against metal as they smashed into this wall or that railing.

It didn't matter.

Kiarra was shouting at me to drop the ones I carried. I set them down as swiftly and safely as I could.

"Daniel, the wolves have to stay here. Get Griffin to take you back," Kiarra nodded to him. "Everybody else, we're needed elsewhere."

With that, I suddenly felt as if the breath had been squeezed from my body as Merrill, Joey and I were flung to a distant shore.

Gavin cursed in Italian as he faced another rogue. One had clawed his back in the initial attack, but Gavin ignored the pain and turned swiftly, decapitating his assailant.

These had been trained well, he realized as he feinted in an attempt to catch his foe off guard. The members of the Council and a handful of Enforcers fought with them, but after the first wave of thirty, another group of thirty rogues joined the fray.

He'd never imagined that so many rogues existed, or that any of them thought to destroy the Council. There'd been no rumblings of such, and those who'd been captured in the past were always questioned carefully before sentencing.

The rogue answered with Italian profanity of his own. Gavin smiled grimly and switched to French.

～

We're breaking too many rules to mention, I sent as we ran for the entrance to the meeting cave. Both vampires assigned to guard the entrance were dead—ash littered the inside of the cave as we raced through.

The tunnel was long and narrow, but somehow the rogues had managed not only to get through, they'd done so without alerting anyone inside the cave. When we reached the Council chamber, the battle had already become deadly.

～

Saxom cursed before destroying most of what was within reach. He'd loosed the rogues under Xenides' command, but worried that he hadn't prepared sufficient forces. How had he not seen that they'd use the Elemaiyan habit of hopping from one location to another?

Saxom snarled and tossed a bookshelf across the room as if it weighed nothing.

～

I'd never seen the Council fight before that night. Never suspected that they'd gained their positions because they deserved them. Flavio fought with an efficiency almost as frighteningly beautiful as Gavin or Merrill did. Wlodek was terrifying as he removed heads from rogues.

Will and Russell fought in tandem, but I'd seen them do that often. Dragon's blades flew as he waded through a knot of rogues. I misted between him and Kiarra, who both fought with blades. With claws flashing, we chased the last of the rogues, discovering that Merrill, Flavio and Wlodek had barricaded the exit from the cave, killing any rogue who thought to escape us.

The last one screamed when he died—Bearcat and Joey had taken him down together. Breathing hard, I nodded my admiration to both.

~

"I'd prefer to demand to know what is going on, but I see that I am outclassed," Wlodek admitted.

He and the others had taken their seats around the U-shaped table, a few looking worse for wear. Two seats were empty—Maurizio's ash littered the floor somewhere, and Saxom hadn't been there for the meeting since he'd gone rogue. He was behind this attack—I was confident in that assumption.

Lion, Kiarra and Dragon faced the Council, with Merrill, Joey, Bearcat and me backing them up. Wlodek's eyes settled on Merrill for a moment before sliding away—I wasn't surprised.

Merrill was Wlodek's child, but Merrill wasn't obligated to Wlodek. I wondered if he ever had been. Perhaps that King Vampire rumor hadn't been a rumor after all.

Too, Wlodek recognized what stood before him. He didn't bow, but didn't assert his authority or threaten. I'd never seen the Head of the Council so nonplussed before.

"The Seer has gone rogue. You know this already," Dragon said.

"What?" Montrose said.

"It's true. The Seer has gone rogue, and he has taken Xavier down with him," Wlodek admitted. "I hear he is in the U.S., but his exact location is unknown. This attack was at his behest, unless I am very wrong."

"You're not wrong," Dragon nodded. "It is our belief that he has allied with our enemy. We fought six rogue vampires before coming here. They are dead, now, but there may be more waiting for his command."

"And Xavier is one of them. I counted him as a friend," Wlodek muttered. He was angry, that was easy to see.

"Xavier is responsible for at least one human death in Corpus

Christi," I said. "He and the Seer are allied with rogue werewolves, there."

"Does the Grand Master know of this?"

"He does," Lion said. "We have formed an alliance with the Corpus Christi Pack, and their Second is in continuous contact with the Grand Master."

"Include me in future correspondence, no matter what form," Wlodek directed his command to Merrill. "Choose the vampires you wish to return with you."

"Brock," Merrill said immediately. "Radomir. Will and Russell."

"Good. Go with Merrill. Report to me often," Wlodek commanded.

"What the hell is going on?" Russell breathed as he walked beside me toward the exit.

"Tell you later," I said.

"I told Wlodek that they were plotting something," Russell said. We'd gathered at Merrill's home in the countryside of Kent. I had no idea it was as close as it was to my ancestral home.

Lion, Dragon, Bearcat and Kiarra were having a meal; Joey, Merrill and I joined the vampires in drinking a bag of blood. There wasn't any need—yet—to let them know we'd changed.

The kitchen island held all of us while we talked; it was two hours before daylight, when Russell and the others would have to sleep for the day. "We've done some damage—likely it'll take time for them to regroup," Lion offered.

"We need some time to rest and prepare," Dragon agreed. He cut his eyes toward Kiarra as he spoke, but she sat beside me, huddled and silent on the barstool. Merrill was concerned, suddenly.

"Brock, take Russell, Will and Radomir to the basement and let them choose their quarters for the day," Merrill said. I blinked. It had come to me in an instant. Merrill was Brock's sire, too.

Brock led the others through a narrow door in the pantry nearby.

When the door closed behind them, Merrill sighed. "It couldn't be helped, my darling," he spoke directly to Kiarra.

~

"Why are they calling him the Seer?" Kiarra's nervousness was plain to all of us. We wisely chose not to point it out.

"He seems to know things. Perhaps his alliance with the enemy might explain that," Merrill said.

"Griffin knew. He didn't tell me." Kiarra wasn't pleased about that.

"He wanted to keep it from you—felt you'd be upset if you knew," Lion attempted to smooth things over.

"I am upset. I'm more upset that I didn't know. Griffin's still trying to run things from Fourth."

This goes deeper than you know, vampire, Dragon sent. I had no clue what he meant, or what Kiarra meant by fourth.

We are ranked, Dragon explained. *Griffin is Fourth. Once, he was First.*

Ranked?

I am Second, Lion is Third.

Kiarra?

First.

What the bloody hell? Is he trying to destroy her?

No. That is not his intent. He was demoted for a reason.

I wasn't convinced.

Lion and I will explain later. I feel it may be best if she leaves the planet for a few days and comes to terms with this.

I'm going with her, then, I fumed.

Lion and I may go as well. Pheligar can bend time to get us back if necessary. Daniel and Merrill will be our eyes and ears while we are gone. Merrill can see to transporting our vampire allies to Texas, he added. *With Griffin's help. Griffin can contact us if necessary.*

When are we leaving? I asked.

"Now," Pheligar appeared. He wasn't pleased, I could see that easily enough. *At least folding space is easier than hopping,* I flung out while being transported away from Earth.

~

"I don't want to talk about it."

Kiarra sat on a comfortable lounge chair on her wide deck, staring at the water below. Joey and Bearcat had chosen to stay with us, but they'd wisely offered Kiarra fruit and cheese for lunch before stealing back inside the house.

"You're brooding," I pointed out. "Let it go, sweetheart. Tell me what this is about. It'll help, I promise."

"It's too painful." Karzac appeared and took a chair next to mine. "We push, she retreats. Every time."

"Karzac," Kiarra sighed before closing her eyes and frowning.

"You cannot carry this forever. While none of us expected this, it was always possible. You must admit that."

"The odds were so small as to be nonexistent," she breathed.

"The trouble is that he managed to become immortal again," Lion said as he appeared and *Pulled* another chair in from somewhere. Settling his large frame on the seat, he breathed the air appreciatively. "Not nearly this warm at home," he added.

"Who managed to become immortal again?" I asked. Of all those present, I was the only one who didn't know.

"Saxom. Fucking Saxom. The-raping-bastard-who-should-be-a-rotting-putrid-corpse," Kiarra stood and cursed.

"Fuck you, Saxom," she shouted into the air. "I curse the day you were born and every breath you ever drew."

Now we're getting somewhere, Lion sent.

"Fuck you, Saxom," I stood and shouted. "I curse the day you were made a vampire and I curse the one who made you, you oily, evil bastard."

"Fuck you, Saxom," Lion stood and roared. "I curse the day you were made a healer for the Saa Thalarr."

"Fuck you, Saxom," Karzac stood and shook a fist at the air. "I curse you for every bit of harm you ever brought to anyone. I curse you for the dead in your wake. But most of all, I curse you for your betrayal."

"Wait," I held out a hand. Now I was getting it. *Saxom was the one who raped Kiarra.* "I'll kill the bastard," I said and stalked into the house.

~

"Adam?" Kiarra set a cup of tea on the small table beside my chair. I sat on the deck again, after pacing in her library for hours. Lion and Karzac had gone earlier. Perhaps they'd talked with Kiarra after I left them on the deck, but I didn't want to pry. Every time Saxom's image swam into my mind, I seethed.

He deserved so much worse than death.

"I should be handing you tea," I sighed before turning to her. "This is nice." I fingered the turquoise blouse she wore—it brought out the color of her eyes.

"It's one of my favorites." She surprised me by sitting on my lap and wrapping her arms around my neck.

"This is nice, too," I settled her head against my shoulder and held her one-handed while I lifted the teacup in the other. "Good tea," I said after sipping it.

"Lion brought it. It's a special blend from his home world."

"I like him," I said. "Honest. Straightforward. Blunt, when necessary."

"He has a big heart," she agreed. "Everybody loves Lion. He was a warrior-priest on Pterak before he joined the Saa Thalarr. It was his duty to protect the innocent. He's still doing that."

"What about Dragon?"

"The Dragon Warlord of the Falchani," she snorted. "There are so many legends written about him, he's almost a god to those people."

"Nothing wrong with that," I leaned in to kiss her forehead.

Don't ask her about her past, Bearcat warned as he and Joey walked out of the house and sat nearby. *She won't tell anybody. Dragon says wait for her to tell us.*

Then we'll wait, I said. I didn't want to upset her any more than she already was, and for her to come to me and voluntarily sit on my lap? I wasn't about to destroy that. "What's for dinner?" I asked aloud.

"What do you want?" Bearcat asked.

"What I'd really like is to taste the food at my restaurants, but that's out of the question," I replied.

"Says who?" Kiarra sat up and blinked at me.

"We'd have to ask Pheligar, and there's no way I'm asking him just to go to a restaurant," I fumbled.

"I can bend time. I know we can go back about three years and be perfectly safe," she said. "What we can't do is risk running into Adam during that time. It's dangerous."

"What if I could tell you when I'd be out of town on assignment?" I said, unable to keep the hope from my voice.

"If you could be sure of that," she frowned.

"I can be sure. I have excellent recall."

"Do we need to make reservations?"

I snorted a laugh. "I own the damn thing," I said. "I'll fire them if they turn us away. Can we go early? There's something I'd like to show you."

"If you want," she said. "Joey, do you and Bearcat want to go?"

"Bear wants to take me to Tulgalan for dinner."

"Then go with Bear. We'll bend time for Earth three years ago. What should I wear?" she asked.

"I'll look through your closet," I grinned.

"I've never worn this. Wolf bought it for me, but," Kiarra frowned at her image in the mirror.

"It's lovely on you."

"I don't usually wear anything I can't run or fight in."

"I sincerely hope we do neither. This is dinner, sweetheart, not Armageddon." The navy silk cocktail dress fit her perfectly, with a low neckline and just the right amount of flare about the knees.

"In my line of work, you should always be prepared for Armageddon, even when invited to dinner."

"I've seen something close to Armageddon a time or two. Dinner was never included."

"Come on, you." She grabbed my arm and folded space.

❧

"I'm surprised you knew where to take us," I smiled down at Kiarra.

"I found where you live by *Looking*," she wrinkled her nose at me. "If you want to go somewhere else, you'll have to drive us."

"The Jaguar or the Mercedes?"

"I've never ridden in a Jaguar."

"Then the Jag it is. But first, you have to see my apartment."

"Don't forget this is three years ago—it's just daylight," she reminded me as I took her arm and led her across the street to the building I owned in London. The top floor contained my living quarters. The underground portion housed my vehicles. Three floors in between, I used for storage. One tends to collect things if one lives centuries, after all.

"No elevator?" Kiarra blinked curiously at me as I unlocked the door leading to the stairs.

"I can hear a human bumbling up the steps long before they arrive at my door," I pointed out. "It's free security."

"In addition to the paid security?" she asked dryly as I tapped a code into a keypad beside the door.

"It's never wise to invest your safety solely on electronic gadgetry."

"True."

She followed me up four flights of steps to my top-floor apartment, breathing a contented sigh when I led her through the door.

"You like?" I asked.

"I love."

"Come now, you were expecting a bachelor pad, minus pizza boxes, weren't you?"

"Well," she shrugged.

The furniture was expensive, contemporary and comfortable. The rugs on the wood floors were hand-made Persians. I'd consulted with a decorator for furniture, pillows and artwork, but the final decisions had been mine.

"It's like walking into an oasis after the desert of your stairwell," she shook her head in disbelief.

"Do you think I want to invite thieves in during prolonged assignments?" I asked.

"I keep forgetting you can't set up shields," she said. "Sorry. Wasn't thinking."

"Come with me," I motioned for her to follow. "I want to show you something."

"Adam, I've already seen John Thomas."

"Not John Thomas, although he is asking to see you," I replied. Without another word, I strode toward my bedroom and the closet beyond.

"Your closet? Sweetie, you have more clothes than I do," she said, staring at rows of suits, shirts, ties and shoes, segregated by colors and hanging in the room I'd converted into a walk-in. "This feels nice," she touched the sleeve of an Italian silk shirt, custom-made to fit.

"I've had plenty of time to collect clothing," I pointed out.

"Really?" The word was dry and filled with humor.

"I didn't bring you here to show you my clothes, as much as I like them," I said. "I brought you here to show you this."

There is an island in the center of my closet, filled with drawers and storage space. A delicately carved wooden box takes up part of that storage. "This is what I wanted you to see," I said, lifting the box from its cubbyhole.

"This is beautiful," she breathed, touching the hand-carved wings of dragonflies and lilies. I'd had it made nearly a century earlier, for a very specific purpose.

"Yes, the box is lovely," I agreed. "But I want you to see what's inside it."

Setting the box on top of the island, I lifted the lid. Lined with silk, the box held rows and rows of jewelry. All kinds of jewelry. Sparkling gemstones of all colors adorned necklaces, earrings, bracelets and rings.

"I don't understand." She blinked at me in puzzlement.

"You know I saw you decades ago."

"You said that, yes."

"I've been buying jewelry every year since then, on that anniversary. For you. All of that will be yours, if you'll marry me."

CHAPTER 14

"A dam, I," she whispered. "You can't have. This is too much."

"This," I pulled a small box from its nest in a corner, "is what I'm asking you to wear tonight." Lifting the lid of the tiny box, I revealed the first thing I'd bought for her. A huge diamond, flanked by sapphires. "If you wear this, it means yes," I said.

"I'm afraid to touch it," she said.

"What are you afraid of?"

"That this is a dream, and I'll wake up."

"Here." I pulled the ring from its bed of satin and held it up, my fingers shaking slightly. "Give me your hand."

With only a moment's hesitation, she held out her left hand. I slipped the ring on her finger. It was a bit loose, but not enough that she'd lose the ring.

"I can adjust it with power," she sighed, staring at the ring on her finger for a moment. "It's beautiful, Adam."

"Then tell me you love me, and say yes."

"I love you, and my answer is yes."

"Right this way, Mr. Chessman." Employees were falling over themselves to get us to a table and seated comfortably. I wanted to smile. I didn't. They didn't see me often—they generally dealt with my business manager during the day. He always said the chef at this restaurant was exceptional. He would be put to the test tonight.

"Adam, there's a vegetarian version of a cottage pie on the menu," Kiarra breathed.

"That's," I frowned, prepared to complain to the chef about so common an item being offered.

"It's wonderful. I want that," she shut her menu with a happy sigh.

"Then you'll have as much as you want." I went back to studying the menu. "I believe I'll have the Beef Wellington."

"Lion and Dragon love that," she said.

"Wine?"

"You choose."

"All right." The wine steward barely blinked when I ordered the most expensive red they had—the Domaine Faiveley Musigny Grand Cru.

Remember—it doesn't take much to get me drunk, she informed me in mindspeech.

I seem to recall that, yes, I replied. *In fact, I'm counting on it.*

Please don't carry me out of here, she countered.

I'll take your elbow like a gentleman. I can't say I'll continue that ruse once I get you into my bed.

You're quite the rake.

I've had nearly a century to imagine what things I wanted to do with you, and how I wanted to do them. Most of them involve sex, I'm afraid.

You're living your dreams?

Oh, the reality is so much better than the dream. Dreams are cold. Reality is warm, my heart.

I will admit that sex is much better than I imagined.

You didn't have much to base it on. This is love. That was violence. There is a vast difference, as you know.

I know. She lowered her eyes. I'd upset her.

"None of that," I tilted her chin with a finger. "I promise I will kill that bastard, and smile when I do it."

"Adam, what if," she began.

"No, none of that, either." She attempted to turn away. I cupped her face in my hand to prevent it.

The meal was excellent. I worked to keep a conversation going, and learned many things. I already knew she was First, but had no clue as to what that really meant. She explained that it meant she might consult with the others regarding difficult decisions, but the final decision would be hers on most things.

"Dragon is a master strategist. Lion has experience in the trenches. I listen to both of them all the time," she said.

"What about Griffin?"

"He only listened to himself," she shook her head. "That's how I ended up with the bastard as my healer, instead of choosing one for myself. Griffin met Amara and wanted her as his healer. Saxom didn't want to retire. He was forced on me, when I didn't feel good about him from the beginning."

"It makes me curious as to why Saxom didn't want to retire."

"There was always a streak of cruelty about him—at least where I was concerned. I hated asking him to heal anything—and I had to ask," she muttered, staring at her hands. "I often went to Karzac instead—he didn't mind and he was kind instead of malicious."

"Karzac appears most knowledgeable," I agreed.

"As I am First among the Saa Thalarr, Karzac is First among the healers. His decisions are final regarding treatment. He can only be trumped by Pheligar, and often they work in tandem on difficult cases."

"Such as yours, recently."

"Yeah. That's the first time my guts have been strewn across the floor."

"I liked it not at all," I grumbled. "Although I am grateful they took me with them when you were removed."

"I figure Pheligar didn't want to hear your howling all the way to the Larentii homeworld."

"Here." I poured more wine into her glass. It was our second bottle, and I intended to consume all of it. "Joey will care for your bumps and bruises from now on. He's looking forward to it."

"I'm comfortable around him," she agreed and sipped her wine. "He has a sense of humor, too. That's important."

"He certainly has that," I agreed. "He taught me to smile again."

"You forgot how?"

"Nearly. Most vampires lose their humanity after a while. Joey restored mine."

"A point in your favor," she held up her glass. I did the same and we drank to humanity, although we were neither.

Her elbow was firmly gripped by my left hand as she wobbled out the door. The valet had already brought the Jaguar around, and it was waiting at the curb. I settled Kiarra on the passenger seat, shut the door and then slid into the driver's seat, the warm leather creaking comfortably about me as I fastened the seat belt.

"How do you drive on the left?" she giggled and then hiccupped.

"Is that a serious question?" I turned the wheel and drove away from the restaurant.

"It just seems wrong," she snickered.

"In this case, the Brits feel that driving on the right is wrong," I parried. "Stop signs? Those are for amateurs."

"Did you just snort in derision?"

"Derision may have been involved."

"Feeling superior, are we?"

"As a British vampire, how could I feel otherwise?"

"How do the Italian vampires feel about that?"

"You see the Council is located in England, don't you?"

"Somehow, I knew that was coming. Adam, I'm drunk."

"I know. We'll be home in a few."

I woke when she slid off the bed in the middle of the night. "Water," she croaked and headed toward my small kitchen. I lay back against my pillow with a satisfied sigh—this was wish fulfillment on my part —that she was in my bed.

She was naked, too—and I enjoyed the sight of her backside as she walked out of my bedroom on her way to get a drink of water. I intended to wait for her return, then convince her to let me love her again.

I waited patiently for her return, until I heard the front door to my flat open. I was out of the bed in a blink and rushing toward the kitchen, claws out, while the question of who might have broken in without setting off the alarm flew through my mind.

Lion's arm came around me like an iron band, keeping me from leaping into the kitchen.

The past is changing, he warned me mentally. I blinked past him into the interior of the kitchen, where my former self from three years ago stalked into the kitchen, likely wondering why the refrigerator door was standing open. Kiarra's hand gripped the top of it while she rummaged among bags of blood, looking for who knew what.

"Adam?" her head popped up over the top of the door and she blinked at the vampire I'd been years earlier. *What was I doing here, then?*

"Why are you dressed?" she frowned. I was dressed—for a Council meeting, it seemed.

"What are you?" the former me growled. "Never mind. Never mind." I watched as he—I—stalked toward her. Lifted a hand as if he were in a trance and traced her face with his fingers. Lion silently placed a hand over my mouth.

I have to get you out of here, he sent. *If the two of you touch, it's lights out.*

I wanted to scream as Lion folded space, taking me away.

❲

"At least she's already given you permission to take her blood," Lion set a cup of tea in front of me. He'd taken me to Kiarra's planet and set me down in the kitchen.

"How did you know?" I asked, still puzzled over recent events.

"Pheligar, who likely got a message from a higher up," he said, taking a seat beside me. "You can be in the same place at the same time, with permission or if you're one of the powerful. You really didn't have permission. That's why she asked about a time when you were away from home—so the former you wouldn't meet the future you. You'd have fought yourself. Wouldn't you?"

"If he put his hands on her. If I put my hands on her," I corrected. "And he—I—did."

"That would have canceled one—maybe both of you. This is stranger than you can imagine," Lion sighed. "I know you recalled that time perfectly—before you went. How things became so twisted, I may never know."

"Is she all right?"

"Kiarra can take care of herself."

"Time is a strange entity," Dragon arrived and took a seat on my other side. "It may be that someone was watching you in the past. Saw you show up at your restaurant with a woman, which you never do. This would involve the powerful, no doubt, but then enemies can be anywhere, and form dangerous alliances."

"I worry that this may be a larger, more dangerous plot than that," Pheligar appeared and *Pulled* in a large chair to fit his height. "It worries me more that I cannot find reasons by *Looking*, and even the Wise Ones are puzzled."

Wise Ones? I sent to Lion.

I'll explain later.

"Well, that's fucked up." Kiarra arrived, looking rumpled and weary. "Adam, we may have to discuss your vampire lust and stamina."

Yes, I laughed with the rest of them.

～

"My love, I have those memories, now," I grinned as I slipped her shoes off. "It felt as if I'd been given the best Christmas gift ever."

"You bit me twice," she pointed out, slapping a hand over her eyes.

"Hush, I'll get you in bed and let you sleep. This time," I said. We sat on the edge of her bed while I worked at removing clothes and shoes.

"You remember that now, because I allowed it. I had to mute the memory when I left you in bed for the day. I can't believe how much danger you were in."

"Stop worrying about it. Lion carried me away from there. Problem solved."

"But what if," she said.

"None of that." I unzipped the dress and lifted it over her head.

"Sweetie, you don't understand. You might have been lost."

"I'm right here," I soothed. "Time for sleep."

"My Lord," The Ra'Ak Prince bowed to Acrimus.

"H'Jerix, I am displeased. I gave you important information, yet the goal was not achieved. A fight was imminent, and she would have attempted to intervene. All of them should have fallen."

"We cannot account for every piece of interference—we cannot see all things," H'Jerix objected. Acrimus cared not that H'Jerix wore his serpent's guise and his words were often hissed. "It is as if our attempt was recognized and thwarted."

"She is dangerous to us. Make her a priority from now on. I care not how you accomplish this—I wish her destroyed."

"May I ask why? You know Saxom will be outraged if he learns of it."

"Saxom is merely a pawn. Mostly ineffective. He is alive for one reason, and you are cooperating with him—for one reason."

"Moxas," H'Jerix hissed.

"This is important to the future," Acrimus growled. "Do not fail me again."

~

"She's still tired, I can feel it," Joey informed me. He was proud of himself—for reading Kiarra's condition from a distance and for folding space for the first time. Bearcat arrived with him, but Joey had transported both of them.

"Then she needs the sleep," I said. I wanted her awake with me, but I hadn't spent the night engaged in the sexual Olympics. Yes, I was—and wasn't—responsible for that.

"I can't believe that happened. Tiger told me," Bearcat held up a hand.

"Does everything go like that—what one knows, the others do, too?" I asked.

"We're a collective intelligence," Bearcat teased. "No, it's not like that—we can have secrets, but once it's out to one of us, the rest of us usually get the information."

"Are you sure you understand what could have happened?" Joey frowned at me.

"I understand that I might have destroyed myself," I said. "Although it's still sinking in."

"What if Kiarra had attempted to intervene? She could have been destroyed, too. I hear the process is rather cataclysmic," Bearcat mused.

"I'm glad I hadn't heard that before," I growled. "This puts a different light on it."

"I hear you're engaged," Joey clapped me on the back. He was attempting to distract me, now, but I ignored him.

"I think you should go ahead and get married," he added. "In Vegas. Go back a couple of years and get married by your favorite rock star impersonator."

"I don't have a favorite rock star."

"I can suggest one of mine."

"No, thank you. I get to hear your music often enough through your earphones."

"Maybe there's a Mozart impersonator, then."

"I prefer jazz. You know that."

"Just teasing," Joey grinned.

"The marriage idea is a good one," I said, ruffling Joey's hair. "Convincing Kiarra may be a different story."

"Convincing me of what?"

"How do you do that?" Bearcat breathed. "We say your name, you show up, no matter what."

"Nexus echo."

"Right."

"It's an old Larentii mind trick."

"Very funny."

"You're going to Vegas to get married, aren't you?" Joey bounced on his feet.

"What?"

"Vegas. Married. Not rocket science," Joey grinned.

"Says you," Kiarra tweaked his ear.

"Wow. Affection. I love it," he laughed.

"Come here, you." She pulled Joey into her arms for a hug.

"And the universe rights itself," Bearcat sighed with satisfaction.

That's how the four of us ended up in Las Vegas, two years prior, inside a tiny wedding chapel. Joey had insisted that Kiarra couldn't wear a rented dress, so he and Bearcat disappeared for a few minutes, then reappeared with an ivory gown in a dress bag.

I believe she slapped his hands when he offered to help her dress. The photographs taken by the photographer were lovely, although half of them captured Kiarra frowning.

The awkward moment came when I produced her wedding band from a pocket, and she discovered she didn't have a ring for me. For a moment, she was close to tears before breathing a deep sigh and pulling something from her low-cut wedding dress.

"What's this?" I blinked—the ring was pale in color, but upon closer examination, I discovered it held many colors, including gold and silver.

A piece of my horn, she responded. *It's the only one of its kind.* She slipped it onto my finger.

"I pronounce you husband and wife," the movie-star look-alike announced. I leaned in to kiss Kiarra; we were married.

~

"You own this?" she studied the manor house converted into a hotel in Dublin.

"It has an excellent rating, and the restaurant gets top reviews." We stood near the gate leading to the property, which was surrounded by an expanse of lawn and gardens. Built of white stone, it had three stories, with a wide terrace in the center and a sunroom on one end.

"You really, really own this."

"Yes. I tried to hire the chef to work at one of my restaurants in London. He didn't want to leave, so I purchased the hotel. He gets to work for me anyway."

"Does he mind?"

"Absolutely not. I gave him a raise when I bought the place. He's quite happy."

"Good. I didn't want somebody spitting in my food."

"All the rooms are updated. Let's see if the largest suite is available for the owner."

"Let's just see if the largest suite is available. I have an alias and a credit card," she said. "We don't need a repeat of last night."

"Understandable. Shall we?" I offered her my arm.

"Absolutely."

~

"Adam, this is nice." Kiarra studied the lawn behind the hotel from our suite window. "It's so green. I've never been to Ireland before."

"I like Dublin," I shrugged. "I imagine I'll like it better, now that I can taste the food and walk the streets in daylight."

"Can we go to Trinity College? I always wanted to see the Book of Kells," she said.

"I'll take you—tomorrow. Tonight, we'll eat, drink and have sex."

"The traditional honeymoon, then?"

"If that's what you want to call it. I'd say my lust is not so traditional. Marriages were often arranged in my day. Justin was lucky that he liked Catherine so much. My parents found three women they thought I should marry. I refused all of them. Poor Justin was the sacrifice for the Chessman boys."

"You really loved your brother."

"I did. My parents, too. Sweetheart, will you take us somewhere?" The idea had come to me from nowhere.

"Anywhere," she said.

"Good." I gave her the address of my ancestral home. Taking my hand, she folded us there.

"He won't sell it, the bastard," I grumbled as we walked past crumbling walls and antique furniture covered in dust.

"He's a bastard for treating it this way," Kiarra agreed. The house was quite dim inside, as there was no electricity. "It's falling down," she added.

"I know, and there's nothing I can do."

"I didn't get you a wedding present," she said.

"I got a ring." I held up my hand.

"Pffft." She waved it off. "I'll do this, sweetie, just for you."

I never expected the glow as she worked, or that it was even possible. I shouldn't have been surprised. Crumbling walls repaired themselves. Dust disappeared. Threadbare fabrics became whole again. Scratches on wood healed—on furniture and flooring. Wallpaper brightened, the colors seemingly new again. I wanted to weep as my family drawing room from the past reappeared about me.

Just as it had been resurrected, so was the rest of the house. My breath caught at the staircase—it had rotted out. Now it looked new, the carpet running down it just as fresh.

"I think I just jacked up the price," her shoulders drooped. "But at least it won't fall down while you're negotiating the price next time."

"I don't know that he'll sell during his lifetime, but I have an advantage over him, there. He can't outlive me."

"Nobody can guarantee that, Adam. Not even one of my kind. You know why."

"I know." I pulled her against me. "This is the best wedding gift I could ever receive."

"You're welcome."

"I don't want to trouble them with this," Dragon studied the video. "Not until tomorrow, anyway. They knew to send it to Anna Madden's address, didn't they?"

"They knew," Griffin agreed.

"How is Merrill taking this?"

"He's upset. That's his third-youngest. *Was* his third youngest. Brock is angry and extremely distraught."

"Filthy bastard. This is always the lowest of tactics, to draw one of us out. We need a way to evacuate the population of Corpus Christi, before it gets worse."

"We need Kiarra."

"She deserves one night with Adam before we lay this on her."

"I know."

"The kapirus is responsible for the remaining deaths."

"I know that as well. I'll call a meeting of the others tomorrow. We'll figure this out. We have to figure this out."

"What is it?" Kiarra knew before I did. We walked into her kitchen after leaving Dublin behind, to find Lion, Dragon, Joey, Bearcat and several others waiting for us.

"We have a message from the bastard," Dragon held up a flash drive.

"Not now," Kiarra breathed and rubbed her forehead. I led her toward two empty barstools and settled her on one of them before sitting beside her. Lion produced a laptop, the flash drive was installed and we watched the video in shocked silence.

"Hello, Kiarra," Saxom said. "Did you think to hide from me? I suspected it was you all along. It is both fortunate and unfortunate that Chessman was sent—it had to be either Russell or him, so Xavier could yank their strings. I received every bit of information on you that Chessman supplied, did you know that?" He laughed. The sound scraped raw nerves.

"I hear you've learned of my presence," he went on, his eyes lighting with something close to insane glee. "You know what I want. I'll do whatever it takes to get it. This is just a taste."

My breath caught when Xavier walked into the frame, dragging someone with him—Jeff, one of the Corpus Christi vampires. The one with medical experience; the one who'd helped save my life after I was bitten by rogue werewolves.

Kiarra began to tremble beside me. I pulled her against me as tightly as I could. We watched as Xavier sliced Jeff's head from his shoulders just as easily as I might lift a pen to write. I held the stone-faced expression vampires are known for while Kiarra wept in my embrace.

Other bodies were shown to us. All drained of blood, several of them werewolf. The kapirus had been quite busy. "This will continue to happen if you refuse to come to me willingly," Saxom chuckled. "I care not for them. I have no desire for them. You know what I want. Make it soon, Kiarra, or more deaths will bloody your hands. In the meantime, as a show of good faith, bring Chessman to his sire. He has offended both of us, and we desire his death. That will buy you time for these."

My heart stopped when Rita's two small sons were jerked forward by a rogue vampire, who shoved them in front of Saxom. "We killed the werewolf guards, as you likely realize. Send Chessman along, and

I'll let these two go," he said. "Chessman must come alone to the ship channel seven nights from now. His death will ensure that these two live."

The children were crying as my barstool scraped back and I stood, furious. If I could have gotten my hands on both of them then, they'd have died. "We have to evacuate Corpus Christi," Kiarra brushed tears away.

"How do you propose we do that?" Lion asked. "Dragon and I have come to the same conclusion, but aside from telling the population the truth—that a madman, a kapirus, rogue werewolves, vampires, spawn and a Ra'Ak are likely waiting to devour them, I'm not sure how to go about it."

"Let me think about this for an hour," Kiarra wiped more tears away. She sounded determined, however. I couldn't help comparing her to many women I'd known, and most of them would have succumbed to a fit of the vapors.

"Adam, come with us," Lion motioned me toward him.

"While Griffin is the best when it comes to *Looking*, Kee's the best at finding viable solutions," Lion informed me. We sat on the front deck in the open air on a beautiful day.

Saxom had ruined all that.

"Jeff was Merrill's third youngest child," Dragon sighed before *Pulling* in a bottle of Scotch and three glasses. "He is obviously upset, as is Brock, Merrill's second youngest." He handed a glass of Scotch to me. I accepted gratefully. I knew Joey was Merrill's youngest, but I had no idea how many vampire children Merrill had.

"Three now living," Lion answered my unspoken question. "When this is over, I'll teach you how to shield your thoughts."

"Didn't you hear? I have to go alone and face Xavier and Saxom," I huffed.

"Bullshit," Lion muttered. "Isn't that what they say in your language? Bullshit?"

"It's an acceptable term for idiotic circumstances," I tossed back the Scotch and held out my glass for more.

"Idiotic and deadly," Dragon nodded, tilting the bottle and splashing more Scotch in my glass.

"There's no way you're going alone to meet those bastards," Lion said, emptying his glass and asking Dragon for a refill. "We don't send one of ours into an untenable situation like that. Saxom knows it, too."

"So he's expecting others."

"He'll use it as an excuse to kill those children. We have to find them first."

"We'll have to split up," Dragon corrected. "And do this simultaneously. Yes, we must locate the children, but part of us will perform the rescue, the rest of us will go to the ship channel with Adam. If we coordinate with mindspeech, we ought to be able to pull this off."

"We're back to the problem of locating the children," Lion said. "Griffin says they're in one of those blank pockets we've encountered."

"I know where they were when that video was recorded," I said.

"Where's that?" Dragon was interested immediately.

"In Roy Cheek's old office at the refinery," I said. "Joey and I went there to hack Cheek's computer. Come to think of it, I'm not sure I ever informed Xavier that we went there instead of Cheek's house to do the hacking."

"He'd expect you to go to Cheek's house?"

"Yes. That's the standard protocol. We lay compulsion if necessary, get the information and then tell the victim to forget we were there. Kiarra pointed me toward Hartshorne Oil, so that's where Joey and I ended up. Cheek wasn't on our initial radar, either, but Xavier did know that he was involved somehow after I messaged him several times."

"I figure he knew all along that Cheek was involved, through Saxom," Lion huffed. "You heard the bastard—he said he suspected Kee was here the whole time. He's been drawing her out slowly. I'm just glad it was you and not Russell who came. Russell would likely be dead already."

"True." I shook my head before emptying my glass again. "I suppose I ought to thank Merrill for that."

"Thank Merrill and Griffin," Dragon said. "While Griffin could have been better at keeping everyone informed, at least he accomplished one thing—getting you to Corpus Christi instead of your vampire sibling."

"I think I have something," Kiarra walked through the door and headed toward us. "You're just not going to like it."

CHAPTER 15

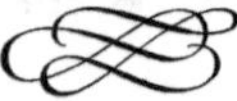

"It's barely formed," Griffin shook his head.

"There's a way, it's just dangerous," Kiarra replied. "Easy enough once, but to jump from one strike to another will require skill and concentration."

"Too perilous," Pheligar said. "I do not approve."

"You'll have to hide the power expenditure in numerous strikes to speed it up," Dragon said. "Risky at best. We can't afford to lose one of us. We don't have enough as it is."

I was confused as I listened to the conversation. Pheligar had transported us back to Corpus Christi shortly after Kiarra sent mindspeech. Again, I marveled at the ability to transport anything across time and space at will.

The image of a loosely formed tropical depression was shown on Joey's laptop as the discussion continued. Currently located east of the Dominican Republic, the weather experts weren't predicting the storm to be a threat. It was early in the season, after all, and it looked to turn northward toward southern Florida, bringing rain with it.

"I understand that," Kiarra argued nearby as I studied the computer image. "I think I can do this. Tell me, do you have any other ideas?"

"Kee," Lion began, "we have six days to get it here. Six days before

Adam has to go to the ship channel. If you don't make it," he shook his head.

"They won't expect this," she countered. "It'll appear completely natural. Even if they consider it, they'll realize how dangerous it is and dismiss the possibility."

"They would be right to think so—it could be suicide," Dragon sighed. "This is impossible," he flung up a hand in resignation.

Joey huddled against Bearcat, who had both arms wrapped around him. He was terrified. I didn't know enough yet to be terrified. Yes, I'd been listening, but still had no idea what Kiarra meant to do.

Merrill and Griffin sat nearby. They hadn't said anything, although Merrill looked grim. "I think," I said, "it's time somebody explained exactly what's going on."

"What?" Lion whirled to face me.

"I admit it—I have no idea what you're talking about. Please tell me —in plain English, if you don't mind." I frowned at Kiarra as I said the words. She intended to risk her life and I was excluded from the conversation. I was her husband and had that right—to voice my informed opinion on the matter. At the moment, it was decidedly uninformed.

"There's a way to get on and off a planet where the Ra'Ak may be, if Pheligar isn't available and there's an emergency," Dragon said. "We *Call* lightning. The expenditure of energy in a lightning bolt can hide the power we use to get on and off a world—but when we do it, we're actually cloaked within the lightning. Our shields keep us from being fried for the brief time it takes for lightning to strike. Kiarra is planning to hop from lightning strike to lightning strike to get to this tropical storm, and then employ more lightning strikes to hide the power needed to form a hurricane and send it in this direction. There's no way to tell if her shields will hold up past the first strike— none of us has ever attempted it. And, as we've pointed out, it is likely suicide to attempt it."

"Are you fucking kidding me?" I stood and shouted.

～

We weren't speaking. I wanted to yell. She wanted to yell back. It was a standoff between us. Neither of us intended to budge. I seethed, she sulked. I glowered, she grimaced. Lion and Dragon had given up their attempts to dissuade her.

Yes, there were questions I wanted to ask, such as when she intended to make this suicide attempt. I held back, because I knew it wouldn't stop with questions. She was playing with my heart, and I suspected she knew it.

Joey was in his bedroom with Bearcat, and he wasn't speaking to anyone, either. I hadn't realized the depth of his connection to her, through her blood, until then.

"Any healer will get that—residue from intense feelings—if they have the blood connection," Karzac settled onto a chair nearby. I'd chosen a seat in the sunroom and stared at the gulf. The sun was setting on the opposite side, leaving the island in twilight. A heavy bank of clouds lay to the east, bathed in gold, purple and blue. I turned my gaze away from the sunset to blink at the healer.

"You're telling me this because?" I growled.

"I'm telling you this because this course of action is the only one she knows to save lives. It upsets her a great deal, and we're not making it easier for her."

"I'm not making this easier for her because it's madness," I snapped.

"You see this as something that affects you. I see it as something that affects all of us. Kiarra is the heart of the Saa Thalarr. Lose her and we lose too much."

"Yet you're willing to let her engage in this foolishness."

"I've seen her overcome tremendous odds before. This isn't a rash decision, vampire. Know this, too—she'll risk herself before she'll risk any of us."

I turned back to the view through the window, and watched as lightning streaked horizontally through the cloudbank. The hair on my neck rose and I was up and racing through the house, shouting Kiarra's name as the sound of thunder boomed around the house and rattled it to the foundation.

◦

"All we can do is wait." Lion set a cup of tea in front of me. "We should have known she'd do it this way—leave without telling us because all we do is argue with her."

"Can you tell if she's?" I began.

"No. Pheligar says no, too. Therefore, either her strongest shields are in place, or she's gone. Joey is numb, Adam. If you have any comfort to give, perhaps now is the time."

◦

I was awake during what might prove to be the longest night of my life. I'd received no word, and there was no return. I'd held Joey for hours, so Bearcat could rest. Shortly before dawn, Bearcat took over, gently asking Joey if he wanted anything to eat or drink.

Food hadn't crossed my mind—Joey and I had clung to one another in shared grief, neither of us speaking our fears or sorrows.

Kiarra had left us both without a good-bye.

"I'll be back," I whispered, kissing Joey's forehead and leaving him with Bearcat.

Rain had come in the night, leaving the deck behind the house wet and gray while seabirds called over rough surf as the sun rose.

The clouds had gone, leaving barely a thin line far to the east. I cursed the beating heart in my chest, then, because it thumped painfully, reminding me of what I'd had for such a short time.

"Adam, come with me," Lion stepped behind me and gripped my shoulder.

"What?" I turned to face him.

"You need to see this," he said and jerked his head toward the house. I followed him inside. Dragon and Karzac sat at the kitchen island, watching the television that hung below the cabinets.

"This storm is developing quickly," the hurricane expert announced. I blinked. There it was, heading straight for the gulf—a newly formed hurricane. Not a tropical storm—it had moved beyond that stage. "Currently it is a category one, but that will likely change in the next few hours as the storm travels over the warm waters of the Gulf of Mexico. At the moment, it is expected to hit Cuba by tomorrow, perhaps as a category two or three. Stay tuned, we'll provide more information as it becomes available."

"Then why isn't she back?" I whispered in confusion.

"I'm surprised she made it this far," Dragon muttered. "But Cuba is the problem. If the storm passes over land, it weakens. She's driving it, Adam, and that means she has to stay with it. I didn't think about this part before—hurricanes are unpredictable. It could land anywhere on the Gulf Coast if somebody isn't directing it. I have no idea what the cost to her might be in the long term."

"This is untenable," I rubbed my forehead. "Still no word?"

"Again, we don't know if she has enough energy to devote to sending a message. I imagine she is doing everything she can to maneuver this thing without it becoming obvious, and who knows how long her shields will hold?"

"Adam, as long as this thing is going around Cuba and heading in this direction, I think we can trust that she's alive," Lion said.

Yes, my shoulders sagged at that news. *She's alive for now*, I sent to Joey.

"The Pack is still in mourning for the four we lost, but they know what killed those four—and Sam Greene," Daniel said. "The Grand Master is sharing the information, which Shirley can corroborate, since she's seen the monsters first hand."

Kiarra had been gone three days, and still the hurricane gained strength and ground its way in our direction, missing Cuba completely and turning toward the west, taking aim at the Texas Gulf Coast.

Night had fallen and a planning session was in the works—the vampires Wlodek sent had been staying at safe houses in San Antonio, but they had arrived and moved into the beach house with the rest of us.

Joey and I had busied ourselves with making bedrooms lightproof for the visitors for the past two days. Russell had grinned sheepishly at me the night before when he and the others arrived—he was wearing jeans, boots and his cowboy hat. I wanted to laugh.

I didn't.

"Doing all right?" Russell asked, taking a seat on the sofa beside me. We'd chosen the media room as our meeting place, and the vampires filtered in, one at a time.

"For now."

"I never expected you to, well, you know."

"Russell, this is the one. I can't explain it better than that."

"Do we know whether she's all right?"

"No."

"Damnation."

"Yes."

"We're hoping that they're still holding the children at the refinery, but we have no new information on that," Dragon began once we were gathered and sitting. "I don't know whether Kiarra will be available, so we'll go with what we have, here. Since this will happen at night, we'll divide our vampire allies and attack both targets simultaneously."

"Shirley has news," Daniel said. "We know a family of shapeshifting coyotes—we have an agreement with them regarding hunting grounds. Shirley offered them rights to prime real estate in exchange for checking the refinery for us. They got in and out fast, but they said there's evidence that humans are being held there, still. There's garbage and other signs of habitation."

"I think we should check that house again—the one where Rita was killed," Merrill suggested. "We don't know that they haven't gone back there."

"I say we check it and the safe house," Russell agreed. I nodded at Russell—he was very good at what he did.

"What about Kyle?" I asked. "Is he safe?"

"Kyle is in San Antonio. He'll be back tomorrow. I asked him to join us," Merrill said. I blinked. Kyle was one of Merrill's three living vampire children. I knew it suddenly, without bothering to *Look*. Somehow, Merrill had known to place Kyle and Jeff here, in the Corpus Christi area. I wanted to shiver at the way things were falling into place.

I didn't want to say anything, but Merrill looked gray. He wore the vampire mask, but there was a tightness to his mouth and a shortness in his words that hadn't been there before. He'd lost one of his children, but that wasn't the only thing that pained and worried him.

He and I—terrified for her safety. Hiding our panic the best we knew how—behind the vampire non-expression.

"Adam, are you still prepared to meet Xavier and Saxom on the ship channel?" Dragon asked.

"More than ever," I nodded. I didn't add that if Kiarra failed to return, there was nothing for me to live for, anyway.

"Your sire's compulsion will no longer hold sway, but it may be a good idea to keep that from him—at least at first," Dragon said. "I suggest that you mist in with those who are going with you, and drop your passengers far enough away so Saxom and Xavier won't suspect. You can walk in from that point, without letting them know how quickly you can become mist. Use it as a weapon, Adam. They won't expect it."

"Good advice," I agreed. "Who's coming with me?"

"I'll come," Bearcat offered. "Dragon and Lion want to lead the group going to the refinery, or wherever we believe the children may be. We suspect the enemy may be concealed nearby, laying a trap, so it's best if they take the majority of our team there."

"I'll go with Adam and Bearcat," Joey said. Nobody made note of the fact that he stumbled over his words.

Russell and Will volunteered for my group. Brock and Radomir would go with Dragon, as would Merrill, Karzac and Daniel. Merrill offered to send Kyle with my group. I accepted. If she returned, I wanted Kiarra in my group, too. Who knew if that might happen?

"That's damn handy," Russell swore in his best Texas accent. I'd misted Will, Merrill and him into the Corpus Christi safe house. Nothing had changed, and there was no evidence that Saxom's rogues had returned. I'd set my passengers down in the kitchen the moment I determined we were alone.

"It is damn handy," I agreed. "I wish I could have misted this quickly in the past."

"It certainly would have saved time," Merrill said. "Did you make these improvements?" He studied the floor and countertops.

"Yes. It's a hobby. Something I wanted to do in my early life, but I can only do this in my spare time, now."

"Excellent work." He ran fingers over the granite countertop.

"Thank you. The Council will knock this down, now," I sighed.

"A craftsman's efforts are never wasted," Merrill said. "If there is even one person who appreciates them. Shall we go to the house where the woman was killed?"

"Yes." I gathered my passengers into my mist again and left the safe house behind for good.

"Packaging for microwave mac and cheese, plus candy wrappers and soda bottles," Daniel said. "That's what they found at the refinery early this morning."

We had two days before the meeting on the ship channel, and had gathered for another planning session at the beach house. "We found nothing at the safe house or the other location," I said. "The scents were old—they haven't bothered to check whether we'd been there. So far, everything still points to the refinery as the primary target."

"Police reported ten more people missing as of last night," Dragon growled. "Probably a food source for vampires and who knows what else. One of those missing is a police officer, and I worry about the investigation leading them near the refinery. More may die if that happens, and they'll move the hostages, forcing us to hunt them again."

"The Mayors of Port Aransas and Corpus Christi are announcing plans for evacuation of the area," Lion said. "Quite a few have left already, since the hurricane is a category four and heading right in this direction. Weather experts are predicting landfall roughly four hours after you're scheduled to meet on the ship channel." He blinked dark eyes in my direction, letting me know that Kiarra still seemed to be in control.

I wanted to sag in relief. I didn't. We had one more day to watch the storm and refine our assault on two locations. So much could go wrong in the interim.

"I can't get through to her. I've sent mindspeech," Pheligar said.

"Sit down," Nefrigar *Pulled* in a comfortable chair for his brother. "Have you fed? I can open the skylight for you."

"I can't remember," Pheligar rumbled. Nefrigar moved the tinted glass ceiling back with a thought, allowing bright sunlight to enter. "Will you delight in the knowledge that you were right and I admit it?"

"Brother, why would I delight in what has brought you misery? Have you approached the Wise Ones recently to learn of any new information?"

"No. I worry that she will spend herself completely so there will be nothing left. The enemy will devour her if that happens."

"I understand," Nefrigar nodded. He seldom employed human gestures, but this one fit the occasion.

"If I had acted in the past, I could step in to protect my mate. As I did not," Pheligar left the sentence hanging.

"You can do nothing, now, except wait."

"You do not understand the consequences, should she survive, brother. If I tell her I muted our M'Fiyah, she will be angry. If I tell her that the Wise Ones once saw our son, she will be angry. How can this be rectified at such a late moment?"

"If she survives, I suggest moving slowly toward a mutually acceptable conclusion. Allow your feelings to show in small increments. She will become used to it. When the time comes, it will readily be accepted."

"You do not know Kiarra," Pheligar huffed and disappeared.

"You have not fed sufficiently," Nefrigar spoke into the air about him.

～

"This one?" I held up a shell for Joey to see.

"Turkey wing—in local lingo. It's more commonly known as a zebra ark."

"Fascinating." I studied the shell in the morning light, cupping it in my hand so as not to damage it. Reddish-brown lines ran in a pattern across a rectangular half shell. It did resemble a turkey's wing, and I understood why it might be named as such.

"Look—a banded tulip." Joey held up another shell, perhaps two inches long, that bore a spire, a tail of sorts and a round body in between. As he'd said, it did have lines banding the surface.

"The storm is causing things to wash ashore that normally wouldn't," Lion joined us in the early-morning light. Joey was barefoot, his pants rolled above his ankles as he walked the soft sand on the beach, while I wore dress shoes and pants. Joey left neat footprints behind while the sand sucked at my shoes.

If I survived the upcoming ordeal, I was resolved to invest in a good pair of trainers and casual pants or button-up jeans.

"I haven't found a whole sand dollar yet," Joey pointed out. "They're all washing up in pieces."

"I worry that Kiarra may return to us the same way," Lion shook his head as he gazed eastward. We could see the clouds approaching with the storm; just that morning, the local news was filled with images of the traffic tie-ups as residents fled the coastal areas.

Local police had knocked on our door shortly after daybreak, informing us of the mandatory evacuation. Merrill placed compulsion and they left us behind, believing the house to be empty.

"Dragon says the hurricane has been upgraded to a category five," Lion said, handing a tiny, white shell to me. "Called a baby ear moon snail," he said and turned toward the house.

The shell was ear-shaped, pale and delicate. "How does anything live in this?" I wondered aloud.

"I'm amazed at how beautiful they are," Joey said, lifting a tiny, whole sand dollar from the surf. "It's as if an artist designed them, instead of nature."

"Perhaps nature is an artist, and goes by another name," I replied.

"Do you think she's okay?"

"I don't know. I hope so. That's what we have left, now. Hope."

"You think we will trouble ourselves over a storm?" Calhoun laughed. "You know we have the ability to weather the winds or leave in a fraction of a second. You have what you want in your sights. We shall have what we want as well."

Saxom frowned at the rogue godling. Calhoun had never said what he wanted. Moxas set up the meeting through the Ra'Ak somehow, and Saxom had grasped at the chance to take what he desired.

If the Saa Thalarr were destroyed in the process, all the better. "I'll make her pay for allowing that filth to touch her," Saxom hissed.

"That is your business," Calhoun waved away Saxom's words. "We want the planet; we have plans for it. It was classified as not worth saving, yet here they are, intending to rescue it."

"They will fail," Saxom muttered. "I'll see to it myself."

"Grand words," Calhoun replied with a sneer. "Prove them."

"Sixty miles an hour," Lion said as we watched short, squatty palms growing outside the media room whip and twist in rising winds.

"Don't wear anything tonight that will blow about and obscure your vision."

"Understood. I'll let the others know when they rise."

"Inconvenient—that vampire habit of sleeping through the day."

"Speaking from experience, it's decidedly inconvenient."

"At least we never worried about getting enough sleep before," Joey yawned beside me. I draped an arm over his shoulders and hugged him. We'd slept badly since Kiarra left us behind.

"Tomorrow at this time, it'll be over," Lion said. "One way or another."

"That's what concerns me," I said.

"Child, I do not want news of your death," Wlodek said, his voice gruff.

"Father, I have no desire for that news to reach you," Merrill responded.

"Then make sure that you and Radomir return to me."

"Of course. Anything else?"

"I greatly desire Saxom's death. And Xavier's. For their betrayal and the assault on the Council."

"I will do my best to see that happens. Have you chosen new members for the Council, to replace Saxom and fill Maurizio's empty chair?"

"Ilaisaane and Nestor are being considered."

"Father, I dislike both choices."

"It cannot be helped; they have a majority of support from the others, and I cannot exert my influence in this matter."

"I understand. We will work around this somehow, should it come to pass."

"If it comes to pass. Be well, my son."

"And you, Father."

"Adam, I'd like to speak with you."

Griffin found me on the top level of the beach house, in a room the former owner had used as a study. It overlooked the gulf and offered a bit of quiet time so I could sort things through in my mind.

"About what?" I turned to watch as he walked into the room. He was tall—taller than I by a few inches, with brown hair and hazel eyes.

"About you—and your family. And why you're vampire," he added.

"I'm vampire because I was attacked by six thugs on a street in London. I'm vampire because they robbed me and left me for dead. Xavier found and turned me before I died."

"So you've been told."

"Yes. Many times. Xavier always thinks I should be a more grateful child."

"You owe him nothing." Griffin said those words with a hiss, accompanied by a swift and violent sweep of his hand.

"What are you saying?" I gave him my full attention, then.

"Do you recall the stories of your uncle? The one who reportedly died at sea?"

"Yes. I never knew him—I was a baby when he disappeared. My father often spoke of his brother Gerald, but I only saw photographs of him. Why do you ask?" This seemed an odd conversation to have on the day my life might end, but I was intrigued, nonetheless.

"He wasn't lost at sea," Griffin said.

"The official reports say otherwise."

"Because the writers of the official reports were instructed to say otherwise. Your uncle was in port during that time. He was turned, Adam. Gerald Chessman was a vampire. He was killed shortly before your turning."

"What?" If Griffin's goal was to shock and infuriate me, then he'd accomplished both those things.

"Just as your great-great-great uncle was turned. That uncle—Maxwell—was a vampire, killed shortly before Gerald's turning. Gerald was chosen because your father was married and he wasn't. Gerald—and you—were targeted deliberately, because Maxwell was a mister. That talent runs in families, as you know. The Council considered whether to take you or your brother, Justin. When Justin's engagement was announced, that decision became easier for them to make. Xavier was instructed to take you. He hired those thugs, then watched and waited for the appropriate moment. All of it planned, to enrich the vampire race."

"That's why he was overjoyed when I became mist for the first time," I snarled. At that moment, I wanted to break things. More than anything, however, I wanted to kill Xavier. I'd always felt guilty—felt I owed him for saving me.

He'd killed me, instead. Yes, Griffin likely knew that I had thoughts of allowing Xavier to kill me after I attacked him and Saxom.

No longer. I wanted to kill both of them. Intended to kill both of them. Anger rose, bitter as the bile in my throat, against the Council as well. They'd toyed with my life. Arbitrarily chose me to make their lives easier. A mister, at the Council's beck and call. It made me wonder what Gerald and Maxwell had done for them—and in what capacity.

I'd never been given full access to Council records. Perhaps this was the reason—that I'd see my uncles' information and complete the puzzle of my life. I didn't know whether I should thank Griffin for this information or curse him.

"I'll settle for neither," he said softly and left the room. I sagged onto a chair and dropped my head into my hands. Had I ever expected such a dramatic turn in my life? No. I was determined, however, whereas before, I hadn't been. If I fell, I would fall fighting against what had taken me. Had used me. Expected me to be grateful for it. I dropped my hands and stared out the window as lashing winds and rain hit the window. My laugh, when it came, was harsh and filled with bitterness.

"It will be raining hard, Son. Dress accordingly." I tousled Joey's hair. Kiarra wasn't coming back. At least for this fight, if at all. Winds in excess of one hundred miles per hour screamed about the house and waves were lapping against tall dunes in front of it. I had no clue how high the storm surge might be, and the ship channel on the opposite side of the island was a poor place to make a final stand.

"This is grim," Joey mumbled. He and I—both afraid to feel. Both of us beyond numb. We had a job to do and we would do it, but we felt as if our hearts had been cut from our chests. The beating there? Merely reflex.

"Sunset," Merrill announced as he joined us. "Child are you prepared?" he placed a hand on Joey's shoulder.

"I guess. I wish we knew more about Kiarra," he said.

"As do I."

"We'll know eventually," I offered. "Joey, are you sure you won't be cold?" He wore a thin T-shirt with a rock band logo on the front over jeans and leather trainers.

"I'll be okay," he shrugged, stuffing hands in front jeans pockets.

"Get us through this, young Joey, and I'll allow you to buy khaki pants and trainers for me."

"Add a few polo shirts and it's a deal," he nodded.

"I'll accept that," I agreed.

"Vampires are awake, get ready to go," Dragon announced behind us.

CHAPTER 16

"We'll drive as far as we can, then go in on foot, or in Adam's case, as mist," Dragon instructed. All of us, including Kyle and two werewolf drivers, had gathered in the foyer, preparing to leave. "We have four hours, before a category five hurricane hits the coast. This needs to be over by then."

"That's for damn sure," Lion agreed. "We'll have to employ power to get all of you out of here, and if we don't find the main enemy by that time, all hell will break loose."

"Let's go, the clock is ticking," Dragon said. He wore his blades strapped to his back over a sleeveless, laced-up black leather vest. The tattoos of red dragons rippled down his arms as he opened the door.

The werewolves had provided us with the best vehicles they could —armored Humvees with tall tires to drive through high water, if necessary.

It was necessary.

Highway 361 was covered by water. Joey's face and knuckles were white as he sat beside me, and I worried that the winds would sweep us off the highway before we reached the narrow road leading to the ship channel.

The road was little more than a path, actually, through a field that the fishermen used to get to prime fishing areas on the channel. The ground was soaked and flooded in places, rendering the road practically impassable. Tall grasses on either side had been beaten down by the rain and winds, and it was difficult to see past a rain curtain of grayness surrounding the vehicle.

We were forced to stop long before I was ready.

"When I drop you out of my mist," I said before we left the truck behind, "Wait for a minute or two and then walk in."

"Adam, what are you doing?" Joey asked.

"Planning a surprise," I growled. Before he could argue, I turned to mist and gathered my small army with me.

"This is impossible. We'll have to hop to a location near the refinery." Lion studied the low bridge leading into Corpus Christi. Covered in three feet of water, it was impassable.

"Do you want to come with us, or turn around and take your chances on the island?" Dragon asked the werewolf driver.

"I'll come. It's suicide to stay on the island," the werewolf shook his head.

"Sam, if you don't want to fight, we can leave you in a sturdy building," Daniel offered.

"I'll fight. Might take my mind off this storm," Sam Sheridan replied.

"Your dad," Daniel began.

"My dad isn't here. I am. I volunteered to drive, and I drove as far as I could. Now it's time to see if I'm a werewolf or not."

Dragon blinked at the twenty-year-old werewolf before nodding in approval. "Then come with us. Do what you can. I don't suppose I have to warn you not to do anything foolish."

"I'll do my best, Mister Dragon."

"Lion, do you want to get us there?" Dragon asked, turning dark, unrevealing eyes toward his fellow Saa Thalarr.

"Oh, yeah. I know just the place," Lion purred.

I should have suspected something when I saw Saxom and Xavier waiting for me, an apparent bubble of calm about them. If I'd been thinking rationally, I might have noticed that their clothing was dry. Rain lashed and pounded everything else, but they were untouched by it.

I didn't notice. At least not then. My anger erupted and I saw both through red eyes as I stalked toward them, the rain and wind pushing me in their direction.

Only seconds behind were Joey, Russell, Will, Kyle and Bearcat. I wanted this finished before they arrived.

How foolish I was.

Half the building is already gone, Lion sent. He and the others walked through the abandoned administration building. *The blank spot is persisting, even in such close proximity.*

Understood, and this place wasn't built to take this kind of punishment, Dragon agreed. *They may have taken the children away already. You know this is likely a trap.* With one end of the building flattened by the storm, the rest of it looked to follow swiftly.

The offices are still intact, Merrill observed.

Let's go, then, Lion responded.

Wait, what's that sound? Karzac placed a hand on Dragon's arm.

"It's a child crying," Daniel snapped. "They're here. Let's go."

They ran down a hall toward Roy Cheek's office, when walls blew apart and disintegrated about them. A nine-foot kapirus would have been bad enough alone in such a storm—it unfolded from a crouch and roared into the wind and rain.

A Ra'Ak's appearance behind the kapirus was so much worse.

Half my claws were sheared away as I slashed at Xavier first.

Someone—or something—had placed a shield about him strong enough to destroy a vampire's claws.

Mine were strong enough to cut metal.

I watched, furious, as Xavier laughed. The storm was too strong and too loud for me to hear him.

Nevertheless, it infuriated me. Another claw shattered as I attacked his shield a second time.

One hand—one arm—almost defenseless.

Adam, stop, Joey screamed in my mind. *They want you dead, but they want to watch you destroy yourself as much as possible, first.*

Will shouted behind us as a roof flew past him before crashing into the shields protecting Saxom and Xavier. There, it was ground to bits by whatever protected them. I blinked in shock—the same thing had destroyed four of my claws.

That's when the rogue werewolves—twenty or more—leapt from covered trenches and attacked Joey and the others. They had a fight on their hands as I turned back to my targets. I couldn't worry about that battle—I had my own to fight. Two yelps came—two werewolves were down.

Had things not happened as they did at that moment, my anger would have remained in control and I would have continued to attack Xavier's shield in futility. The thing in our favor, perhaps, was that it took Saxom and Xavier by surprise even more than it did me.

"What the hell?" Daniel shouted as the black-scaled kapirus lunged toward him, fangs bared and ready to snap his head from his body.

The eye? Lion sent.

Everything had gone still and silent in the space of a blink.

Nothing moved.

No winds blew.

A few bits of debris floated down from a cloud-covered sky.

Watch out! Dragon's mindspeech sounded. His dragon roared at the Ra'Ak, which coiled and prepared to strike.

~

"This makes everything so much easier," Saxom sneered as the shield dropped about him. Xavier stepped from his protective bubble to stand beside the Seer.

Adam, what just happened? Joey's mindspeech reached me. Sounds of fighting continued behind me, so I knew Joey survived, at least.

"It's the eye of the storm," Saxom laughed. The sound grated while my anger cleared slightly and a thought formed slowly in my mind.

This couldn't be the eye.

The hurricane wasn't scheduled to make landfall until four hours from now. That meant the eye wouldn't pass over land until sometime afterward.

"You're both fools," I hissed at them before I charged, my hand extended, my remaining claws ready.

~

The kapirus snapped at Sam, who'd become werewolf the moment the monster appeared. Daniel had leapt aside already, leaving Sam vulnerable behind him.

The huge, black lion roared and charged, crashing into the kapirus. Both of them fell across debris from the building while the Ra'Ak's head snaked forward, determined to kill the Saa Thalarr battling the kapirus.

~

Xavier screamed compulsion at me to stop. I might have laughed—if there'd been time.

He was counting on controlling me.

He and Saxom, both.

His compulsion slipped away as easily as a raindrop slides across a windscreen.

Saxom shouted his compulsion, followed closely on the heels of Xavier's. He never finished his command.

His head rolled away before the final words left his lips. I savored a moment of grim satisfaction as Saxom began to flake.

Adam!

My name was a cry. I blinked as Xavier turned on me, fangs bared, claws ready. My right hand was toward him—the hand missing four claws. I shouted as he flew at me.

Merrill's claws took the kapirus' head too swiftly for most to see. Lion rolled away as the Ra'Ak snapped at him.

Dragon leapt as the Ra'Ak's head turned in his direction.

Did she know how this would end? Had she seen it, somehow?

I recognized the blade in Kiarra's hand when she appeared.

This was no steel blade.

This was her unicorn's horn. It gleamed a rainbow of colors, even in such gray light. There was no time to appreciate its beauty.

Xavier was on me, his claws slashing toward my throat.

He never made it.

With a single thrust of her horn blade, Kiarra skewered him.

I recalled Karzac's words as I watched my sire die.

If that touches evil, the evil dies.

The light left Xavier's eyes. I stepped forward to embrace my love.

Two giant serpents erupted from the wet ground about us.

"Take the children to safety," Karzac shouted at Merrill, Daniel and

Sam. He'd gone looking for Rita's sons while the others battled monsters. Few knew until later that four rogue vampires were left flaking behind the healer.

Karzac was First among the healers for a reason.

Dragon breathed fire, forcing the Ra'Ak to back away for a moment.

"This way," Merrill shouted, pointing toward a whitewashed petroleum storage tank nearby. "We need to be on the other side quickly."

Sam Sheridan didn't need further encouragement. Snatching one of the children from Karzac, he ran.

Karzac folded space with the second child, while Merrill grasped Daniel's arm and flew toward safety.

Dragon jerked aside as the Ra'Ak's deadly head snaked forward. The moment the Ra'Ak recoiled, Dragon leapt.

Even their scales are poison, filtered into my mind. I blinked in shock. Calling the Ra'Ak giant serpents paid them no justice.

Fifty feet long or more, with bodies at their thickest large enough to swallow a rhino. Copper scales gleamed as they moved, their heads spiked with lengthy, dangerous barbs.

The teeth, when their mouths opened to roar, were numerous, sharp and deadly.

One Ra'Ak for each of us.

Had they suspected and chosen to lie in wait for us?

"Adam!" she shouted at me a second time. I couldn't stop myself—I jerked my head in her direction.

Her horn blade flew toward me.

She'd tossed her protection to me. I caught it quickly.

Just not quickly enough.

The Ra'Ak she faced lunged in, almost too swiftly for me to see. Watching in horror, I heard her scream as the monster sank deadly, poisonous fangs into her body. I barely turned in time to stab the second, who intended to do the same to me.

Holding up a hand in reflex is a useless gesture. I had no time to think, and never considered going to mist. My love was dead—she died as I turned to reach for her. I barely had time to blink before the explosions came.

I'd seen spawn dust. Watched as their chunks flew in every direction. The younger ones felt like a sandstorm.

The larger ones required skill or a strong shield to survive.

When a Ra'Ak dusts, unless you have thick steel or strong shields between you and the blasting chunks, you will not survive.

I had neither of those things.

All I recall is the light so many speak of when they die.

The storage tank was battered and had collapsed on one side—the side facing the Ra'Ak.

Dragon had waited to strike until the others had reached the safety of the opposite side. "I'm glad that's over," Lion frowned at the mud covering his clothing. Chunks of the Ra'Ak's dusting were everywhere. "Pheligar has a cleanup waiting. You were right, brother. The Ra'Ak was here. Do we have information on Adam, or why the storm stopped when it did?"

The hurricane had vanished, and the winds had slowed dramatically. Lightning formed in clouds hanging low over the gulf, but those were far to the east and looked to be receding.

"Dragon," Bearcat appeared nearby, holding Joey up with both arms.

"Bear?" Dragon's voice suddenly held fear.

"Two Ra'Ak on the ship channel," Bearcat dropped to his knees, Joey falling with him. "Adam and Kiarra are gone."

Joey's Journal

Merrill and I returned to his brownstone in New York.

He wasn't speaking to anyone.

Radomir reported to Wlodek on the events in Texas. He knew that Adam was dead and Merrill in deep depression.

Bearcat promised to come for me in two weeks.

Merrill wasn't the only one in mourning.

⁓

"I am the Ear," he said, causing Griffin to jerk his head up at the sudden appearance.

"How may I be of service?" Griffin bowed his head respectfully.

He and the others knew of the three messengers. Most had never seen them, including many in the Hierarchy.

"You will retire, effective immediately," the Ear commanded.

"But I am not," Griffin sputtered. This was the opposite of what he expected might happen.

"Wisdom cares not that you are not ready. He knows that you saw deaths and the capture of the children. You did nothing to prevent them. Belen and Thorsten have already been advised of your retirement. We will not interfere with your power—or your friendships. That may change, however, so do not press your luck."

The Ear disappeared, leaving a seething Griffin behind.

⁓

Joey's Journal

"Kee knew," Bearcat said beside me. "No challenge was issued—by her or by the Ra'Ak. A challenge neutralizes a Saa Thalarr's blood."

"So, because a Saa Thalarr's blood will kill anything that takes it without permission, the Ra'Ak that bit her died?"

"Exactly. She timed it right, too, because there was a slight delay— enough time for Adam to stab the second Ra'Ak with her horn. Both dusted at the same time. I didn't have shields strong enough to cover them and the rest of you, too. Their bodies were blasted to bits, being that close to the epicenter, so to speak."

"What about the hurricane? Everybody thought that would kill her."

"There's been some talk. Pheligar won't speak to anybody right now, so we didn't get the Larentii opinion on this. One of the more popular theories is that she kept hopping from lightning strike to lightning strike—so fast that none of them had time to affect her."

"That would require days of frenetic activity with no rest," I pointed out.

"And that's the argument against that one. Another theory is that she employed Adam's talent of turning to mist. A lot can go through mist without affecting it at all. Bullets, winds, you name it."

"That sounds more like it," I sighed.

"She stopped it, too, at just the right time. That took a lot of power. Didn't make any difference in the end, though."

"Yeah."

"All that time, too, the Ra'Ak were using the refinery as their hiding place. That was the deal Roy Cheek made with them—he offered them empty petroleum storage tanks as housing. They shielded those and we never suspected there were that many of them. It was in their plan all along to get the refinery shut down and Cheek and the workers out of the way. When Saxom showed up, he and Xavier used the administration building as their hideout."

"I thought there was only supposed to be one Ra'Ak—according to the rules." Yes, I remembered my lessons from Bear, Karzac and the others.

"That was a world not worth saving, remember? The rules get thrown out the window for the most part. It doesn't have anything to do with the blood, though. That holds true, no matter what."

Joseph? The voice entered my mind like the softest velvet.

Nobody called me Joseph.

Cool hands came from behind and covered my eyes. Soft hands. Smaller than mine.

"What?" I turned swiftly and almost fainted from joy.

Kiarra grabbed my arm when I almost fell from my barstool.

Adam was the one who lifted me and set me on my feet.

I only managed one word before the tears came.

"How?"

~

"I can't tell you, because we don't know," I shrugged and accepted the glass of Scotch from Lion. When Kiarra and I appeared in her kitchen, surprising Joey and Bearcat, the news spread like wildfire. Everybody showed up, eager to learn how we'd survived.

The truth was—we hadn't. Both of us died. I know that, as does Kiarra.

Someone, or more than one, perhaps, in a much, much higher position, had taken an interest. Someone very powerful wanted us to live.

Therefore, we lived.

What I did know is this—Kiarra had been offered a promotion. She had taken an impossible situation and resolved it, at the cost of her life and her love.

She'd refused. Told Belen that she wanted to be where she was—First among the Saa Thalarr.

He said the invitation to join the Nameless Ones was open anytime she wanted to take it. She thanked him and we'd gone to find Joey.

Three weeks had passed since our deaths. I can't explain where we were in that time, because I have no memory of it.

What happened after our reappearance is this; Merrill was declared a friend of all Saa Thalarr and accorded special privileges. In fact, I'd invited him to dinner at one of my London restaurants the following week. He'd been overjoyed at our survival. I didn't lie to myself by believing he wasn't mostly overjoyed at Kiarra's resurrection.

"But what's this?" Dragon held a glass of Scotch in his hand as he came forward to examine me closely.

I didn't turn down the offer for my promotion. "Fourth, in Griffin's place," I nodded. "He retired, and I was offered his position."

"What's your fighting animal?" Lion asked, grinning hugely.

"I chose a black gryphon," I said. "Griffin held the brown and gold gryphon. I wanted black, to honor my Lion friend." I held up my glass to Lion.

I didn't think it was possible, but his grin widened.

Xenides studied the lists of names before him, while Saxom's last mindspeech played continuously in his mind.

Make them pay, Saxom sent, just before his life ended. Xenides was resolved to obey his sire's command.

A year has passed since the incident on the Texas Gulf Coast. I've gone on assignment twice in that time. I'd only just returned recently, to find Kiarra waiting for me. Pheligar stood behind her when I arrived.

"I'm pregnant," she blurted when I went to embrace her.

"What?"

"Four months. Happened just before you left," she said.

"I thought we were sterile," I said, forgetting my manners and my good sense for a moment.

"We're supposed to be," she snapped, turning her back on me and walking away.

Adam, this is your child—something you never thought to get. What sort of fool are you? Pheligar's mindspeech shocked me for a moment—he seldom bothers speaking to anyone.

He was right, though.

It's a boy child, he added.

"My heart?" I stepped toward Kiarra, my hand held out in apology. "Is that Justin there?" I pulled her against me.

"Is that what you want?" She sniffled as she looked up at me.

"Yes. Please say we can name him after my brother."

"We can name him after your brother." She huddled into my embrace.

"We're having a baby," I breathed. "Does Joey know?"

She laughed.

The End

More information may be found regarding Xenides' war with the vampires and other races of Earth in the Blood Destiny series, beginning with *Blood Wager*.

Information regarding Adam's first assignment with Joey can be found in the short story, *Tracking Merrill*, in the anthology *Other Worldly Ways*.

9 781634 780704